"What's the purpose of this board meeting?"

Cade put half a cup of dog food in Patches's bowl, then stepped outside to get water from the faucet next to the porch. "To convince the members of the board that—despite the events of the weekend—I am still the right person to lead the company. I want to show them that my marrying you was not a foolish action."

Laurel looked at him through the screen. "You're not going to try and pretend we're in love, are you?"

Cade stepped back onto the porch. "Quite the contrary. I want to show them we have a workable business arrangement." Noting Patches still hadn't touched her food, Cade put some kibble in his palm and rubbed his scent into it.

"So there will be no kissing, no fake lovey-dovey stuff?" Laurel asked, her delicate brows arching inquisitively.

"None," Cade confirmed. Although he wouldn't mind kissing Laurel again. Not at all.

Dear Reader,

We've all been there. Had a secret crush on a guy who was already "taken." Helped out a dear friend who was in so much trouble she didn't know what to do. Made a hasty promise we later wished we hadn't, but still felt honor-bound to keep. All are situations that can be handled individually, without too much trouble. But what happens when all these things occur at once, when life gets very complicated and there are no easy solutions to be had? I wondered.... And that is how this story began.

I took one maid of honor—Laurel McCabe. Gave her the task of protecting her very good friend—in this case, the bride. And added one very ticked-off groom, Cade Dunnigan. I put them in a situation no three people should ever have to face, and then sat back to watch what they would do.

The bride followed her heart, despite the fact that doing so would likely cause a scandal unlike anything ever seen in Dallas society. The groom decided he would claim his inheritance—and his rightful place at the head of the family company—no matter what that entailed. And the maid of honor....well, she was caught smack-dab in the middle of all the chaos and reminded of the solemn promise she had made. It didn't matter that she wished she had never given her word. She had. So, like it or not, she had to follow through on her "Texas wedding vow."

I had a lot of fun writing this book. I hope you enjoy reading it. For more information on this and other titles, you can visit me at www.cathygillenthacker.com.

Sincerely,

Cathy Gillen Thacker

A Texas Wedding Vow

CATHY GILLEN THACKER

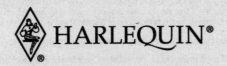

HARLEQUIN®

TORONTO • NEW YORK • LONDON
AMSTERDAM • PARIS • SYDNEY • HAMBURG
STOCKHOLM • ATHENS • TOKYO • MILAN • MADRID
PRAGUE • WARSAW • BUDAPEST • AUCKLAND

ISBN 0-373-75116-8

A TEXAS WEDDING VOW

Copyright © 2006 by Cathy Gillen Thacker.

Printed in U.S.A.

Chapter One

"Where is she?" Cade Dunnigan asked from the front steps of Unity Cathedral in Dallas, Texas.

Not sure how to answer that, even if she was the maid of honor, Laurel McCabe looked upward to the April evening sky. It should have been a perfect night to celebrate the impending nuptials of one of her very best friends. The hot-pink and white crepe myrtles that lined the church grounds were in full bloom. The rush-hour traffic that had clogged the city streets earlier had eased, and dusk was settling around them like a soft, warm blanket.

Cade now stood in front of her, so Laurel had no choice but to look into his ruggedly handsome face. His irritated glance scanned her wavy, shoulder-length brown hair, continued moving over her from head to toe, before returning deliberately to her eyes. "You said she would be here half an hour ago."

The groom-to-be was the kind of take-charge, kick-butt man Laurel usually avoided. Maybe because he reminded her of her five impossibly commanding, know-it-all older brothers.

"Everyone is waiting to go on with the wedding rehearsal," Cade fumed, his lips curving in a frown.

Laurel drew a deep, enervating breath, doing her best not to notice how well his broad shoulders and solid male build filled out his sage-green suit, coordinating shirt and tie. Fabulous looks, and fashion sense, too. What was Mary Elena *thinking*, running the other way? "I know that, Cade," she replied wearily.

"And?"

Laurel didn't want to tell him what Mary Elena Ayers had really said. Especially when she was certain her friend would change her mind as soon as she got over this temporary bout of prewedding jitters.

"She's…" Laurel paused, doing her best to ignore his increasingly uptight attitude, and her own undeniable awareness of him. Mary Elena had known Cade for years, but they had only started dating a ridiculously short one month ago, before the startlingly fast engagement. Laurel had met him just the day before and been instantly wowed. Pewter-gray bedroom eyes dominated his straight nose, sensual lips and masculine jaw. He was quick-witted, energetic and determined. Had he not been about to marry her very good friend, Laurel might have thrown her own hat in the ring. But he was. So he was strictly off-limits to her. Which was a good thing. Cade Dunnigan in wounded-bear mode was not someone she wanted to tangle with.

Cade shoved a hand through his thick, sun-streaked blond hair. The action didn't do much to mess it up, Laurel noted. Maybe because the short, spiky strands looked as if they had been styled by a quick pass or two of a towel over his head, then let dry as is, every which way. The style—if you could call it that— was sexy, tousled, touchable. Very touchable.

"Mary Elena's what?" Cade demanded when Laurel didn't immediately continue.

Laurel started. What was wrong with her? It wasn't like her to move in on another woman's territory, even in abstract fantasy. "She's…not feeling…like herself…today," she said finally. Otherwise, Mary Elena would be answering her cell phone. Or making some effort to let someone know where she was, and when she could be expected to arrive. She wasn't. Which meant her jitters were obviously getting worse….

"What the devil is that supposed to mean?' Cade demanded.

How did you tell a six-foot-one-inch Texan who ran his family company that he had most likely just been stood up on the second most important night of his life thus far, the first being his actual wedding day? Would he believe Laurel if she told him she felt it was just a momentary glitch in what looked to be a long, if uneventful, marriage to Mary Elena Ayers?

"It's complicated." Laurel did her best to cover for her friend. "Sort of a woman thing." She revealed as much as she could, while still maintaining her friend's confidence.

Cade paused, struggling to make sense of that. "You mean… she's…?"

Too late, Laurel saw he had concluded it was a monthly hormonal change. She blushed fiercely in response.

"Why didn't she just tell me she wasn't feeling well?" he continued in concern.

"Her, um, cramps came on rather suddenly." Only they weren't of the feminine nature Cade was imagining. Rather, the type that stemmed from nerves and sent Mary Elena running for the nearest lavatory.

"Is she going to be okay?" Cade asked.

"I'm certain of it," Laurel declared. It was just nerves. Mary Elena had told her so.

Making no effort to hide his unhappiness with Laurel's actions, Cade stepped closer, gave her a measuring look. "Where is Mary Elena now?"

Laurel took a deep breath before answering. "Last I saw her, she mentioned something about going home to lie down," she said quietly, inhaling the soapy-fresh scent of his skin and hair, and the brisk masculine fragrance of his cologne. Aware that her heart was racing, she took a step back, widening the distance between them once again, and folded her arms in front of her. She had to stop reacting to him like this! Cade Dunnigan was taken!

Oblivious to the direction of her thoughts, Cade frowned again. "Her father just checked with the staff at their residence. She isn't there."

Darn. Deep down, despite her friend's assurances to the contrary, Laurel had feared Mary Elena was running away— at least from this evening's festivities. Especially after Mary Elena had gotten the call from Manuel Garcia on her cell phone. The two had pretended to talk about whether or not the planting of the new azalea bushes in front of the Ayerses' Dallas mansion was going according to schedule, but when the tears had welled up in Mary Elena's eyes and her voice had begun to tremble, Laurel had suspected other things were being said on the other end of the connection. Not that Laurel could fault her friend for confiding in the handsome young gardener. Manuel treated her with soulful kindness. It was clear he had quite a crush on her.

"Her father said he hasn't seen or heard from her since breakfast," Cade continued, even more irritably.

Laurel wasn't surprised by that. Lance Ayers had been pressuring his only daughter to "get her future squared away" for months now—he hadn't stopped until Mary Elena had agreed to the arranged marriage and accepted Cade Dunnigan's engagement ring. Her running off this afternoon was probably the result of the unrelenting pressure from both men. It hadn't mattered that Cade had been an old—if casual—friend. Mary Elena hadn't loved him, and she had confessed to Laurel this afternoon that she feared she never would, no matter how much they had in common or how much time passed. But none of that was Laurel's to reveal. Especially since she knew her friend would eventually do what her father wanted, anyway. Mary Elena always did.

"Maybe she'll call Mr. Ayers soon," Laurel said finally, knowing she would have felt a lot better if Cade had behaved as if this marriage were a love match made in heaven. But according to Mary Elena, he had been approaching it in the same businesslike manner that her father had. Clearly, a move that had disaster written all over it from the get-go. But maybe this no-show tonight would get Cade's attention, make him understand he was going to have to be a lot more romantic in his approach to their marriage. Especially if he wanted a chance at making Mary Elena as happy as every bride deserved to be.

Cade appraised Laurel frankly, suspicion etched in his face. "What else aren't you telling me?"

Tons. "Nothing," Laurel fibbed, struggling between her loyalty to her friend and her conscience, which demanded she be truthful no matter what.

Cade's eyes turned an even deeper gray. "You understand," he stated clearly, looking deep into her eyes, "I have to be married by midnight tomorrow to collect my inheritance?"

Yet another idiot who valued money above love. Sighing, Laurel planted her hands on her hips. "Why are you telling me this?" she demanded.

"Because—" he flashed her a crocodile smile "—you are the maid of honor. And as such, the closest person to Mary Elena at the moment."

She defiantly lifted her chin. "So?"

"So…" Cade arched his brow in return "…I want your word that Mary Elena is going to be here tomorrow evening for the ceremony, or I'm calling off this wedding here and now."

Laurel's hand flew to her chest. "You can't do that! Not without at least talking to her," she cried. The public embarrassment and humiliation would crush a tender soul like her friend.

A muscle worked in Cade's jaw. Abruptly, his patience was at an end. "Look, I have to get married. If not to Mary Elena, then to someone else. So unless you're volunteering to take her place if she doesn't show up at the last minute, then—"

"Fine." Laurel cut Cade off impatiently. Like it or not, she knew it was her duty as maid of honor to see the bride made it to the ceremony on time. She was a McCabe, after all. McCabes did not shirk their responsibilities. And that went double if they had given their word. "If I can't get Mary Elena here by tomorrow evening, I'll take her place," she promised.

"And marry me," Cade stated, making sure they understood each other.

"Yes," she vowed in exasperation, deciding she would do whatever it took to end this conversation.

Leaning close, Cade warned softly, "I'm going to hold you to this, you know."

Tension rippled through Laurel's slender frame. "I figured you would," she replied, just as decisively, knowing if she weren't so sure she would win it would be foolish to take on the ruthlessly determined CEO in this battle of wills. "But it's not going to be necessary," she continued flatly. "I've known Mary Elena since we were kids. She is not going to stand you up tomorrow."

In the end, duty and an innate sense of familial responsibility would make Mary Elena follow through on her promise. Laurel was sure of it.

"WHAT DO YOU MEAN you're not coming to the cathedral?" Laurel demanded of her friend, twenty-two hours later. She had spent the day fruitlessly trying to track the bride down in person. "You can't back out of the wedding at this late date."

Mary Elena's voice took on a stony resolve on the other side of the line. "I've thought about it all night, Laurel. I can't marry a man I don't love."

Aware this situation now had disaster written all over it, Laurel rubbed her temples with her fingertips. "Then at least come and tell him that in person."

"If I show up, Cade and Daddy will try and talk me into it, and make me feel so guilty I'll fold!" Mary Elena wailed. "I can't take that chance."

Tension stiffened Laurel's frame, even as she struggled to remain calm. "Where are you now?" Was that airport noise in the background?

"Houston Intercontinental. I've got the tickets for the honeymoon Daddy was giving us. Tell Cade I'm sorry," Mary Elena added hurriedly, her voice steely with determination, "but I'm using them. I have to get out of town for a while."

Laurel couldn't exactly blame her for running, given the mess she was leaving behind. She started to speak, but was drowned out by more airport noise, announcements of flights. The connection ended just as Cade walked in, a determined expression on his face. Laurel's heart sank.

"Where is she?" he demanded.

Laurel could hear the string quartet starting in the chapel. Guests would be arriving any minute. She inhaled a shaky breath.

Time to find out just how much of a sense of humor Cade Dunnigan had. "Funny thing," she began bravely.

Cade's brows drew together above stormy gray eyes. "She's not coming, is she?"

Laurel drew herself up to her full five-foot-five height. She met his implacable gaze head-on. "No," she said calmly, all the while praying Cade would not hold her to that oh-so-foolish promise she had made the evening before. "She's not."

He shrugged, looking disappointed but not surprised. Then he flashed her a wicked smile. "So, prepare to become Mrs. Cade Dunnigan in about forty-five minutes, give or take."

The sounds of the prelude music continued to drift in from the sanctuary, adding to the unreality of the moment. Laurel took a step backward. "You can't be serious."

Unfortunately, he was.

Cade looked her up and down, taking in her pastel chiffon maid of honor gown and obviously finding it wanting. "You're backing out on your word?"

A McCabe's word was everything, Laurel knew. Always had been. Always would be. Still, it wasn't very gentlemanly of Cade Dunnigan to hold her to such an impetuous—and wildly inappropriate—promise. So Laurel did what she always did—she tried to talk herself out of trouble her too-big heart had gotten her into. "Well. I…I didn't think—"

"And you don't have to think now," Cade interrupted. He took her wrist and steered her across the room to the dress hook on the wall, where the wedding gown was hanging. "Get out of that bridesmaid outfit and into this." He thrust Mary Elena's beautiful gown into her hands.

Laurel thrust it right back. "Don't you have someone else you can call to help you?"

"Last night, maybe." Apparently tired of holding the embroidered satin dress with its voluminous skirt and heavy train, Cade placed it back on the hook mounted on the wall. "Not tonight. And with a church quickly filling with guests—" he nodded authoritatively in the direction of the chapel "—time's a-wasting."

Laurel tried to ignore the musical strains of the string quartet. She struggled to recall how long the prelude music had been slated to last, before the wedding party had to start lining up. Forty-five minutes? Thirty? Not that it really mattered, since the outcome of this mess was not in doubt. Laurel glared at Cade, letting him know she expected him to get a grip. "I can't marry you."

Cade's nostrils flared. "Perhaps I didn't make myself plain. You have to marry me."

Laurel scoffed, pretending an ease she couldn't begin to feel. "Or what?" she demanded.

Cade's frown deepened. He leaned closer, further invading her personal space. "Or I sue you—and your very wealthy father, Sam McCabe—for breach of promise and the loss of my inheritance."

Laurel knew what few others did—that her father's "wealth" was all tied up in his privately held software company. To get the cash out her dad would either have to sell McCabe Software Solutions outright or go public, neither of which he planned to do. He liked calling his own shots way too much. "Can you do that?" she asked Cade.

He tilted his head and stared at her. "I don't know." He took the wedding gown and veil off the hook and handed them over once again. "Want to find out?"

Laurel definitely did not want to drag her father into this. He was angry enough with her right now. And like it or not, she *had* made Cade a promise. "We're just talking a wedding, right?" she ascertained lightly. "Not a real marriage. Just something to satisfy the terms of the will so you can get your inheritance."

Cade released a short, exasperated breath. "Do I look like I want to stay married to you any longer than absolutely necessary?" he demanded.

"No." Laurel mimicked his low, arch tone. "You do not." Thank heavens!

"Good." He nodded grimly. "Then we understand each other."

"This is just going to be a temporary measure," she repeated, as much to reassure herself as make clear the terms of their new agreement.

"Right," he said.

"How long?" Laurel asked.

He shrugged, all masculine carelessness once again. "We'll have to ask the lawyer who drew up the terms of the will. We can do that Monday morning, first thing."

Laurel bit her lip, sensing disaster. "Is this even going to be legal?"

"It will be as soon as we sign all the papers."

Laurel looked down and saw that he had an application for a marriage license already filled out in her name. Their eyes met, held. "Come prepared for anything, don't you?" she murmured dryly.

Cade smiled, looking every bit the assertive CEO he was. "Always."

The door flew open and Lance Ayers stormed in. Instead of his usual western-cut suit and string tie, he was clad in a black tuxedo and snakeskin boots. Black Stetson in hand, the Texas oilman glared at Laurel. "Where in blue blazes is my daughter?"

"She dumped me," Cade answered.

Lance's white eyebrows furrowed. He looked even more upset, but somehow not as surprised as either Laurel or Cade had been. "When?"

Cade shoved his fingers through his spiky, dark gold hair. "Ten minutes ago, according to Laurel."

She nodded. "I spoke to Mary Elena on the phone. It's official. She is not showing up tonight."

Concern flickered in her father's eyes. "Where is she?"

Laurel hesitated, not sure whether she should say or not, but not wanting him to worry unnecessarily, either. "The airport," she finally revealed. "Mary Elena said something about taking a few days to sort things out before she talks to anyone about what she's done."

Lance shook his head grimly. "I never should have given her the tickets for the honeymoon yesterday."

Cade's face registered surprise. "What honeymoon?"

Lance scowled. "The one you were too busy with work to plan."

Abruptly, Cade looked as irked with Mary Elena's father as Lance Ayers was with him. "I couldn't have gone," he explained.

Lance regarded Cade with silent blame. "Is that why Mary Elena refused to marry you?"

"You'd have to ask her, but since she didn't tell me about the honeymoon you had planned for us," Cade replied mildly, "I doubt that is the reason."

Figuring she could set the record set straight about this, at least, Laurel spoke up. "She decided she didn't want to marry someone she didn't love." And despite the mess they were all in now, Laurel didn't blame her for that.

Both men frowned in a mixture of disapproval and frustration. Laurel was glad she hadn't been up against the two of them. On this much, they were certainly a united front. Which confirmed what Mary Elena had complained about to Laurel—that the two were pressuring her unduly to go along with what had been, from the very first, their brilliant plan to merge two wealthy families and ensure both Mary Elena's and Cade's future.

Lance Ayers jerked at the knot of his black satin bow tie with one hand and waved his hat with the other. "I'll tell the guests the wedding is off."

Cade moved to intercept him before he reached the door. "It's not off." Cade paused, letting the weight of his words sink in. "I'm marrying Laurel instead."

Lance looked shocked, then enraged. "Not on my dime, you're not. This wedding was planned for Mary Elena!"

Cade shrugged his broad shoulders. "You're right—you shouldn't have to pay for this. Send all the bills to me, including the ones for the wedding gown and veil, and I'll take care of them."

Lance shook his head. "I can't believe she did this to you. After all you offered her!"

"Me, either, but I'll survive." Cade's voice was determined. "One way or another I am getting my inheritance."

"Even if he has to marry me to do it," Laurel muttered beneath her breath.

Lance Ayers looked at Laurel. "How did you get roped into this?"

She sighed. "Long story. Suffice it to say—" she glanced

back to Cade and waited a long, meaningful moment "—our marriage won't last long."

"No kidding," Cade muttered swiftly.

Lance shook his head. "I blame Mary Elena's mother for this. Filling her head with all those romantic notions!"

Unfortunately, Mary Elena's mother had died five years before. And as always, Mr. Ayers was more focused on his latest business deal than he ever had been on his only child. "You want me to make the announcement to the guests?" he asked.

Cade shook his head. "I'll do it. Meantime, tell the wedding planner to make sure all the guests are seated, and we're going to be minus a maid of honor—unless you know someone who'd like to fill in at the last moment?" he asked Laurel.

She shook her head. She wasn't about to drag any other woman into this, whether she could fit into her maid of honor dress and was willing to be drafted or not. Bad enough Laurel was being forced to participate!

Lance nodded, contrite now that he had calmed down. "Consider it done. And for what it's worth, Cade, I'm sorry. Mary Elena should never have embarrassed you this way."

Cade waved off the older man's concern. "You just worry about your daughter."

Lance exited the room and closed the door behind him.

Once again, Cade and Laurel were alone.

"MAYBE THIS ISN'T SUCH a good idea," Laurel said.

"You won't get an argument from me there. We're still doing it, however. How do you get into this thing, anyway?"

Laurel's shoulders stiffened. "You don't need to help me."

Seeming to relish the difference in their heights, and the advantage his additional eight inches gave him, he looked down at her with a taunting smile. "You're saying you can get into this gown alone?"

Laurel's insides clenched at the potent fantasy his offer evoked. That was all she needed—to be in a state of undress with him nearby. No doubt noticing that everywhere she was soft, he was hard, everywhere she was female, he was male. Allowing him to help her out of one dress and into another would lend an unmistakable aura of sexuality to their situation, and surely no good could come of that! "I'm saying," Laurel countered, scowling even more, "you can send someone else in to help me."

Cade scoffed. "And give you a chance to run out on me, too?" he countered, his low sexy voice doing strange things to her insides. "No way. I am not letting you out of my sight."

Despite her desire to stay cool, calm and collected, Laurel's heart took on a quicker beat. Cade had a point. Given the chance to run, she just might. "Trusting, aren't you?" she said sweetly. Determined to irritate Cade as much as he was irritating her, she blinked at him coquettishly.

"Hey!" Cade angled a thumb at his chest. "If I'm suspicious, it's for very good reason." With maddening nonchalance, he reached behind her and undid the zipper of her dark rose bridesmaid dress. His capable fingers radiated warmth through the cloth to her skin. "Good thing the two of you are about the same size."

Not quite. Laurel knew she was one bra size larger than Mary Elena. Which meant she was going to be spilling out of the top of the bodice of the strapless dress. "Just so we're clear," she cautioned tartly, "this marriage is going to be an in-name-only, over-before-we-blink type of thing."

"I'm not offering any fringe benefits." Cade paused and then smiled, as though he already knew exactly what it would be like to make hot, passionate love to her. "Unless you make that a condition of your cooperation, that is."

"Absolutely not!" she countered, shivers of awareness sliding over her skin.

"Then it's agreed," he stated casually, while Laurel hung on to her own composure by a thread. "No sleeping together. One kiss at the altar, perhaps another at the reception."

Laurel stared up at him, her throat dry. She had to hand it to him. He had not only taken this unexpected turn of events in stride, he was ready to play the ruse to the bitter end. "I think just the one will do." Given her attraction to him, she figured that would be hard enough to forget.

Mischief twinkled in Cade's eyes. "We'll see what the situation calls for," he promised.

Laurel's fingers began to tremble. She slipped the heavy gown off the padded dress hanger. Panic surged deep inside her, giving way to incredibly exciting and sexy and totally out of the question fantasies. "I'll let you know when you can kiss me or not," she insisted, telling herself she was most definitely not going to get roped into any wildly arousing or potentially heartrending romantic drama with him. This marriage they were about to embark on was a means to his inheritance, that was all. "Now turn around and close your eyes, until I get this gown on. When I tell you I'm ready, you can do the buttons in the back."

Cade swung around impatiently. "You're getting a little bossy, aren't you?"

"If that isn't a case of the pot calling the kettle black, I don't know what is," Laurel muttered right back, struggling into the dress. It wasn't an easy task, given the voluminous folds. She tripped over the layers of organza petticoat beneath the satin skirt. She would have landed facedown on the floor had Cade not turned just in the knick of time and caught her in his strong arms. His gaze dropped over her sheer rose bustier, matching French-cut panties, garter belt and stockings. "Nice undies," he drawled.

Laurel felt herself flush the same hue as her maid of honor gown. "They're the wrong color for the wedding dress." Although the lacy undergarments nicely matched her too-warm skin.

Cade frowned, his eyes moving over the exposed curves of her breasts. "Are they going to show through?"

The way her nipples showed through the lace? Laurel swallowed hard, even as his glance dropped lower still, to the shadowy vee between her thighs. Why had she ever chosen such outrageously sexy underwear for this evening? Pretending that revealing herself this way was an everyday occurrence, she said with much dignity as she could, "No. The satin is too thick, thank goodness. Would you just let me go and help me into this?"

Making absolutely no effort to release her, Cade continued to stare at her. "I thought you didn't want my help."

"Obviously—" Laurel splayed her hands against the hard chest and shoved away from him "—I have changed my mind."

A knock sounded on the door, followed by the wedding planner's imperious voice. "Five minutes!"

"Be right there!" Cade shouted back, stepping behind Laurel to hurry the process along. "Damn, this dress has a lot of buttons," he said as he closed them with practiced ease.

Damn, it was tight across the chest.

Laurel stared at herself in the mirror, taking in the strapless bodice, nipped-in waist, full sweeping skirt and detachable train. She was going to have to wear her own shoes—there was too much of a size difference there—but thankfully her deep rose evening sandals wouldn't show beneath the voluminous folds of the gown.

"You're going to need this, too." Cade handed her the veil, and attached tiara.

Laurel took a deep breath. Aware that she looked—and felt—very much like a real bride at this very moment, she threaded the tiara through her upswept hair, arranged the veil over her shoulders and pulled it down over her face. "Maybe we can just leave it like this for the entire ceremony," she said, turning to Cade hopefully. "That way no one will know it's me instead of Mary Elena."

"Not very likely," Cade muttered, appearing unwilling to tear his gaze from her face.

"A woman can hope." Laurel sighed, wishing he didn't look so handsome in his black tuxedo and crisp white shirt.

"Hoping for the impossible gets you nowhere, haven't you heard?" Cade muttered. Another knock sounded. He held out his arm and Laurel took a deep breath. They headed for the door.

They made it as far as the chapel vestibule, before she lost her nerve. Or found her mind. She wasn't sure which. All she knew for certain was that she did not want to go on, not one more step.

Cade tightened his grip on her arm. "Don't even think about bailing out on me now," he warned, all master and commander.

"Can't help it," she murmured right back. This evening was

no longer a surreal means to an end. It was too real. And she knew just how Cade's first runaway bride felt. Like she absolutely had to get out of there. Pronto. Before she made an even bigger fool of herself.

"Just think of it as a dress rehearsal for when you really tie the knot with the guy you love," Cade whispered in her ear, as the wedding guests turned their way, did double takes and began to gape.

Laurel dragged her heels—to no avail. Cade was tugging her along. "Somehow I don't think my parents are going to see it that way."

Cade tucked her closer still. "Maybe they'll never have to know," he said with a slight shrug.

Laurel's smile felt frozen on her face as they continued slowly, purposefully, up the aisle. "Now that would be a difficult feat to pull off."

Cade stopped smiling at their guests long enough to look her in the eye. "Why?"

Laurel swallowed. "They're seated in the second row."

Chapter Two

The last thing Cade Dunnigan wanted to do was tangle with Laurel McCabe's famously overprotective father, especially now. "You couldn't have told me this earlier?" he muttered so only she could hear.

"I forgot," she whispered back.

"You forgot," Cade repeated, wishing she wasn't so very beautiful, and that he hadn't just had a glimpse of her in a state of undress that was going to haunt him for many nights to come.

Smart, accomplished women had been a part of his life for as long as he could remember. His wealth attracted them in droves. But none of them had what the innately impetuous Laurel had— that feisty personality mixed with a dazzling beauty that kept his gaze returning to her again and again.

Laurel McCabe was the kind of pampered, protected social-ite Texas was known for. Her thick, wavy, shoulder-length hair with the sideswept bangs was the rich color of maple syrup. Her nose was slim and straight, her lips soft and lusciously full. She had one of the most beautiful complexions he had ever seen, and her wide-set blue eyes reminded him of the summer sky on a bright, sunny day. The curves on her perfectly proportioned frame were as near to heaven as Cade could imagine. And thanks to the fact he had just helped her into her wedding dress, he knew exactly how lush her breasts were, how slender her waist and cur-vaceous her hips. Minutes later, his body was still humming at the memory of her softly rounded bottom, long lissome thighs and cute little knees. His only comfort was the fact she had been so busy being embarrassed she hadn't seemed to notice his immediate, potent arousal. Not that his desire for her mattered in the least, since theirs was going to be a marriage in name only, Cade told himself decisively.

"Or maybe I just didn't want to remember that my parents were in attendance," Laurel continued emphatically.

That, Cade could understand.

"Because when my dad gets wind of this," she lamented softly, with the first real regret she had shown all evening, "he is going to blow a gasket."

As Cade and Laurel strode past the aisle where Sam and Kate McCabe were seated, he saw their eyes widen at the sight of their youngest child in a wedding dress and veil.

Laurel turned her head away and pretended not to see the expressions on her parents' faces as she and Cade continued up the aisle. Not that they were the only ones sitting there in shock and awe, he noted with chagrin. Literally everyone in the chapel was blinking in amazement and doing jaw-dropping double takes. Well, it couldn't be helped. He had an agenda to fulfill, a legacy to nurture and protect. He hadn't expected the task ahead to include pressuring an unwilling woman to be his bride, even temporarily. But thanks to Laurel McCabe's false promises, he'd had no choice but to take her as his wife, the objection of her family and their friends notwithstanding.

As they reached the altar of the historic downtown church, the reverend—known for his cool composure under the most volatile of situations—merely lifted one eyebrow and said a single word. "Cade?"

"I'll explain everything, reverend," Cade promised. Still keeping hold of Laurel, he turned to face their audience. "Family, friends, honored guests. I have two announcements to make. Sadly, my wedding to Mary Elena Ayers is not going to take place this evening. Happily, my marriage to Laurel McCabe will. Reverend, let us continue."

"You call that an explanation?" Laurel muttered under her breath.

Out of the corner of his eye, Cade saw her father start to stand up. To Cade's relief, Kate McCabe pulled her husband right back into his seat, leaned over and whispered something in his ear.

"That was more like a statement of the obvious," Laurel continued to speak accusingly in a voice only Cade could hear as he lifted her veil and kissed her cheek.

He shrugged as he took her trembling hand in his and carried it to his lips. "They're a smart group. They'll figure out our marriage is only taking place because Mary Elena left me at the altar. Heck, by Monday, every man who's ever been wronged by a woman will be cheering me on."

Temper surged in Laurel's pretty eyes, letting Cade know his new bride was no pushover, never had been. "And everyone who knows me will be trying to get me to the loony bin!"

Clearing his throat, the reverend stared them down. "Cade, are you sure this is what you want to do?" he asked.

Cade nodded. "Absolutely. Now let's get this show on the road."

The next few minutes passed in a blur as Cade and Laurel suffered through the ceremony that Mary Elena Ayers and the wedding planner had designed. Cade was barely aware of the vows he was repeating. He sensed Laurel was having trouble concentrating on the words, too. That was confirmed when the minister had to tell her—twice—to put the ring on his finger.

Fortunately, the reverend wisely left out the part of the ceremony where he invited anyone who knew just cause for the two of them not to be joined together to speak then or forever hold his or her peace.

The next thing Cade knew, the reverend was looking at them soberly, and pronouncing them—against his better judgment, Cade was sure—husband and wife. "You may kiss the bride," he concluded.

Laurel turned and glanced at Cade.

He knew she expected him to make it short and sweet and utterly meaningless. Indeed, that had been his plan, too. Until he saw the warm flush of color on her cheeks and the willful look in her eyes that dared him to just try and do anything else. All his life, Cade never had been able to resist a challenge. And Laurel McCabe was one challenging woman indeed.

LAUREL THOUGHT THE ceremony couldn't get any worse. She was wrong.

Oh, it started innocently enough. Every bit as aware of their "audience" as she, Cade took Laurel masterfully into his arms. So glad the ceremony part of the occasion was nearly over, her impetuous promise to help Cade get his inheritance kept, she looked up at him. Their eyes locked in a mixture of victory and relief. His pewter-gray eyes glinted as if he could barely believe he was going through with this. Laurel knew exactly how he felt. "Any chance we could skip this part?" she whispered as Cade's head lowered purposefully to hers.

"Okay by me, probably not by them," Cade murmured back.

Then his lips were on hers… And all pretense stopped. Laurel was inundated by so many sensations at once. The clean masculine scent of him, the minty taste of his mouth. His lips made a long, provocatively thorough tour of hers, extracting an incredibly sensual response from her. Laurel's heart slammed against her ribs, her knees weakened treacherously and her hands curled around his biceps. She clung to him for support as she experienced the kind of thrill she had always read about, dreamed about, but never really expected to feel. She knew very well that this was all for show. The problem was, it didn't feel that way as their lips fused in a kiss that was filled with passion and heat, want and need. The situation threatened to get swiftly out of control, Laurel realized, as Cade's lips continued to press firmly, evocatively against hers. Her breasts were crushed against the solid wall of his chest. Heat built in her middle, then moved outward in radiating waves. For so long she'd wanted nothing more than for someone to tear down the walls around her heart. Now it was happening. Way too fast.

Knowing she had to stop this—now—if she were to stop it at all, she broke the sweet caress and stepped back on legs that shook beneath the satiny folds of her wedding dress. For a second, Cade looked as shocked and taken aback by the desire that had flared between them as she.

The string quartet started the recessional. Aware that she was tingling everywhere they had touched, as well as everywhere they hadn't, Laurel plastered a smile on her face, took Cade's arm. Given the way they had just let their bodies get ahead of their hearts and minds, he was only too happy to rush her back down the aisle. The one thing Laurel was glad about as she and Cade headed for the anteroom just off the chapel, where they would await the lining up of the guests on the steps for the traditional throwing of rice, was that her parents appeared to have left the church sometime during the ceremony.

"How dare you kiss me like that!" she breathed the moment she and Cade were through the door.

"Exactly what I would like to know," a deep voice intoned from the other side of the room.

Cade shut the door behind them.

Laurel and her new "husband" squared off with her parents, Kate and Sam McCabe. The handsome couple had been married twenty-seven years and wanted to see all six of their children married. Just, Laurel was darn sure, not quite this way.

To her father and mother, marriage was serious business, a lifelong commitment deserving much care and consideration. It would never be a joke, or a means to an end.

They had made that clear to her brother Riley not too long ago, when he'd impulsively wed nurse Amanda Witherspoon on a dare.

Laurel didn't need to see the worry in her mother's eyes or the frown on her father's face to know her parents still felt the same way.

"I told your father there surely had to be a very good explanation for what has been going on here this evening," Kate said, fitting her petite frame against Sam's side. She took his hand in hers. "Otherwise you would never have done this."

Laurel had known her mother—a psychologist who specialized in grief counseling—would be the parent more likely to cut her a little slack here. "Actually, there is." She drew a deep breath, not sure how to phrase it. Cade locked eyes with her, whether because he was willing to let her take the lead with her parents or was simply curious as to what she was going to say, Laurel didn't know. She swallowed and looked back at her father. "It wasn't a real marriage. It was more like a favor to a friend."

Sam looked at his wife. "I told you we should have stopped this before they ever said their I do's," he told her grimly.

Kate touched a hand to the flipped up ends of her honey-blond hair, and fastened her understanding blue eyes on her only daughter. "And I told you it's a private family matter, best handled without an audience." She sighed. "I know you're angry at your father, Laurel, for what happened last week—"

"What happened last week?" Cade interjected curiously.

"Nothing," Laurel said.

"I wouldn't call it that," Sam muttered, looking even more aggrieved.

Kate shook her head in silent commiseration. "Laurel lent her car to a friend who—"

"Stole it," Sam said.

"We don't know that," Laurel insisted, the heat of embarrassment sweeping over her face.

Sam arched a dissenting brow. "What we do know is that some of its parts have already surfaced for sale on the Internet. So we think it was taken across the border and chopped up." Sam looked at Cade, speaking man-to-man as he brought him up to speed. "If this was the first time Laurel had been duped, or used by someone claiming they needed her help, it would be one thing," he grumbled.

"But it wasn't," Kate revealed sadly.

"And since Laurel can't seem to differentiate between those who need help and those who would only use her generous nature for their own gain, I insisted she quit flitting from job to job and cause to cause and come to work for McCabe Software Solutions." Sam looked at Laurel sternly. "I still expect you to report for training at eight o'clock Monday morning."

"Fine," she said stiffly. She hated being treated like a child, and a difficult one at that.

Cade shrugged. "I have no problem with it, either."

Laurel turned to him, indignation soaring through her. As if she needed him to give her permission to do anything—married or not! "Like you'd have anything to say about it." She scowled.

Abruptly, Cade looked as implacable as her father. "I would if I were really your husband."

"Well, thank goodness you're not," she snapped.

"Did we miss something?" Kate McCabe cut in with a questioning glance at both of them.

Laurel exhaled loudly and explained in a low, disinterested tone, "I only married Cade so he could get his inheritance. He has to be married by midnight to claim it. We'll be meeting with his lawyer on Monday to wrap up the details. So you really don't have to worry about any of this, Mom and Dad. It's going to be over before you know it."

"She's right." Cade backed Laurel up firmly. "What happened here tonight was just a formality."

"Maybe to the two of you," Sam countered sagely. "It may not look that way to the business community as a whole."

A river of unease swept through Laurel.

"What do you mean?" Cade asked warily.

Sam shrugged. "I read in the business pages you are trying to substantially expand Dunnigan Dog Food with a new flagship store slated to open in a couple of weeks."

"Two to be exact," Cade confirmed.

"What impact do you think your antics tonight will have on that?" he asked bluntly.

"Very little," Cade answered matter-of-factly, "since Dunnigan Dog Food is a privately held company."

"A company that," Sam added, without missing a beat, "relies on the public to purchase its products."

Cade paused.

Laurel blinked. "There wouldn't possibly be a boycott over something like this…would there?" she asked her father.

No one answered her. No one needed to. Laurel knew it could happen. Why hadn't she thought about this before she walked down the aisle? Why hadn't Cade? she wondered in frustration.

"Whether they do or don't may be irrelevant," Sam said, speaking as one CEO of a privately held company to another. "Mary Elena's father, Lance Ayers, is a member of the Dunnigan Dog Food board, isn't he?"

Cade nodded, his expression now as grim as Laurel's dad's. "As well as my uncle George Sr., cousin George Jr., Dotty Yost, Harvey Lemmon and myself." He clamped his lips together. "What's your point?" he asked Sam.

"Successful businesses require a steady hand at the helm. Right now, yours does not look all that unflappable. Set to marry one woman, show up with another. Not good, son."

Reluctantly, Laurel had to concede her father had a point.

Cade's shoulders and chest suddenly looked hard as a rock beneath his tuxedo jacket. He stared at Sam. "You're not suggesting I stay married to your daughter?" he said in disbelief.

"I'm stating," Sam continued, his concern over the situation unabated, "you've both made a terrible mistake, one that is not going to be as easy to overcome as you may currently think."

"YOUR DAD DOESN'T MINCE words, does he?" Cade asked Laurel after her folks had departed.

She shrugged, the high color in her elegant cheeks the only discernible sign she was upset by the dressing-down they had just received. "Not usually, although I thought he was pretty circumspect this evening."

"You call that circumspect?" Cade felt as if he'd been taken to the woodshed. Worse, he knew he deserved Sam McCabe's wrath. He had no business marrying Laurel for just a few days. If there had been any other way to save the company that he, his uncle and cousin had inherited from his grandfather and father, Cade would have chosen that route. But there hadn't been, and with the clock ticking, Cade had had no choice but to pursue any plan, no matter how lamebrained it appeared on the surface, that would enable him to meet his responsibilities and achieve his own dreams.

"You ought to hear my dad when he really gets going." Laurel sat down on the velvet-covered bench next to the wall and spread her skirts out around her. She touched a hand to the tiara perched atop her head, making sure it was still in place before continuing, "Just be thankful my five brothers weren't here this evening to witness this fiasco. They don't pull punches, either. Not to mention the fact that they've never liked—never mind approved of— one of my boyfriends yet."

Another wave of guilt and something akin to jealousy swept through Cade. Another point he hadn't considered. "Do you have a boyfriend?" he asked, hoping she didn't.

Laurel studied Cade with misgiving. "Luckily for us, no, I don't. Although had I had one before I married you, I daresay he would no longer be my boyfriend now." She bounded to her feet, her satin skirts swishing. "Any chance we can get out of going to the reception this evening?"

Cade shook his head, aware—like her—he privately wished they could. "We're the hosts of the party. We have to be there," he told her.

Temper flashed in Laurel's blue eyes. "You owe me big time for this." She looked out the window and saw the guests lining up on the sides of the stone steps that led down to the waiting white limousine.

Cade knew, as did she, they couldn't dally much longer. "It'll be worth it in the end," he promised.

Laurel tossed her head. "Maybe for you."

Cade resisted the urge to take her in his arms again and see if a second kiss would be even half as good as their first. "For both of us."

Her delicate brow arched. "I see how you benefit. I don't see how I do."

He reached out to straighten her veil. "You have the satisfaction of knowing you kept your word, that your solemn promise means something."

She rolled her eyes at the mere suggestion that her actions had, in any way, been laudable. Never mind selfless and noble.

"Except when I'm standing up in a church before the minister and everyone, promising to love and cherish you forever," she said wryly. "Then, it doesn't mean squat."

Cade couldn't disagree with that. His single-mindedness, where business was concerned, had gotten him into trouble once again. "Look, I never meant to hurt you."

"You haven't. Yet." Laurel regarded Cade steadily, her independent nature clear. "Just make sure you don't."

He nodded. "Understood."

"Promise?"

"Absolutely. You have *my* word on that."

A knock sounded on the door. The wedding planner stuck her head inside. She glared at Cade as if he were the lowliest, most fickle scum on earth. "The limo is waiting. So are the guests."

Suddenly feeling as if they were on the same team, instead of unwilling adversaries, Cade held out his hand to Laurel. "Ready?"

She took it in hers and squeezed tightly. "As I'll ever be."

"TELL ME THAT'S NOT a local news crew," Laurel murmured as the limo approached the hotel where the reception was to be held.

"It can't be for us," Cade said.

Laurel met his eyes. "You sure about that?"

"I am," he replied.

Problem was, Laurel soon noted, Cade was wrong.

"Hey, Dunnigan? What's the deal?" the woman with the microphone in her fist shouted as Cade stepped out of the limo and offered Laurel his hand. "Thought you were supposed to marry that oil heiress, Mary Elena Ayers, tonight!"

"Yeah," the reporter next to her, a man in a suit, echoed. "How'd you end up with a computer software company heiress instead?"

Laurel started to sink back into the limo. Cade kept his grip on her hand and reached in with his other to propel her all the way out. "Keep your head held high," he whispered in her ear, as he guided her onto the sidewalk.

"Long story," Cade commented to the reporters. "All you need to know is we're very happy."

"Rumor has it that it's a money match," the woman said.

Cade winked. "Love. Business. They're all the same to me. See you later!" He propelled Laurel through the lobby of the grand hotel and swept her down the long marble hall to the ballroom, where they could glimpse their guests already milling about. "How did they find out about us already?" Laurel whispered, slowing her steps to a crawl.

Cade shrugged, appearing in no real hurry to join their "reception" either. "Probably a slow news night. And like it or not, we're a heck of a human interest story."

Laurel came to a dead stop, her momentary desire to cooperate with Cade fading as fast as it had appeared. She pivoted toward him and she regarded him suspiciously. "You expected bad publicity out of all this, didn't you?"

Cade slouched against the wall. "I hoped it wouldn't happen."

She stepped back even farther, not caring who saw them. "But you knew it might."

He rubbed his handsome jaw contemplatively. "Let's just say I had all last night and today to think about it and decide what to do if you were unable to come through on your original promise to me, which was to deliver my bride to the church on time. Like it or not, this was the best option available to me. Which tells you," he emphasized in a rough tone, pushing away from the wall and sauntering closer once again, "how little choice I had."

Laurel drew a deep breath, aware they were still alone, knowing that wouldn't last. "This is all happening so fast."

"I know." Cade rested his hands on her shoulders. Sympathy lifted the corners of his lips. "I'm sorry. If I could have avoided putting you through this, I would have." He let her go, but kept his eyes on hers. "But we're in the middle of it now."

"So we have to soldier through," Laurel finished.

"Yep. At least try and look like we know what we're doing."

Farther down the hall, at the entrance of the ballroom, a man in a tuxedo stepped out. Laurel recognized him as Cade's uncle George. He was followed by Cade's cousin, George Jr. Both were handsome and blond, and had the Dunnigan good looks. Neither seemed particularly physically fit.

George Sr. simply shook his head in mute disapproval. "This was not what your father wanted," he told Cade.

"Then Dad shouldn't have put that ridiculous stipulation in his will," Cade retorted.

"You and I and the rest of the board members are going to have to talk," the older man said. George Jr. nodded in agreement.

"We will," Cade promised with the authority of an experienced CEO. "On Monday, three o'clock, my place."

George Sr. nodded. His expression turned even grimmer. "I'll spread the word, see everyone is there."

For Laurel, the next few hours passed in a blur. They ate dinner, suffered through the toasts, cut the cake and danced the first dance. The first chance they got, they exited through a side door and made for the staff entrance of the hotel, where a nondescript black hotel limo waited to take them home.

It was, not surprisingly, pouring rain as they stepped outside and got quickly into the car. "Thank goodness the hotel staff kept the reporters away from us." Laurel struggled to contain her expansive skirts as Cade settled on the bench seat opposite her.

"It's their job." He turned and looked as they passed several news vans and the white wedding limo they had been supposed to leave in, and headed down the block toward the freeway that would take them to the Highland Park mansion Cade had grown up in.

Laurel shook her head and tried not to think about what was going to happen next. She was glad he wasn't sitting next to her. Whenever he touched her, she got all fluttery and warm inside. "I can't believe I'm going to be on the news."

Cade relaxed against the back of the seat. "The story will die down quicker than you can blink," he predicted, all complacent male.

Tension flooded Laurel anew. "We hope."

Gray eyes narrowing, Cade studied her relentlessly. "The only way it would keep going is if we added fuel to the fire. We're not going to do that. I know Mary Elena and her father don't want any publicity."

"That's for certain," Laurel agreed, nerves jangling. "This whole evening was humiliating enough. I felt like an imposter."

"You and me both." Cade jerked off his tie and stuffed it in the pocket of his tuxedo.

Laurel regarded him curiously. "You never wanted to get married, did you?"

"Not particularly."

Her heart was beating too fast again, and it was his fault. "Why not?" she challenged softly, not sure whether she was asking for Mary Elena—or herself.

Cade's jaw hardened. It appeared, Laurel noted, he'd had to defend his position before. "Because passion is highly overrated, in my opinion."

"Passion or love?" Laurel countered.

He moved restlessly on the seat. "They're one and the same, aren't they?"

Laurel couldn't say. She'd thought she was in love a few times, only to realize later it had been more like an infatuation. As for passion, well, that too had passed her by. She'd never felt much of anything in that regard, if you discounted the kiss she'd been given at the conclusion of their wedding vows, and Laurel blamed that on adrenaline and nerves as much as anything else. She was sure if Cade were to kiss her again she would not feel the same rush of excitement and pleasure. Not that he was going do so. From here on out there would be no need for that. The only thing she would be getting from him would be a quickie divorce.

Determined to prove why Cade Dunnigan had been bad news for Mary Elena and was even worse news for her, Laurel kept up the third degree. "Have you ever been in love?"

He grinned, as if he knew exactly why she was being so chatty. "No."

That worried her. Why, she couldn't say, exactly. It wasn't as if the two of them were really married in anything but the strictly legal sense. "Did Mary Elena know that?"

"Of course. We were honest with each other, at least about that. Neither of us expected that we would ever be madly in love with each other. Our marriage was an arrangement meant to suit us both."

Except, Laurel thought, her friend had still wanted to love and be loved. "Were you planning to stay married to Mary Elena?" she asked quietly.

His jaw tightened. "That was certainly the assumption, but we never discussed it. Perhaps we should have. I do know she eventually wants children, as do I."

"Wow."

"What?"

"No wonder she ran."

Cade flexed his shoulders and folded his arms across his chest. "She didn't tell you any of this?"

Mary Elena hadn't really wanted to think about her upcoming wedding, never mind discuss it. "All I knew was that she had misgivings from the beginning, but you and her father had apparently put those to rest. Or so she thought," Laurel amended hastily, "until yesterday."

Recognition glimmered in Cade's eyes. "There's something you're not telling me, isn't there?"

That Mary Elena might be in love with the Brazillian gardener she'd been secretly teaching English to for some time now?

"What else was going on with her?" Cade asked.

Laurel shrugged. No way she was going to allow him or Lance Ayers to pin Mary Elena's bolting on Manuel Garcia. "You'll have to ask her, when she comes back." If she came back. Mary Elena hadn't seemed in any hurry to do that when she had spoken with Laurel on the phone. Laurel looked out at the passing scenery. "Can I go back to my apartment?"

The implacable boss man was back. "Not wise. I think—for legal reasons—we need to spend at least one night under the same roof." Her heart skipped a beat. "Don't worry," Cade continued affably, reading her mind. "The place has seven bedrooms. You can take your pick."

Really. "What if I want yours?" Laurel challenged.

He deliberately misread her intentions. "Hey—" he spread his palms wide "—if you want to share…"

Laurel fought the warm flush creeping up her neck. "No. I meant, what if I want the master bedroom. Are you prepared to move to another one?"

"I don't know." Cade tilted his head. His eyes gleamed mischievously. "I guess I'd have to think about it."

She didn't. The last thing she needed was to be sleeping where he usually slept. But sparring with him this way was working to keep the tension at bay, so darned if she wouldn't keep up the sass, just for the hell of it. "Gentleman to the end, aren't you?"

He grinned proudly, all untamable male. "Absolutely."

Short minutes later, the limo turned into the driveway of a sprawling rose-brick Tudor with beige trim. Towering live oaks shaded the immaculately tended lawn on either side of the pebbled sidewalk leading to the front portico. Beautiful rose bushes—in full spring bloom—lined the entire front of the house. The rain had slowed to a soft, steady thrumming, so water glistened everywhere. "It looks pretty slick out there," Cade noted, as he got out of the car and lent her a hand. "You better be careful."

"I'll be fine." Laurel took his hand and did her best to contain her skirt with the other. As soon as she was upright, she let go of him again. "You watch your step."

Cade gave the driver two folded hundred-dollar bills. "Thanks for helping us give those reporters the slip," he said with a smile.

The chauffeur tipped his hat. "Anytime, Mr. Dunnigan."

Laurel lifted her dress with both hands as she and Cade moved up the walk toward the dark house. The air was damp and scented with rain, flowers and wet grass. As she took the three steps to the portico, skirt still in hand, Cade asked, "Want me to carry you over the threshold?"

Behind them, Laurel heard the limo drive off. "I don't think so."

"Sure?" he teased gently. "Might be fun."

It might be romantic. That, she didn't need. Not when she was already standing there in one of the most beautiful wedding dresses she had ever seen in her life. She couldn't afford to start thinking about the way Cade had kissed her earlier, or the fact she was—even temporarily—his wife. "Let's just go inside."

He shrugged in obvious disappointment. "Suit yourself." He strode across the slick stone to the front door, lifted a small polished brass cover and punched in the security code on the keypad beneath. He swung open the door, lifted his hand as if to usher her inside, then stopped suddenly. "Oh, no!"

Laurel was about to say, "Oh, no what?" when she heard something, too—a galloping sound accompanied by some alarmingly heavy breathing. She stepped back in a panic onto the rain-slicked porch just as something big and black leaped through the air toward her out of the darkness. Already slightly off balance as she was, the weight of the sleek black animal hurling against her chest sent Laurel tumbling all the way back. She fell in the rose bushes edging the front porch, the big dog landing on top of her. Paws on her shoulders, he licked her aggressively beneath the chin.

Laurel couldn't help it, she began to laugh—despite the fact that Cade looked anything but amused by his hopelessly enthusiastic pet's antics as he grabbed the dog's collar and pulled him off her. What an end to a most unexpected evening, she thought, and the icing on the cake was the mortified look on the formerly self-assured Cade Dunnigan's face.

Unable to help herself, she lifted a brow and ribbed Cade mercilessly. "Not exactly the wedding-night kisses I was expecting to have to fend off."

Chapter Three

Cade had to hand it to his new "wife." Not many women would have come through such an incident with their sense of humor intact. But then, he was fast beginning to see that Laurel McCabe was one exceptional woman, able to take just about anything in stride.

"Cute," he complimented her with a wink. "But just for the record, those weren't the kind of wedding-night kisses I had in mind for you, either."

Laurel made a face at him. "Very funny." With rain splattering her face, hair and shoulders, she accepted Cade's help. His grip on her wrist was as gentle and implacable as the palm he pressed to the small of her back when he brought her to her feet. Serious now, he said, "You have my most sincere apologies for what just happened."

Laurel looked as if she didn't doubt that for a moment. Nor did she seem to blame him for Beast's enthusiasm. Another happy fact, since most women would have.

"Just out of curiosity…is that a dog or a horse?" she asked, as Beast galloped excitedly back toward the open portal, then paused at the threshold, dramatically swinging his large, handsome head in the direction he wanted them to go.

Arm wrapped around her waist, Cade guided Laurel to the door. "Black Labrador retriever."

Abruptly realizing her veil and tiara were askew, Laurel did her best to straighten both and restore order to her upswept dark hair. "How much does Beast weigh?"

"One hundred ten pounds, give or take. He's sweet as can be, but also dumb as a post sometimes. Hence his knocking you into the bushes."

"No kidding," Laurel said dryly.

"The good news is he apparently likes you."

"Sweet." Abruptly realizing something was dripping down her collarbone into the bodice of her dress, Laurel wiped dog slobber from beneath her chin.

She thought about wiping her hand on her dress, then wiped it on Cade's shirt instead. When he grinned indulgently, Laurel continued, "But couldn't you have warned me what lay ahead?"

Cade would have if he hadn't been so busy admiring the way Laurel looked in her dress that he'd lost all sense of time and place. And that had been his fault. "I forgot he was inside," he explained casually. "Normally, he barks when I come home, he's so excited to see me. He didn't, which means he was probably asleep when we arrived."

Laurel chuckled and shook her head, seemingly content to stand there on the porch for a moment and enjoy the misty April evening, with the rain pouring softly down. "If he treats burglars the way he treated me, I can't say he's much of a watchdog," she remarked.

"Oh, you'd be surprised how protective he can be and how fierce he sounds when he is defending his turf." Cade stepped closer to remove a leaf from Laurel's hair. "But he's also experienced enough to know the difference between friend and foe, and seeing the way we were together automatically signaled to him you were someone to be welcomed, not scared away." Cade inhaled the fragrance of rain-damp skin, crushed roses and perfume. "Hence the rather boisterious greeting. Although I must say that was an unusually affectionate introduction. Normally, he's content to sit and wag his tail and wait to be petted."

"What made me so special?" Laurel queried dryly, glancing over at Beast.

"I don't know. You'd have to ask him," Cade drawled as he

took her by the arm once again and steered her toward the portal. "Maybe he just liked the swishing sound of your dress."

Laurel rolled her eyes and Cade switched on lights as they stepped across the threshold. The majestic entryway was two stories in height. Tucked beneath the curve of the sweeping staircase was a large round dog bed. A twelve-inch bone and a stuffed toy shaped like a frog were sitting on top of it. For good reason. It was his dog's favorite place to simultaneously hang out and guard the establishment. "Beast. On your cushion. Now!" he pointed.

Cade watched with satisfaction as Beast loped over and plopped down obediently. Picking the stuffed frog up with his teeth, he swung it around his head excitedly. It made a rivet-rivet sound. Her cheeks blushing with pretty color, Laurel watched him command his dog to "Stay!"

Looking suddenly uneasy about the prospect of spending the night with Cade, she said, "Tell me you didn't really name your dog Beast."

Knowing exactly how she felt—his six-thousand-square-foot house was suddenly seeming a little too cozy to him, too—Cade explained, "My dog's registered name is Cavalier Wyndham Crossroads."

"That's a mouthful." Beneath the teasing words was a matter-of-fact prompting for the whole story.

He tried not to fantasize what it would be like to really bring Laurel here as his bride. Not easy, given the fact she was still in a wedding dress, he in a tuxedo, and both were now sporting gold bands on their left hand. "The kennel that bred him named him. His parents' names were incorporated into his official moniker. But obviously, that was not anything I wanted to call him, so while I was thinking about it and trying out different names, I affectionately called him Big Ol' Beast, and somehow that seemed to fit him more than anything else I could come up with. Eventually, it got shortened to Beast."

Laurel backed up slightly, not stopping until there was a good three feet between them. "Only a guy would come up with something like that."

Only a guy, Laurel thought, would think them spending the night together under the same roof was no big deal.

For her, it was a very big deal. For reasons that had a lot to do with the dress she was wearing and the gold band now on her left hand. After walking down the aisle on Cade's arm, nervously speaking vows and attending a three-hour wedding reception in their honor, it was impossible not to feel married. Even if she knew, in any real emotional sense, it was just a farce.

Cade flashed her a bad-boy smile. 'Thank you—I think the name is perfect for Beast, too." He paused to survey her. "You know, you are a mess," he told her.

Laurel dipped her head in regal acknowledgment and went into a mock curtsy. "Thank *you*."

"I mean it." Cade ignored her wry tone as he came closer still, looking her over from head to toe in a way that made her senses sizzle. "Your hair is kind of damp in places. You've got mud and leaf stains on your dress. It's also ripped." He stepped behind her and ran a hand from the nape of her neck across one shoulder blade, moving her veil gently aside. Contrasting with the tantalizing heat of his fingers was the assault of cool, air-conditioned air. "And—oh God—you're bleeding!"

"What?" Laurel started, as much from his touch as from his declaration.

"Your back," Cade continued, his low voice laced with concern. "It looks like you got scratched by some thorns." He moved in for a closer look, his breath tickling her spine like a ghost. Again his fingers ran lightly over her skin as he plucked at the ripped fabric. "Don't you feel that?"

You better believe she was aware of his touch, Laurel thought. Even more so now than when he had been helping her into her wedding gown. "Yes."

Cade frowned and stepped in front of her again. "Better get that cleaned up," he told her soberly. "It could become infected."

"Good idea," Laurel replied dryly, "except I don't think I can reach it."

"I'll do it for you," he offered, the picture of lazy male assurance.

Determined not to let him see how much his nearness was affecting her, Laurel lifted an insouciant brow. "No way."

He straightened, his eyes holding hers. "I'm not trying to seduce you."

"Good." Laurel ignored the shimmer of sexual attraction between them. "'Cause there's no way in hell that is going to happen." She was much too smart to let her heart be broken by this business-minded man.

"Just so we're clear," he teased, moving closer still.

"You bet we are." She glanced away. "I don't have anything to change into. I left my bridesmaid dress at the church."

Cade shrugged. "I'll find something for you to wear."

She let her eyes rove over his tall, solidly built frame and powerful shoulders. "That ought to be interesting."

His smile guaranteed it would. "Want me to unbutton you?"

He was close enough she could feel his body heat and breathe in the brisk, masculine fragrance of his cologne. "Only because I can't do it myself."

Once again, she felt his nimble fingers moving efficiently down her back. No one could say he wasn't experienced in undressing a lady, she thought. He unhooked and unbuttoned like a pro.

Finished, he led the way to the stairs. "I'll show you to a guest room and bath upstairs."

Laurel swept after Cade, aware her dress was gaping down her back. Realizing too late that they should have waited to undo it until she got the clothes she was going to change into, she followed him, holding the front of her dress to her chest with the palm of her hand. That worked fine until she actually reached the sweeping stairs. Then her plentiful skirts, and the petticoats beneath, threatened to trip her. She paused on the first step and tried to gather the heavy satin with one hand while holding the front of her dress with the other.

Abruptly aware she wasn't right behind him any longer, Cade paused midway up the staircase. Seeing what the problem was, he dashed back down to her side. "Trouble with the dress?"

"Obviously."

Cade's eyes twinkled mischievously. "Want to go ahead and take it off here?"

Damn, but this man had earned every bit of his let's-get-right-down-to-business reputation. "You wish."

He waggled his brows in comic fashion. "I'll give you my jacket to throw on."

At Cade's unabashedly frank look, Laurel felt herself blush to the roots of her hair. "You *really* wish."

"All right then. Since you give me no other choice." He came all the way back to the landing. Before she could draw a breath, he had one arm beneath her knees, the other circling her spine. The next thing Laurel knew she was being swept up in his arms and held against his chest. "We'll do it this way then," Cade said.

She wreathed one arm around his neck and held on to the front of her dress with the other. "Must you always make things so difficult?" she asked, not sure when she had felt quite so vulnerable and excited all at once.

"See, there's where we differ." Cade carried her as if she—and the wedding dress—were light as a feather. "To me, this seems like the easy way." He reached the top of the stairs.

Laurel glowered at Cade as she struggled to get a handle on her soaring emotions. "You can put me down now."

Ignoring her request, Cade strode on down the long hall with bedrooms on either side.

Without warning, Laurel had an inkling what it would be like to really be Cade's wife, to wake up in his bed every morning, to lie in his arms every night. "Is something wrong with your hearing—or are you just trying to be annoying?" Maybe if she kept the banter going, she wouldn't think about the fact this was their wedding night. He was her husband. She was his wife.

A determined look on his face, Cade strode into a beautiful green-and-white guest room and set her down halfway between the bed and the door. "There you go."

"Thank you." Laurel swallowed.

She tried not to think how romantic this situation was, or could have been, she amended swiftly, if it were anything but the only means to Cade's inheritance.

"I'll get you something to wear."

While she waited for him to return, Laurel perched on the edge of the bed and looked around. Clearly, Cade hadn't taken her into his bedroom, a good sign that he intended to keep things on the up-and-up. There was simply no way he would have slept in a bedroom with feminine Queen Anne style furniture.

Several minutes later, she heard him whistling. Cade strode in, carrying a light blue dress shirt, a pair of gray jogging shorts and a first aid kit. He had removed his tuxedo jacket and cummerbund. His starched white shirt was open at the throat, his sleeves rolled up. The shadow of a beard lined his face. He looked sexy and in firm control of the situation. "How and where do you want to do this?"

Laurel's parents had often wondered how she got herself into such crazy predicaments. Right about now, she was wondering that herself.

"Here on the bed or in the bathroom?" Cade continued.

Laurel forced herself to stifle several obvious puns. There was enough sexual electricity between them without ratcheting it up another notch. "Bathroom," she said brightly, as if her mind weren't on all the hot possibilities that were never going to happen, anyway. If only because she was smart and self-protective enough not to let them.

She led the way into the luxuriously appointed bathroom, and couldn't help but groan as she caught a glimpse of herself in the mirror. Her tiara and veil were still slightly askew; her upswept hair was coming undone. The rain had caused her bangs and the tendrils of hair that framed her face and nape to curl every which way. There was a smudge of something that might have been mascara or mud across one temple. Her cheeks were pink, her eyes unmistakably aglow with excitement. She looked ripe for the taking, which was the last thing in the world she wanted to be. What was it her parents had said about not allowing herself to be taken advantage of anymore?

Cade plucked at the skirt of her gown. "You want to take this off first?" he asked.

And be seminaked in front of him once again? Laurel quickly took out the pins holding her tiara and veil in place; dropped them all on the bathroom counter and went back to holding her dress against her chest. "No."

Cade took spray-on antiseptic out of the first-aid kit, as well as a tube of antiobiotic cream. Laurel shut her eyes and suffered through the application of both, counting backwards from ten— in Spanish—all the while.

"I don't think there's a way to bandage it, unless we use long strips of gauze and tape," Cade said finally, jerking Laurel out of her self-imposed reverie. His fingers moved lightly over her shoulders once again. "But since it has stopped bleeding—"

"I'm sure it will be fine," she replied, ignoring the flutter of desire deep inside her. Suddenly, she was having trouble drawing air into her lungs. And from the look of it, so was he.

"Well," Cade said finally. "I better take care of Beast. I'm sure he has to go out again before I put him down for the night." His manner became purely social once more. "You need anything else?"

My equilibrium. "Just sleep. Thanks." Laurel gave him a brisk, purposeful smile that was every bit as counterfeit as the vows they had said.

Another pause. He brushed a lock of hair from her cheek, tucked it behind her ear, and this time made no effort at all to disguise the desire in his eyes as he gave her a slow, sexy smile. "Then I'll leave you to it," he said.

CADE WAITED AS LONG AS HE could the next morning, but when eleven o'clock came and Laurel still hadn't stirred, he knew he was going to have to wake her. He looked at Beast, who was sprawled on the sunroom floor. "What do you think, fella? Is she going to be a morning person? Probably not, or she'd already be awake."

Figuring what he had to tell Laurel might go easier if he brought her breakfast in bed, he headed for the kitchen, where he pulled out a tray and filled it with a glass of juice, a fresh cup of coffee and one of the cherry Danishes he and Beast had picked up on their morning walk to the corner bakery. For good measure, he added a small pitcher of cream, a sugar bowl and a rose from one of the bushes out front, tucking a copy of the *Dallas Daily News* under his arm. Beast followed him up the stairs, as eager to say good-morning to their guest as Cade was. He paused outside her door, knocked, and when there was no response, went on in.

Laurel was sprawled on her side. She had her head on one pillow, another clutched to her chest. She looked sweet and enticing, and so deeply asleep he hated to wake her.

As if sensing the presence of man and dog, she breathed deeply, shifted and ever so slowly opened her eyes, the simple act bringing more pleasure to Cade than he had ever imagined possible.

Not that he was here to fantasize about what it would be like to really make her his, since that clearly was not going to happen. "Beast and I brought you some breakfast," he said.

Laurel shoved the hair from her eyes and struggled to sit up. She had brushed her luxurious brown locks out the night before. They fell in soft, tousled waves to her shoulders. Cade waited until she was situated, then fitted the tray across her lap. Looking up at him, she yawned and rubbed the sleep from her eyes. "You didn't have to do this."

Cade watched her stir cream and three lumps of sugar in her coffee. He supposed there was no time like the present to lay it all out on the table. "Actually, I sort of did."

He waited until she glanced up before he continued matter-of-factly. "The family attorney called." A full day ahead of schedule, Cade thought. "He'll be here in forty-five minutes. He wants to speak to both of us about my inheritance."

Laurel's brow furrowed. "What does that have to do with me?" she asked curiously.

Exactly what Cade would like to know. Belatedly, he realized he hadn't thought the situation through as thoroughly as he should have. Had he done so, he would have realized going in that Texas was a community property state, and his inheritance was now part of that arrangement.

Not that he expected Laurel McCabe to take him to the cleaners. He did not see her as that kind of woman.

"I'm sure Roy Worley will tell us when he gets here. In the meantime, you should see these." Cade handed Laurel the lifestyle section. News of their hasty marriage was reported under the headline I Do, I Don't, I Do.

Laurel lifted a brow, then frowning, began to read the article aloud. "'Cade Dunnigan made Dallas history last night when he surprised guests there to see him marry oil heiress Mary Elena Ayers by announcing that marriage was off, and another one—to software company heiress Laurel McCabe—was on. No one even knew Laurel and Cade were dating, a guest at the nuptials said. Nor was there any indication that the father of the original bride, Lance Ayers, objected to the last-minute replacement. Although the father of the substitute bride, Sam McCabe, was plenty unhappy. And it's easy to see why. Rumor has it Cade Dunnigan only married Laurel McCabe to get his hands on his family money.'"

Laurel stopped reading and put the paper down. She swore softly. "My parents are going to flip when they read this."

"That may be why the cell phone in your purse has been going off all morning long."

"I take it you didn't answer it?"

Cade shook his head. He wasn't touching that with a ten-foot pole.

"Good." Laurel breathed a sigh of relief. "Because whatever they have to say, I don't want to hear it."

In her position, Cade probably wouldn't, either.

In retrospect, he realized there was a lot he hadn't considered when he had pressured Laurel into marrying him the evening before. Fortunately, theirs wasn't a union that was going to last any longer than necessary.

"WHAT DO YOU MEAN, there are further stipulations to the terms of my inheritance?" Cade asked Roy Worley half an hour later, as the three of them gathered in the living room.

There had been no time to drive Laurel to her Dallas apartment to pick up more clothing, so she was still wearing his shirt, fresh from the dry cleaners, and the jogging shorts that showed off her long, spectacular legs. Cade was dressed casually, too, in shorts and a T-shirt. Roy Worley was wearing a golf shirt and slacks.

"Shouldn't I have known about this when the will was read five years ago?" Cade continued, disturbed.

"I'm going to let your father tell you his reasons in his own words." Roy took a videotape out of his suitcase.

Cade popped it into the machine and hit Play. Seconds later, his father appeared on the screen, bigger than life, as commanding, wily and strong-willed as ever. "I imagine you have a lot of questions, Cade. So here goes. I left you controlling interest in Dunnigan Dog Food because I think you are best equipped to run it and take the company into the new millennium," Donald Dunnigan began. "I insisted you be married in order to receive your inheritance because I think every one of us, Cade, is meant to be with a certain someone. Just as your mother and I were meant to be together. I also think that our three divorces and four marriages shook your faith in the institution of marriage, and made you think that matrimony might not be worth it after all. Well, I'm here to tell you that it is."

His father cleared his throat before continuing. "Your mother's and my mistake was splitting up every time the going got hard, and then letting our pride keep us apart, until we came to our senses once again and remarried. I want you to avoid this pitfall, Cade, and go the distance the way your mother and I should have. Therefore, I am stipulating that you will retain your inheritance only if you stay married to your new bride for a period of the next thirty-three years. Your mother and I figure if you hang in there that long, you'll want to stay together, and tackle every problem or challenge that comes your way together, as she and I should have. Should you choose not to do this, or even embark on anything approaching a sham marriage, then the shares I am willing to you will revert to the company and be divided equally among the nonfamily board members. Hence, you will no longer have control of the company your grandfather and I built."

Donald Dunnigan paused. "I imagine you're very unhappy with me now, Cade. That's okay. It'll pass as soon as you realize how valuable a real and lasting marriage is. So, good luck, son. Your mother and I love you very much and always will."

The screen went black.

Aware the blood had drained from his face, Cade glowered at Roy Worley. "Tell me this is a joke," he demanded grimly.

Roy shook his head. "It's no joke."

Cade looked at Laurel. She was so silent and pale that Beast went over to lie at her feet and look up at her in concern.

"Why didn't you tell me this?" Cade asked the family attorney furiously.

"Because I couldn't," Roy said. "Your father left very strict instructions. I followed them to the letter."

His emotions in turmoil, Cade shoved both hands through his hair. "Why would he do something like this?" But even as he spoke, he knew.

"Your father was afraid you would marry just to get the money, and then just as quickly divorce. Given what happened yesterday, your father didn't appear to be that far off in his prediction."

"There must be some way around it," Cade said desperately.

Roy Worley shook his head. "I assure you there isn't. Your father's will is iron-clad, Cade. I don't know what the two of you were thinking when you went into this hasty union last night, but if you want to retain your inheritance, you two better get serious about this marriage, and fast."

Chapter Four

Laurel thought her life had been out-of-control crazy the evening before. That was nothing compared to the way she felt now. "I can't stay married to you for thirty-three years!" she told Cade furiously as soon as Roy Worley had left. She glared at him suspiciously. "Is this why Mary Elena took off? Because she got wind of this condition to your inheritance?"

"I didn't know, so there's no way Mary Elena could have." Cade drew a breath, shook his head in stunned defeat. "Thirty-three years," he repeated in disbelief.

"I wish I had known this before you talked me into walking down the aisle with you," Laurel fumed.

"That makes two of us," he retored.

"Because there is no way I'm pretending to be your wife for anywhere near that long." Laurel flashed him a tight, mocking smile meant to put him in his place. "So you better get used to living on less." She started to storm past.

Cade clamped a hand on her shoulder and hauled her back in front of him. Simmering with frustration, he gave her a narrow glance. With his shock fading, he marshaled his resolve. "It's not that simple," he told her soberly.

Laurel looked around. Clearly, he was used to the finer things in life. The house was luxurious to a fault. "I'm sure you will find a way," she told him sweetly.

A new worried light came into his gray eyes. "If it were just me, sure, but…" He swore as he looked out the front window.

Curious, Laurel moved to his side and saw four limousines pulling up at the curb, one after another. This couldn't be good. "What's going on now?" she asked, bracing for the worst.

"It looks as if we're about to be paid a visit from the DDF board of directors." Cade frowned as his uncle George got out of one limousine, followed by George Jr. Next came Mary Elena's father, Lance Ayers. Then two more people Laurel vaguely recalled seeing at the wedding, but had not met. All five of them had very serious looks on their faces.

"Not 'we,'" Laurel corrected. Stubbornly, she kept her eyes locked with his, even as she stepped away. *"You."*

"Not me," Cade countered, challenging her all the more. He stepped closer, his tall strong body exuding so much heat he could have started a prairie fire all on his own. *"Us."*

Laurel angled a thumb at the center of her chest. She couldn't let herself get drawn into this pretend marriage, emotionally or intellectually. Especially when she knew how physically attracted she was to him! To do so was just asking for trouble. And trouble was something she did not need. "Listen up, hotshot," she snapped defiantly, "I don't have anything to do with your family's company."

"You do now that you're my wife," Cade vowed, advancing on her so deliberately and methodically he took her breath away. "Help me out here, Laurel, and follow my lead. I promise I'll more than make it up to you."

"By—?" Laurel questioned, telling herself she had not just stumbled into a lion's den.

Cade shrugged and kept his eyes locked with hers. "We'll figure that out later."

"It's not much in the way of promises," she taunted.

"It's the best I can do right now," he told her in a flat, businesslike tone.

Which was exactly why Laurel knew she should reject Cade's offer. And would have if it hadn't been for the raw desperation in his eyes. She knew how it felt to have your back against the wall. To have everyone close to you watching, waiting, for you to fail. She didn't want that to happen to her, and she didn't want it to happen to Cade, either.

Not that his problems were hers, temporary marriage or no. Still…

She had always been a sucker for the underdog.

A fact that had always, without fail, gotten her into more trouble than she could handle…especially now.

"Are you going to help me or not?" Cade demanded impatiently.

Laurel knew she shouldn't.

"Fine, I'll help you," she said, caving in impulsively. She tossed her head and gave Cade a scathing once-over. "But you will pay," she vowed. "For using me this way."

He flashed her a mischievous grin, the picture of masculine relief. "I don't doubt that for a second."

It would have helped Laurel's ego had he seemed the least bit apprehensive about that, instead of looking as if he were relishing the chance to go toe-to-toe with her in a battle of wits and wills.

"Remember," Cade told her with a smoldering glance just before he opened the door, "we're newlyweds."

What the heck was that supposed to mean? Laurel wondered, clueless as to what Cade Dunnigan actually expected from her.

"SORRY TO INTERRUPT YOUR…uh…honeymoon," George Dunnigan Sr. stated gruffly as he walked into Cade's mansion.

Cade imagined that was true. If there was one thing his uncle liked to avoid it was uncomfortable family situations. Hence, George Sr.'s inability to deal with his only son's laziness and greed.

"If you can call it that." George Jr. flashed a disagreeable smile that indicated he couldn't wait to push Cade out of the CEO slot and assume the helm of DDF himself. A move that would soon be possible if the other board members of the privately held company backed Cade's cousin in the upcoming leadership vote instead of him.

"I must say," Dotty Yost complained as she handed a videotape to Cade. "I have never seen such a hullabaloo about anyone's romantic mistake." As usual, the petite sixty-something woman was wearing a flowered rayon dress and heels. A strand of pearls encircled her neck. A big hat, with flowers on the brim, covered her short, silvery gray curls.

Harvey Lemmon came in next. The tall, rangy, seventy-something man with thinning blond hair wore the same suit he had for the last ten years, not because he couldn't afford a new one, but because he hated to spend money on anything he didn't really "need." Harvey had made his fortune in dollar stores—he owned thirty in the Dallas–Fort Worth area alone. Another two hundred fifty were spread out over Texas. Harvey was always concerned about pinching pennies.

Last in the door was Lance Ayers. The retired oilman and father of the bride who had bolted before the nuptials could take place looked calmer than he had the evening before, but no less concerned about everything that had happened since. He was a bottom line guy, Cade knew. At the end of the day, Lance wanted to know he had made a substantial profit on whatever business deal he was involved in. He didn't much care how he got to that bottom line.

Aware Laurel hadn't yet met everyone in the room, Cade paused to make introductions, then guided everyone to the formal living room.

"I know we agreed to meet on Monday, but given the amount of publicity your last minute exchange of brides caused, we all felt we should meet today," Lance told Cade as he took a seat in one of the Louis XV-inspired chairs.

"It was in the newspapers, and on the TV news last night, too." Dotty handed over the videotape she had brought with her, before she took a seat on the brocade sofa. "I'm worried about lawsuits."

"From whom?" Cade asked, not all that surprised. Dotty's late husband had been an attorney with a reputation for suing anything that moved. That was how he had made his fortune. Consequently, Dotty was always worried about getting sued herself.

Lance looked at Dotty. "My daughter and I have no desire to sue anyone," he assured the only woman on the DDF board of directors firmly.

Harvey handed over the newspapers. "I'm worried the impact all this bad publicity will have on our bottom line. If there's a boycott of Dunnigan Dog Food we could be in trouble."

No kidding, Cade thought.

"Why would anyone boycott Dunnigan products?" Laurel asked curiously, as she sat down next to Cade.

"Because women buy dog food and might not like the idea of Cade substituting one woman for another, as if they were different colored socks or something," Uncle George explained kindly.

"Face it, cuz," George Jr. interjected snidely, his innate nastiness coming to the fore, "your hasty marriage has brought DDF into the limelight in a most unflattering way."

"Temporarily," Cade said, slipping his arm around Laurel's waist. He noted with relief she did not pull away from him, as she would have had every right to do, but instead leaned into him as cozily as any newlywed would be expected to. "My wife and I intend to fix that."

"How?" Dotty said, relaxing slightly.

Cade looked each board member in the eye. "By settling down to a quiet life and working hard to bring DDF into the future as the thriving, growing company we all know it can be."

"Does that mean you're still planning to go ahead with the opening of the first DDF store in two weeks?" Uncle George asked skeptically.

"Absolutely," Cade replied.

"Are you sure that's wise?" George Jr. demanded. "Given all that's happened in the past twenty-four hours, maybe you should put it off indefinitely, Cade."

Cade knew his cousin would like nothing more than for him to fail.

"I can't do that," he explained patiently. "The space for the flagship store has already been leased, interior work is under way. It would be a huge drain on company finances if we were to back out now."

"Then maybe you should put someone else at the helm, to deal with reporters during the publicity blitz," Uncle George suggested.

Cade knew exactly whom his uncle had in mind. "I'm not stepping down as acting CEO," he said firmly. "Nor will I do anything else that will make it look as if our company is in turmoil. We'll vote for permanent CEO the day after the opening of the flagship store, as scheduled. Until then, you all will have time to think about it and decide if you want me at the helm."

Cade spent more time calming everyone down, promising they would meet at the regularly scheduled weekly meeting on Monday afternoon, then showed them the door.

"Thanks for backing me up," he told Laurel after everyone had departed. "There's a lot at stake here."

She lifted a brow and sent him a sharp, skeptical look, but all it did was intrigue him. "For me, too," she pointed out quietly.

Once more, Cade was flooded with guilt for having pulled Laurel into this. The awkward silence lengthened as they gazed at each other. "If there were any other way—" he began apologetically.

"Why isn't there?" she interrupted. Even more fire came into her eyes, making her look simultaneously sexy and unapproachable as hell.

Cade slid his hands in the back pockets of his cargo shorts. He did not want her to walk out on him. Aware his insides were twisting like a pretzel, he watched the color climb in her cheeks again. "Because Dunnigan Dog Food is a privately owned company," he explained reluctantly, wishing he weren't in a position to have to beg for her cooperation, but that was exactly what he planned to do if necessary. The legacy left to him meant that much.

"Dotty Yost, Lance Ayers and Harvey Lemmon each own ten percent of the voting shares," Cade continued, pleased to see Laurel was listening intently. "My uncle George owns fifteen percent, his son, George Jr., another five percent, and I own twenty percent on my own. My dad left me thirty percent of the company on my thirtieth birthday—today—which, when combined with mine, controls one half of the company voting rights. I get to keep those shares as long as I remain married to you. If I am not married for the next thirty-three years, the voting shares from my father get spread among the three nonfamily members of the board."

Laurel studied him with care. "Why would that be such a bad thing?" she asked quietly.

She seemed to know instinctively, Cade realized, that he at least was not motivated by greed.

He moved closer. Deciding to lay all his cards out on the table—it was the only way he figured he could get Laurel's trust—he admitted sorrowfully, "Because Dunnigan Dog Food has been losing market share for the last ten years. As is, we can't compete with the advertising budgets of the big brands. If I don't turn things around—soon—the company my grandfather started, and my father grew, will eventually become extinct. I don't want to see that happen."

Laurel spread her hands wide. "You don't think everyone else who was just here feels the same way?"

Cade sighed, wishing like hell that were the case. He walked back into the living room and began collecting the coffee cups and soda glasses their guests had left behind. "Harvey, Dotty and Lance will do whatever they think will earn them the most money, including sell out to a competitor. Same for Uncle George and George Jr. I'm the only one who is putting my heart and soul into this. The only one who believes that Dunnigan Dog Care Centers could be 'the place' for dogs everywhere, if only we can get our flagship store up and running."

Cade was willing to do whatever was necessary to achieve that goal. "If I can prove my ideas are sound, and show enough profit and income potential in the first store, then I think I can get Dotty, Lance and Harvey to vote with me, to continue expanding the company. If not, then I'll sell this place and try and buy them out, using the profits from this house. But that's going to take time, Laurel. And time is what I'm asking you to give to me."

"You're right," Laurel said with a sympathetic sigh as they carried the dishes to the kitchen. "There is a lot more to this situation than I realized."

The sound of another car door opening and shutting in the drive had Beast bounding off his dog cushion. He let out a resounding bark and trotted over to the front door. "Now what?"

Cade muttered, as the two of them returned to the foyer, glanced out the front windows and saw a tall, fit man with the same color hair as Laurel's getting out of a battered pickup truck.

She groaned. "You know him?" Cade asked.

Laurel nodded. "That," she said with a beleaguered sigh, "is my oldest brother, Will."

"WHY HAVEN'T YOU BEEN answering your cell phone?" Will demanded, blunt as ever.

Laurel sighed. Will's eighteen year stint as a navy fighter pilot had made him tough as nails. Her oldest sibling practically oozed discipline. His failed marriage—undertaken hastily when Will was about her age—had broken his heart. And although his success as owner of an exclusive charter jet service had made Will a wealthy and very eligible man, he showed no signs of settling down again anytime soon. Probably because, Laurel figured, he was as afraid of making another mistake and getting his heart stomped on again as she was.

"Because I didn't want to talk to anyone in the family," Laurel said.

Will folded his arms in front of him. "I can see why you'd be embarrassed. That was some stunt you pulled last night. However, it did accomplish one thing."

Laurel braced herself for the next assault. "And what would that be?" she asked sweetly.

"Your marriage got Mom and Dad to back off—at least for the moment." Will towered over her, disapproval etched on his ruggedly handsome face. "That doesn't mean, however, that the rest of us agree with what you're doing, little sister. You should have had better sense than to take this dude up on his offer regardless of the inheritance he was waving beneath your nose. But no matter. What's done is done. For the moment, anyway. We have to soldier on. Sooner or later we all make fools of ourselves."

"Is that what you think I've done?" Laurel regarded him incredulously. She didn't know whether to deck him or simply show him the door. "Made a fool of myself—in front of every-one—for money?"

Will shrugged. "I don't know what else you'd call it, stepping in for the runaway bride that way. Fortunately, the damage done to your reputation is not irreparable. There's still time to turn the whole sordid tale into some sort of publicity stunt on Cade's be-half. For instance, you-all could say he was striking a blow for jilted bridegrooms everywhere when he married you that way."

"Interesting angle," Cade said, rubbing his jaw in a thoughtful manner. To Laurel's frustration, he looked as if he respected her brother. "I hadn't thought of approaching it that way," he murmured.

Laurel's temper flared. "Don't you dare side with my family!"

Cade shrugged. He and Will exchanged man-to-man looks that were both thoughtful and considering. "Well, sooner or later, you are going to need a way out of this mess I got you into," Cade said practically, turning his attention back to Laurel. "And if we could do it with your reputation intact, so much the better."

Laurel didn't mind when Cade acted passionately. Being driven by your feelings was something she not only understood but had personally experienced. Being manipulated as a means to a desired end was something else entirely. She batted her eye-lashes at Cade coquettishly, then pretended to swoon. "You're so much more gallant than I would have expected."

Ignoring Laurel's sarcasm, he turned back to Will. "I never meant to put Laurel in such a difficult situation," he said. "Had it not been for my midnight deadline—"

"Let's not forget your stubborn insistence on holding me to my promise," she interrupted, stepping between the two men.

"You mean you agreed to marry him before yesterday even-ing?" Will said.

Laurel flushed. She saw no way out of her verbal mess except to admit, "We knew there might be trouble Friday evening. I thought—erroneously, I now see—that I could help avert it, but I promised Cade I'd marry him if Mary Elena failed to show up at the church. And since I had given my word…I followed through."

Will studied her. Promises made—and kept, come hell or

high water—were something else he understood, and respected. "Did you tell Mom and Dad that?" he asked kindly.

Laurel sighed and pushed her fingers through her hair. "Let's just say Mom and Dad weren't of a mind to listen to anything I had to say last night. I expect that is still true today."

Her brother nodded agreeably. "I can't say they're exactly happy with you right now."

Laurel rolled her eyes. "No joke."

"But Riley, Brad, Lewis, Kevin and I all told them you'd come to your senses as soon as you settled down."

Laurel felt her temper spark once again. "What did you do? Have a family meeting about me?" She did a double take when no denial followed. "How could you?"

Will shrugged. "We had to decide what to do."

Resentment swept through Laurel, making her want to avoid not just Will but her entire clan. "The McCabes always circle the wagons, right?"

"We love you, Laurel."

"You just don't trust me to make sound judgments," she deduced bitterly.

Will sighed. "You have to admit some of your decisions up to now have been…suspect."

Without warning, Cade wrapped his arm around Laurel's waist and he eased her against him protectively. "I know we just got married," he murmured dryly, "but if you want me to punch him in the nose for you, just say the word."

Laurel leaned against him gratefully. "I'll kick him in the shin myself if it comes to that," she muttered. Glad to have someone on her side, for once, she continued meaningfully, "Fortunately for all of us, it's not going to come to that, since Will is leaving now."

Her brother straightened his spine, looking every bit the ex-military man he was. "I'll be glad to go if you come with me, Laurel."

She tossed her head indignantly. "I'm not going anywhere with you, Will, or anyone else in the family," she announced haughtily. "So I'd appreciate it if you passed that word along." Out of the corner of her eye she saw Cade smile.

"You can't seriously be thinking of continuing on with this farce!" Will exclaimed.

"Why not?" she retorted. "Cade already asked me to stay on for the next thirty-three years."

"You don't love him!" Will thundered, obviously upset.

"So?" she countered, unconcerned—at least for the moment. "Not every marriage is based on love."

"Fine." Her brother threw up his hands. "You can talk to Dad about this when you show up for work tomorrow."

Suddenly, that really did not seem like a good idea. "I'm not going to be working for McCabe Software Solutions," Laurel decided. Unable to help herself, she continued impulsively, "I'm going to be helping Cade with the Dunnigan Dog Food business."

"You're going to work for him?" Will asked, incredulous.

To her relief, Cade only pulled her closer to his side. "Yes," he said, without batting an eye. "In fact, Laurel starts first thing tomorrow morning."

Will scowled. "Doing what?"

"Assisting me," Cade stated.

Her brother shook his head. "Dad is going to be very unhappy with you," he predicted grimly.

"It won't be the first time." Deciding too much had been said and decided upon without due thought already, Laurel pushed him toward the door. "Give everyone my regards," she said cheerfully.

Will shook his head, looked at Cade. "You better treat her well, or I promise you, you'll be facing the wrath of all the McCabes."

"AND I THOUGHT MY relationship with my family could be aggravating at times," Cade said as soon as they were alone again.

Laurel ducked her head in embarrassment. She glided away from him. "Sorry you had to witness that."

"No problem." He tore his gaze from her sensational legs, figuring it was time this conversation took another tack. "You put up with the visit from the board of directors this afternoon." He shrugged as she swung around to face him once again. "I figure it's only fair I do the same for you."

Laurel raked her teeth across of her lower lip. The fragrance of her hair and skin filled his senses. "Did you mean what you said about me working at your company?" she asked, looking perplexed.

Cade shrugged, unable to think of anything at that moment that he would like more. "It's up to you, of course," he told her casually, "but frankly, with the grand opening of the flagship store coming up, I could use the help. Plus, your presence at DDF would go a long way toward showing the board of directors that you and I are serious about making this marriage work for however long we need it to do so."

Just that quickly, some of the light left Laurel's blue eyes. Looking eager to get out of there—and away from him?—she shoved her bangs to one side. "Do you have a car I could borrow? I need to go to my apartment and get some of my stuff."

Cade imagined she would want to get out of his clothes, even if she did look spectacular in yet another of his starched shirts, with the sleeves rolled up to her elbows and the first two buttons undone. She'd cinched his navy athletic shorts tight around her waist, and though they came to midthigh on her, they still exposed plenty of showgirl-perfect leg. The only shoes she had with her were the evening sandals she'd worn at the wedding the night before.

He watched as she bent down to slip off the slouchy sweat socks she had borrowed from him, and put on her sandals again. It was all he could do to swallow, and his voice was hoarse as he told her, "You can take your pick of vehicles." He led her to the garage, which housed a Porsche, a Land Rover and a Mercedes. "Just don't lend it out to anyone, okay?"

Her eyes glinted in response to his teasing tone. "I'll try not to," she responded just as drolly, then paused to study the selection. "I'd like the sedan."

Just what he had figured she'd want, Cade thought. He handed her a set of keys to the Mercedes. As their fingers touched and he felt the softness of her skin once again, a jolt of desire swept through him. Had they not been married, had he not needed her cooperation so badly, he would have used the opportunity to pull Laurel into his arms and kiss her again. Slowly. Patiently. But knowing he couldn't afford to mess up their tenuous agreement with an ardent impulse, he curtailed his need to hold her in his arms once again and see where the passion simmering between them led. There would be time for exploration later, after he was made permanent CEO of DDF.

"So, what are you going to do while I'm gone?" she asked casually, slinging her evening purse over her arm as she headed for the foyer. When she turned to look at him, the soft edges of her lips turned up in a slight smile.

His heart warming at the sight of her, Cade followed his "wife" as far as the front door. "I'm going to get back to work. We've got a lot to do in the next two weeks."

Laurel nodded and breezed out the door.

With Beast at his side, Cade watched her drive away. Then forced his thoughts back to the pressing business at hand. He went to his study, sat down at his desk and picked up a notepad and pen. As he began to organize his thoughts, he wrote out the to-do list that was part of every effective executive's life. As usual, he divided the tasks between the work and personal areas of his life, concentrating first and foremost on the company his family had founded. Before long he had six items on his list of tasks to be completed.

DAMAGE CONTROL—BUSINESS

1) Sell the marriage—media, community, family, friends.

2) Host dinner for board members. Restaurant?

3) Continue with plans for flagship store.

4) Grand opening of flagship store.

5) Board vote on new CEO.

6) Get board to approve my plans for business expansion.

His thoughts about work organized, Cade turned to his personal agenda and started writing a list of six items for that, too.

DAMAGE CONTROL—MARRIAGE
1) Move Laurel into the house.
2) Speak with Laurel's parents, Sam and Kate McCabe.
3) Convince Laurel to assist with the dinner for board members.
4) Work out the sexual aspects of the relationship…
5)
6)

Try as he might, Cade could not fill in the last two items on the list. Besides making peace with Laurel's family, putting on a united front for everyone else that would make them both appear reliable and trustworthy, and deciding whether they were going to sleep together or not he couldn't think of anything else he needed to do. He stared at the list a little while longer, then decided the heck with it. Business beckoned, and it was a call he could not ignore.

Chapter Five

Beast was waiting at the front door when Laurel got back several hours later. The Mercedes sedan she had borrowed from Cade was stuffed to the roof with everything she figured she would need during the next few weeks. Laurel carried in her suitcase and purse and set them down in the foyer. Tail wagging, Beast came over to check out both items.

"Hey, fella." She petted his silky black head, grinning when he licked her bare knee in greeting. "Mmm. Doggie kisses." Beast licked her knee again, then sat back on his haunches and looked up at her expectantly.

"So where's your master?" She didn't hear anything—the house was so still it was echoing. "I hope Cade's around, because otherwise I am going to have to carry all that gear in by myself."

At the mention of Cade's name, Beast jumped up again, inclining his head at Laurel as if urging her to follow.

"Are you going to help me find Cade?" she murmured when the big Labrador trotted purposefully through the hall that ran the length of the house, through the kitchen and the sunroom to the French doors overlooking a beautifully landscaped swimming pool.

"Ah, you want to go out, don't you," Laurel noted. She opened the door. Beast loped across the cement patio to the edge of the pool. He barked again, letting Cade know they had company.

Cade stopped swimming midlap and glanced toward Laurel,

then changed direction and swam across the width of the pool to her. He stopped at the edge and stood up in the four-foot-deep water, revealing magnificent chest and shoulder muscles. He wore swimmer's goggles and pushed them up on his head. "Get everything you needed?" he asked.

Trying not to be distracted by his powerful build, she nodded and admitted cheerfully, "Enough to hold me until we get this mess sorted out." Damn, the man was buff! And from what she could see beneath the shimmering surface of the water, those swimming trunks he had on didn't hide much. Her imagination was going wild.

"Want me to help you carry it in?" he asked.

Oh, my. Was it hot out here or what? Barely able to keep from fanning herself, Laurel smiled. Suddenly, enlisting Cade's help did not seem like such a wonderful idea, not when she was feeling so hot and bothered. She wrinkled her nose and let him off the hook. "You're busy."

"And you're my wife," he replied with easy cameraderie. "What kind of husband would I be if I weren't a gentleman?" He climbed out of the pool, water streaming from his body.

Laurel immediately realized two things. Her "husband" was every bit as fit and muscled in his lower half as he was above the waist. His sleek black nylon racing trunks hugged him like a lover and demonstrated just how incredibly well-endowed he was. Talk about too much information, Laurel thought, flushing and turning her glance away as he toweled off his long, solid body with brisk strokes. She was going to be dreaming about this for days—and nights—to come!

"So you swim a lot, obviously," she observed inanely.

Cade slanted her a curious look. "How do you know that?"

"Um…the way you moved in the water. Plus I think Mary Elena might have mentioned something about you going through University of Texas on a swimming scholarship."

He regarded her like a genial host. "Do you swim?"

Aware she could very easily make a fool of herself if she didn't get a grip, Laurel forced her voice to take on an oh-so-casual tone. "I work out on an elliptical trainer. Or I did." She frowned, wondering how she was going to work off this surge of Cade-induced adrenaline. "I guess I'll have to find something else to do to stay fit now that I'm here." She paused, aware she hadn't seen the entire house yet. "Unless you have one?"

"Actually, we do," he drawled. "I'll show you where the work-out room is, after we carry your stuff up." He wrapped the towel around his hips and slid his feet into beach shoes. "Car in the drive?"

Laurel nodded.

Pretending not to be the least bit turned on by his stunning physique, she led the way. Beast trotted along next to them, tail wagging. Cade stopped when he saw the packed interior of the car. He had the same look on his face that her father and brothers used to have when they moved her into Jester dormitory. "It looks like more than it is," Laurel said hastily.

To his credit, Cade recovered quickly. "I'm sure we'll get it done in no time," he said, taking the first of what looked like a dozen armloads. He waited for her to fill her arms, too. "But first things first. You have to choose a bedroom."

A task easier said than done, Laurel soon realized. The upstairs had seven bedrooms aside from his, each with its own bathroom. "Wow, they're all so different," Laurel observed, bypassing the Asian-inspired, over-the top Victorian and cool contemporary design schemes for a cozy cottage-style bedroom at the far end of the hall. It had white furniture and sunny yellow-and-white linens that immediately brightened her mood.

"My mom was really into decorating." Cade carried his arm-load of clothing in and hung it in the generous closet. He watched as Laurel did the same. "Aside from my father, that was my mother's one true passion, and one she stuck with a little more regularly than she did her marriage."

Laurel caught the note of hurt in his wry tone. She searched his face. "Your dad was right, wasn't he? On the videotape? Your parents' constant drama did affect you." It had made him guarded. Cynical. Unwilling, she feared, to emotionally commit.

Cade shrugged. "It made me realize feelings like that are best contained," he told her practically.

Laurel didn't think so. But then, she'd always had the model of her parents' enduring, happy marriage to follow.

"If my folks had run their relationship like a business," Cade concluded firmly, "they would have been a lot happier."

Well, that explained why he had gotten engaged to Mary Elena the way he had, Laurel thought. And it also revealed why he was willing to stay married to her. Cade didn't want any more than what they had right now. An agreement with no emotional involvement, no real risk to their hearts. And maybe, she thought to herself sagely, that was what she should expect to get out of this, too.

FORTY-FIVE MINUTES LATER, Laurel's suite was cluttered with clothes and belongings yet to be put away. Her stomach growled, reminding her she hadn't eaten in hours. With Beast at her heels, she went in search of her husband. He was dressed again—in shorts, a loose-fitting, tropical-print shirt, and deck shoes befitting the warm April evening. He had showered after his swim, and the fragrance of soap and shampoo mingled with the masculine fragrance unique to him. He looked tan, fit and sexy, sitting behind the carved mahogany desk in his study. Without warning, she felt her heart flutter again.

Laurel swallowed. Get a grip! "Um…Cade? About dinner…"

He gave a careless wave without bothering to look up. "You go ahead."

Laurel slid her hands in her pockets of her capri pants and ventured a little closer. Wearing her own clothes again gave her confidence. Made her feel more in control of the situation. And if they were going to live here together, they needed to work out some sort of system to coexist comfortably. Trying to avoid each other, pretend they weren't sharing space, was not the way to success. She tried again. "You want me to cook?" They might not be a couple in the normal sense, but they could at least break bread together when they both happened to be here at mealtime.

This time Cade did look up. Frustration etched his handsome face. "Do whatever you want. I'm going to be working."

Laurel got it.

Except…

"Cade, it's your birthday. We should really do something to mark the day."

He stopped typing on his keyboard and rocked back in the chair. "I think we did do something to mark the day—last night—when we got married in the nick of time," he drawled. Then, seeing her concern, he stopped joking around and continued softly, "Seriously, I'm fine. I just want to work tonight. You could do me a favor, though."

"Sure." Laurel figured since he was giving her a place to live, a car to drive and a temporary job, she could help him out.

"Order us some dinner." Cade moved his glance away from her once again.

As long as he didn't consider her a servant slash wife, she amended silently to herself. "What would you like?" Laurel asked.

Cade was still totally mesmerized by the document on his computer screen. "Anything. Doesn't matter."

"Chinese? Greek? Tex-Mex? Italian? Barbecue?"

"Kung Pao chicken and an order of spring rolls."

At last, a decision. "White or brown rice?" Laurel asked.

"Both. There are delivery service menus in the kitchen, in the drawer next to the phone." With a distracted look on his face, Cade plucked his wallet out of his back pocket, opened it up and handed over several one hundred dollar bills before turning back to his work. "This should cover it."

No kidding, Laurel thought as she took the money off the edge of the desk. "Am I buying for the week or just tonight?" she asked dryly. His attitude about a lot of things only confirmed her idea that they lived in different universes.

"Tonight. We'll get something for tomorrow night tomorrow."

Laurel figured Cade would come out of his study long enough to eat with her, especially since the aroma of the food she had ordered was amazing. She was wrong. He just nodded his thanks when she told him dinner was there, and told her to go ahead without him.

Beast, however, was only too happy to follow her to the kitchen. Laurel saw the food and water dishes in the corner. The pantry held a large metal bin, with a sack of Dunnigan Lite large-breed dog food inside. She poured a scoop into his dish and added clean water to his bowl, before settling down with her container of Mongolian beef. "So this is what it's going to be like, huh, bud?" she murmured, chin in hand.

Beast thumped his tail in acknowledgment.

Laurel sighed. She had worried about the physical and emotional intimacy of sharing space with a man she barely knew. What a laugh! This was going to be worse than living alone. Much worse.

CADE HAD FIGURED HE was prepared to have Laurel living in the same house as him, just as he had been braced to have Mary Elena around. However, he had not expected to have this immediate physical and emotional reaction to Laurel. And after just thirty-six hours as man and wife, he was not quite sure what to do about it. It had been all he could do to stay in his study the afternoon and evening before. As for sleep…well, there hadn't been much of that. All he could think about was Laurel getting ready for the wedding, wearing his clothes, coming out by the pool, sauntering into his study…. Never mind the way she had kissed him back at the conclusion of the ceremony!

Of course, that had been his fault, for laying one on her in the first place. Just as this morning was his fault, Cade admitted readily, as he strode down the upstairs hall and stopped just short of her bedroom door. He should never have volunteered to give her a job, even if it had gotten her temporarily out of having to go to work for her father….

But he had done that, too.

So they were both going to have to live with it.

"Are you ready to go?" he asked her as she finished putting on her perfume. It was already seven-thirty, and he liked to be at the office by eight. "Or do you want to catch up with me later?"

"I'm ready." Shoes in one hand, purse in the other, she raced out her bedroom door looking every bit the dazzling beauty she was. And it wasn't just the feminine features of her face, the silky waves of her lustrous brown hair, her supple curves or her slender, petite frame. It was the way she moved, with such grace and energy. The way she smiled. The way, when she looked up at him, she really seemed to see him. When he was around her, even for a few minutes, he could feel his barriers lowering. Not good for someone trying like hell to keep things on an even keel emotionally. Cade didn't want the soaring highs and daunting lows that seemed to come with passion. He didn't want to feel much of anything, for this woman in his life. And yet it was happening.

He frowned and focused on what could be readily discussed: her rather inappropriate attire. "That's what you're wearing to work?"

Laurel blinked. "A sundress is not okay?"

It might be in less corporate, business-casual environment. The women at DDF headquarters wore discreetly tailored slacks or skirts and blouses. The men dressed like Cade, in starched shirts, slacks, loafers. Today he had on a tie and jacket because he had a board meeting later, but that was about as dressy as it got. Laurel looked as if she was going to a cotillion. Worse, the spaghetti straps of her pale yellow sundress with its fitted bodice and full, flaring skirt seemed just loose enough to slip off her shoulders from time to time. That might not be a problem had she not the prettiest arms and shoulders he had ever seen. It had been hard enough keeping his mind on business the day before, without having her constantly underfoot. He would just have to keep her busy.

"Do you want me to put a suit on?" Laurel asked, as she bent down to slip on ridiculously high-heeled sandals.

"Uh, no." Cade dragged his gaze away from her sexy calves and trim ankles. What was wrong with him? After all, he had seen women with great legs before. Women with a figure to die for.

Laurel moved so he had no choice but to look directly into her eyes. "Then what's the problem?" she demanded.

The problem, Cade thought to himself, *is that I desire you like*

I have never desired any woman before. And a desire that potent was dangerous. It could let him get off track, and that was something he couldn't afford to do right now, he reminded himself firmly. This marriage was a business arrangement, and a temporary one at that. Knowing he needed to tell her something, Cade said finally, "The high-rise we're housed in can get a little cold this time of year. You know how it is in big commercial buildings."

Laurel nodded, smiling at him with relief. "Right." She dashed back into her room, and came out with a lacy yellow cardigan the same shade as her dress. "Okay, I'm ready!" she said.

The question was, was he? Cade wondered as they headed down the stairs. Laurel was going to be one hell of a distraction during the upcoming business day.

Beast was lying on his cushion next to the stairs, where he would stay until they got home at suppertime to feed and care for him. Laurel and Cade said goodbye to him, then headed out to the garage.

"What am I going to do today?" she asked as she climbed into the passenger side of the Porsche.

Cade hedged. "I haven't exactly figured that out," he told her honestly, watching as she tucked her skirt around her and settled into the smooth leather seat. "In fact, if you've had a change of heart about actually working there, I'd understand."

Her reaction wasn't long in coming. Narrowing her eyes, she asked, "You don't think I could possibly be of any value at Dunnigan Dog Food, do you?"

He fitted the key in the ignition and turned to look over his shoulder as he backed the car out of the garage. "I don't even know what you do for a living."

She shrugged, all innocence. "I majored in business in college."

"And since?" Cade pressed.

Laurel hesitated, looking none too happy as she admitted, "I've worked for six companies in four years. Everything from business consulting to telemarketing and property appraisal."

Such broad experience could be a good or bad thing. "Why so many changes?" Cade asked curiously, heading up the entrance ramp to the expressway.

"I haven't found anything I like." She looked down at her lap and pleated the fabric of her skirt between her fingers. "And to be perfectly truthful, I keep getting fired because my personal life always ends up interfering with my professional duties."

This really did not sound good, Cade thought, as he carefully merged into the heavy traffic headed toward downtown Dallas. "Maybe you should take your dad up on his offer to work at McCabe Software Solutions."

The mutinous look was back on her face. "And hear a lecture every single day about why I should never have married you? I don't think so. Besides, I don't even like computers. Dogs, on the other hand, I do like."

"We don't have dogs at company headquarters, except Beast, occasionally, when I know I'm going to have a very long day. Then I take him with me so I can walk him in the park down the block. But otherwise…" Cade turned onto Commerce Street.

"We're getting off track here," Laurel complained, as he flashed the parking tag that allowed him to enter the garage without taking a ticket from the attendant on duty. "What exactly am I going to do today in terms of assisting you?"

Cade headed for his usual parking place, next to the elevators. "I'm not really sure yet." He eased into the space and turned off the ignition. "Maybe you can help out in the mailroom."

"You're kidding," Laurel said after they'd both emerged from the car. She studied his expression over the roof of the Porsche. "You're not kidding." Disappointment tinged her low voice.

Cade refused to back down. "It will give you a chance to get to know everyone," he explained.

To his relief, Laurel did not dispute the logic of that. Nor did she appear irked with him for not trusting her with anything important, thus far. They both knew his actions were justified. He literally did not know what she could do; it was up to her to show him. Then, he figured, they would see.

"How many people actually work here?" she asked as they entered the building.

Relieved to be able to talk facts and figures about the company he was so proud of, Cade said, "We employ three thousand people, one hundred of them here at headquarters."

Laurel stepped into the elevator ahead of him, her skirt swishing. "Will the board members be here?"

Cade drank in the sweet, floral fragrance of her perfume. "Later today."

"But not this morning?"

He punched the button and watched the door close. Trying not to think how intimate it felt to drive into work with her like this, he murmured casually, "George Jr. and George Sr. might. It depends if they have a golf date or not."

Laurel grasped the metal handrail when the elevator lurched upward. The small space was warmer than the outside air. Pretty color flushed her cheeks. "Do they have jobs?"

Cade thought about his grandfather's dream to have both his sons working for DDF and splitting the power, proceeds and work equitably, all the way down the line. Sadly, it hadn't come to fruition in his father's generation, and did not appear to be in his own, either. "George Jr. is supposed to be in charge of marketing."

Laurel studied Cade in a way that made *him* feel warmer. "I gather you don't think he's doing a good job," she murmured.

Glad they had the elevator to themselves—a rarity this time of morning—Cade nodded. "You gather right," he said grimly.

"Then why is he in that position?" Laurel pressed, more curious than ever.

The million dollar question. Cade offered a wry smile as the elevator slid to a halt. "Same reason you were almost working at McCabe Software Solutions today," he told her, struggling to keep the mood light, despite the fact that Laurel had quickly and effectively located the burr under his saddle. "Nepotism. My uncle George lobbied hard for my cousin to have the position, and my dad gave it to him. I won't be able to make any substantive changes in the executive staff until I am voted permanent chief executive office and president of the company."

"But then you will?" As they waited for the door to open, Laurel moved nearer, her shoulder gently brushing his.

Once again he was filled with the overwhelming desire to take her into his arms and kiss her. It required every ounce of self-control he had to remain where he was and appear unaffected by her closeness. "I will definitely make changes," he replied, firm in his resolve. Their eyes met, held. "When I take the helm," he said slowly, deliberately, "anyone who isn't pulling his weight will be gone."

Gosh, that was harsh, Laurel thought, as she and Cade left the elevator on the fourteenth floor and stepped into DDF headquarters. But not at all unheard of in the cutthroat world of business where bottom line, profits and net results were everything. If a CEO couldn't manage the company and trim the budget as needed, he or she would not be there for long.

"You'd fire me, too, wouldn't you?" she murmured while they approached the receptionist's desk.

"In a heartbeat," Cade confirmed cheerfully.

Good to know, Laurel thought. Was the same true of her position as his wife? More to the point, if the situation were reversed, would she be as quick to fire him? And given the circumstances, why did it matter, since Cade had said all they really had to worry about was the CEO vote coming up and getting DDF back on solid ground. Once that had happened, he would deal with his inheritance situation. In all likelihood there would be no thirty-three years of marriage—*or* anything else—between them, if she and Cade got their wish, anyway.

Noting how he seemed to be in total business mode now, Laurel watched as Cade nodded at the receptionist and kept right on going to the first door on the left, marked Mailroom. Laurel struggled to catch up as he held the door for her and swiftly made introductions. "Laurel, Benjamen Delgado. Laurel is going to be helping you today, Benjamen." Cade smiled at the clerk, patted Laurel on the shoulder, then headed off, laptop briefcase over his shoulder. The door shut behind her.

She looked across the room at her new co-worker. Some four or five years younger than her, he was short, stocky, with olive skin and inky-black hair and eyes. He shut off his iPod player and took the headphones from his ears. "Nice to meet you," his said, thrusting out his hand.

"Likewise." Laurel smiled to ease the awkwardness. "I guess you know—"

"That you married the boss at Unity Cathedral on Saturday night?" Benjamen interrupted with youthful exuberance. "Oh yeah. The whole office is buzzing about Mr. Dunnigan exchanging one bride for another." He paused, gave her the once-over. "You're a lot prettier in person than the picture in the newspaper," he told her appreciatively.

"Thanks." Laurel grinned. "I think."

Benjamen picked up a stack of envelopes and began sorting them quickly. "You're really going to work in the mailroom?" he asked her inquisitively.

Laurel set her purse and sweater in the corner. "Cade thinks this would be a good way to introduce me to everyone in the company."

The mail clerk inclined his head. "I guess that makes sense."

"Actually, I think he just wanted to get rid of me," Laurel admitted drolly. "He offered me a job in the company, then didn't know what to do with me, so decided to stick me here."

Her honesty resonated, as she had hoped it would. Benjamen laughed. "I'm sure you won't stay here long," he soothed. "No one does. Me, I'm out of here next month, as soon as I finish my degree. They've promised me a job on the sales force. So..." he sorted the last letter "...you want to push the cart around or what?"

Laurel looked at the overflowing metal pushcart. "I'll do the first delivery, if it's okay with you. Then maybe we can switch off later?"

"Whatever works." Benajmen grinned amiably and showed her the chart on the wall that detailed the layout of the various offices. He held the door for her. Laurel took a deep breath and moved on out.

The reaction she got from everyone else in the company was pretty much the same. Everyone knew who she was. Everyone was surprised to see her working in the mailroom, but cordial nevertheless.

Glad she wasn't having to face the kind of resentment she would have encountered at her father's company, Laurel went about her job as cheerfully as possible. Her cart was nearly empty when she reached the executive corridor. George Dunnigan Sr.'s office was empty, but George Jr. was in.

"Hello, Laurel." Cade's cousin smiled. He was seated at his desk, playing a game of blackjack on his computer, in plain sight of anyone walking by. "I didn't expect to see you here today, never mind pushing a mail cart." Standing up, he motioned her inside, then shut the door behind them, enclosing them in the luxuriously appointed space.

Unlike the other offices Laurel had seen thus far, which were decorated in businesslike shades of black, gray and cream, George Jr.'s office was done in a shimmering gold, reminiscent of a famous New York real estate tycoon. "What's Cade trying to do? Humiliate you? I thought he'd got his fill of that with Ariel."

Who the heck was Ariel? And what did that have to do with her? Laurel wondered. She looked at George Jr., too stunned by his unexpected rudeness to speak, even if he was now technically her family, at least as long as she was married to Cade.

"Listen." He clapped a too-familiar hand on her shoulder, clearly happy to cause trouble wherever he could. "I'm going to tell you what I suspect your family already has—you can do a lot better."

Laurel pried his hand from her skin. "I really don't think this is any of your business," she told him, struggling to maintain her composure.

"I disagree." George Jr. flashed an oily smile. "Thanks to your hasty marriage, we're family now. I just have to wonder what Cade promised you to get you to agree to such a potentially embarrassing arrangement. A portion of his inheritance—maybe in the form of stock in the company? No, he would never part with that. DDF means too much to him. Probably just money, right? A lot of money."

With effort, Laurel kept her voice pleasant and ladylike. "I'm not going to discuss this with you."

George Jr. gripped the metal handle and used the cart to block her way out. He stared at her as if a great deal were at stake for him, too. "I don't blame you for being defensive," he commiserated smoothly, as if he really had her best interests—and not his own—at heart. "Anyone in your situation would be. You just need to be aware that Cade may seem a gentleman on the surface, but deep down there's nothing but cynicism and calculation where his heart should be."

At that, Laurel's good manners went right out the window. "Sure you're not describing yourself now?" she replied tartly.

George Jr. laughed, a little too heartily. Again his gaze was too intense for comfort. "If you don't believe me, ask his ex-fiancée, Ariel. In the meantime, you want my advice? Get out while the getting is good."

"Exactly what I plan to do." Laurel grabbed hold of the cart. When Cade's cousin tried to stop her again, she put all her weight behind the mail cart and ran over his foot with one of the wheels.

George Jr. swore and hopped backward, grabbing his shin. Laurel yanked open the door—and came face-to-face with her brand-new husband.

"Mind telling me what is going on here?" Cade asked.

Not about to make the scene in the DDF offices Laurel bet George Jr. wanted her to make, she smiled and said breezily, "Just delivering the mail, and chatting with your cousin here."

Cade's eyes narrowed in suspicion. He nodded, clearly not believing her for one second, and looked past her. "I want to talk to you about the new marketing plan for the store."

"Sure thing, cuz," George Jr. replied, managing to brush Laurel's leg with his as she exited the office.

Ignoring the deliberate touch, Laurel hurried back to the mailroom. She had just loaded the cart for the second time when she heard a commotion at the front reception desk.

"You cannot see Mr. Cade Dunnigan without an appointment," the receptionist was saying.

Laurel stuck her head out the mailroom door.

"I'm telling you it's an emergency," the fifty-something woman at the desk insisted. Unlike the others in the office, who were all dressed in some variation of business-casual attire, the interloper was wearing a long-sleeved navy T-shirt, jeans and sneakers. She had a red bandanna tied around her neck, and a jaunty, white straw cowgirl hat settled over her gray curls.

"I'm going to have to ask you to leave," the receptionist said firmly, despite the fact the gate-crasher was near tears.

Laurel had never turned her back on a person in distress and wasn't about to start now. She didn't care what the rules were! Leaving the mail cart behind, she stepped out into the elegantly appointed hallway. "Perhaps I can help. I'm Mrs. Cade Dunnigan. Laurel."

"Oh, thank heavens," the woman exclaimed with real gratitude as they shook hands. "This is such an emergency! I'm Frances Klenck, president of the Dallas–Fort Worth Golden Retriever Rescue group. Law enforcement has just taken custody of forty-seven dogs at a puppy mill. We have to pick up all the dogs in two hours, at the animal shelter in Denton. We need vehicles, food, money and people willing to take animals on an emergency basis and see them through whatever medical treatment is necessary until we can find proper homes for them. Since Dunnigan Dog Food is headquartered right here in Dallas, I was hoping to get the company's assistance."

Cade strode down the hall, looking tall and imposing. Obviously, he had caught the gist of what was going on. "We will be happy to donate food for the animals. But I'm afraid that's all we can do."

Maybe it was all *he* could do, Laurel thought. She, on the other hand, was merely operating in a makeshift capacity here. "I can help."

"Laurel…" Cade warned.

"Seriously. Benjamen can handle the mail delivery." Laurel turned back to the volunteer. "I'll go with you."

Frances Klenck looked at Laurel's pretty yellow sundress. "You're sure about this? These dogs have not been kept in anything near optimal conditions, and none have been cleaned up yet. To say they're a little rank and mangy at the moment is an understatement."

"She has a point," Cade cautioned. He regarded Laurel with mounting impatience. "You've never done anything like this."

He was beginning to sound like her father, always warning her away from potentially difficult situations, Laurel realized. Always acting as if she wasn't strong or smart or savvy enough to cut it, when she absolutely was! "How do you know?" she demanded, incensed.

Cade's brow lifted in challenge. "Have you?" he retorted.

Darn him for putting her on the spot. "Well, n-no," Laurel stammered. Not with dogs, anyway. But she had come to the aid of many a person in trouble!

"You might not be able to handle it," Cade continued, as if the outcome of this not-so-private tête-à-tête was already decided.

And she might not be able to keep herself from decking him if this kept up. Laurel folded her arms in front of her and regarded her husband mutinously. "I can handle it just fine," she told him with sugary sweetness. What she couldn't seem to handle was Cade. The way he was challenging her, and acting as if he could manage her life, was making her mad.

"I didn't mean to cause a fight," Frances Klenck interjected hastily.

"We're not fighting," Laurel and Cade said testily, in unison.

By now, a crowd had gathered. Realizing the last thing they needed was an audience for any newlywed discord, Laurel looked at Cade. "Where is the food you want to donate?" she asked simply.

He paused. "The closest place from here is probably the flagship store in Highland Park," he said finally.

Sounds easy enough, Laurel thought. "Do I need keys to get in there?"

Cade shook his head. "I have to go over there anyway, to check on progress." His mind made up, he put a possessive hand on her back. "I'll take you."

Chapter Six

"You are not getting involved in this," Cade told Laurel the moment they were in his Porsche, en route to the Denton animal shelter.

He was trying to manage her life, just like her family always had. No way was Laurel going to allow that. "I have news for you," she told him stormily, not about to let him take up where her father, mother and five older brothers had left off. "It's not up to you to decide that."

Cade arched a brow. "It is if you're living and working with me," he said.

"Then maybe," Laurel countered, mocking his implacable tone, "it's time I stopped doing both."

Cade's jaw set. Obviously, he didn't like her threatening to walk out on him and his problems any more than she liked him ordering her around. "You want me to remain your bride?" she continued contentiously. "You'd better start respecting my decisions."

He slanted her a self-assured look. "Even if they're the wrong ones?"

As they reached a red light, Laurel turned to face him, intending to let him know to cool it. As their eyes clashed, he smiled and touched her face, brushing his callused thumb across her cheek. She had a sharp suspicion he was thinking of kissing her as thoroughly as he had before, and the sharper suspicion she would be lost if he did try to coax her into submission that way. Forcing her pulse to slow, she insisted, "They aren't wrong."

Cade frowned as the traffic light changed and he had to drive on. "You have no idea at all what you're getting into here," he groused as he proceeded cautiously through the busy intersection. "It's going to break your heart."

"Mine or yours?" she retorted. Was Mr. All Business All the Time a bigger softie than he was willing to let on?

"I can handle it," he promised staunchly.

If so, why was he suddenly looking so worried? Laurel wondered.

"I guess we'll see about that," she predicted with a great deal more confidence than she felt.

"You, on the other hand…" Cade shook his head.

Unnerved by the conviction in his low voice, Laurel shifted uneasily in the butter-soft leather seat. "Underestimating me and my ability to help others is a mistake. Ask anyone who's done it."

"Have you ever been to a poorly run puppy mill?"

"No."

Cade's voice reverberated with a cynicism that stung. "Have you ever seen any dogs who've come from one?"

Double no. She swallowed.

"The authorities don't go in and take dogs for no reason, Laurel. Generally speaking, if they feel they have to remove them, it's because there has been abuse or neglect."

Laurel was silent. "Have you ever seen dogs in this condition?" she asked at last.

He nodded, his expression grimmer than ever. "It wasn't a pretty sight."

No wonder he was so upset, she thought.

"So this is what we're going to do," Cade continued firmly. "We're going to go in there and assess what the dogs need that DDF can supply, make arrangements to see it's turned over to Frances Klenck and her army of volunteers, and then get out and go back to the office. You got that?"

Laurel arched a cantankerous brow. "I got that it was an order and I don't take orders."

Cade cocked his head and gave her a thorough once-over. "You will in this instance."

Want to bet? Laurel thought as the strains of "The Yellow Rose of Texas" suddenly filled the car. Glad for the respite, she fished her cell phone out of her shoulder bag, hit a button and pressed it to her ear. No one answered her greeting, but Laurel thought she heard crying on the other end. "Mary Elena?" she guessed.

Cade kept his attention focused on the road.

"How are you? Where are you?" Laurel continued.

"I'm in Miami," Mary Elena replied in a voice thick with tears. "I was going to get on the cruise ship, but Daddy's canceled my ticket and revoked all my credit cards."

Oh, dear. "Don't you have any money you can draw on?" Laurel asked, aware Cade was now listening in.

"I've got enough cash for a few days," her friend admitted miserably. "That's it. Laurel, Daddy's so angry with me. He told our accountant to cut off all my funds."

That must mean he was pretty angry, Laurel knew. Lance Ayers had always given his only child everything her heart desired—at least in material possessions—and then some. His willingness to let her lead her own life was something else entirely. Like Laurel's own father, he felt he knew what was best for his daughter, better than she did. Their mutual trouble dealing with overprotective fathers was one of the reasons Laurel and Mary Elena had quickly become such fast friends. "You've talked to your dad, then?"

"Not yet," Mary Elena admitted reluctantly. "I've been afraid to try, but Daddy called and left about a dozen messages on my voice mail, telling me about everything that's been going on."

"Then you know that Cade and I...?"

"Got married? Yes. Laurel, you didn't have to do that," Mary Elena scolded. "I mean, I know I left you in a terrible spot, but to marry him in my place—without love—that's a horrible mistake!"

Tell me about it, Laurel thought, considering the stream of orders she had just gotten from her "husband."

"You need to get it annulled right away."

Laurel rubbed at the tension building in her temples. "I can't do that."

"Surely Cade can get his inheritance some other way if he really tries!"

"Apparently, he can't," Laurel admitted reluctantly, ignoring the implacable expression of the man sitting beside her. She turned her attention to the passing scenery. "According to his father's will, Cade has to be married, and stay married, for the next thirty-three years."

"Thirty... Laurel, you can't possibly be considering staying hitched to him!"

Her own attitude exactly—at first. Now, Laurel was horrified to find she was considering staying on indefinitely. If only to see where the sparks between them would lead. How nuts was that?

"Just for a while," she answered.

"Now I really feel awful," Mary Elena wailed, sounding even more upset.

"You did what you had to do," Laurel told her calmly. "I got myself in this mess."

Her friend sighed, her attention now focused on something other than herself. "You've really got to work on that helping-other-people-to-your-own-detriment thing, Laurel."

"No joke." It had taken marriage to a man she had no business being attracted to, but Laurel was beginning to see she did have some issues that needed to be addressed. She didn't want to talk about that with Cade listening in, however.

"What are you going to do?" Mary Elena asked.

I'm going to try to keep my emotional distance and not let Cade kiss me again, Laurel thought. *Try to figure out why I don't want to say no to him on much of anything.* Except the dog situation, of course. There, she was going to do what her heart dictated. Period. "I'm going to muddle through until we get everything sorted out."

"This is all my fault," Mary Elena moaned.

"Actually, I think I did this to myself. And it's a lesson to me to never do it again," she stated firmly. She'd be lucky to get out of the situation with her heart intact. "But let's not talk about that." She ignored the fact that Cade was absorbing every word she said. And more importantly, didn't say. "Let's talk about you." Laurel pushed on resolutely. "What are you going to do? Have you talked to…?"

"Manuel?"

"Yes."

Another sigh. "He's been calling and leaving messages on my voice mail, too," Mary Elena confessed reluctantly.

"Have you phoned him back?"

Silence fell, and Laurel thought she heard more crying. "Yes," he friend said finally.

"And?" Laurel asked gently, her heart going out to her.

"It's such a mess," Mary Elena sniffed. "My father fired him."

Perhaps not such a bad thing, under the circumstances, Laurel thought. "I'm sure Manuel will find more work," she soothed.

"Not with the poor references Daddy's giving him. He said that unless I come back home and start behaving myself again, Manuel can forget about ever working in Dallas, period."

Lance Ayers was just powerful enough to pull something like that off. "Oh, dear."

"Manuel's being very brave about it, but I'm angry," Mary Elena continued indignantly.

"Maybe you can talk to your father, get him to change his mind, or at least give Manuel a better recommendation," Laurel said.

"Daddy's going to have to if he wants me to ever speak to him again!" Mary Elena declared.

"Atta girl," Laurel murmured.

"In fact, I'm going to call Daddy right now and speak to him about it," Mary Elena added, even more defiantly.

"If there's anything else I can do…" Laurel said, knowing her friend had been there in crises for her, too.

"I'll call," she promised. "In the meantime, you watch out for yourself."

"In what regard?" Laurel asked cautiously.

"In regard to Cade Dunnigan! I swear, he and Daddy both have business models and cash registers where their hearts should be."

Whereas she, Laurel thought, had a lonely void waiting to be filled.

"So what did Mary Elena say?" Cade asked as soon as Laurel cut the connection and put her phone back in her purse. He turned the Porsche into the animal shelter parking lot. "Is she coming back to Dallas?"

"She's thinking about it," Laurel said. Telling herself she needed to be driven by practicality and not emotion, she asked, "Do you want her to come back?"

He shrugged and continued to look as unmovable as a five-ton boulder. "I have a few things to say to her."

Ouch. "Such as…?" Laurel pressed when he didn't go on.

Cade's glance narrowed. "I think that's best left between Mary Elena and me, don't you think?"

Yes and no, Laurel thought. She knew she had no reason to be jealous, but she was. Maybe because Cade had originally planned to say "I do" to Mary Elena, not her. Laurel didn't enjoy feeling like a runner-up, even though she knew there was no love involved in either situation, and honestly, how silly was that? It wasn't as if there was any love on her part. Just a basic physical attraction, pure and simple, simmering between them. And that, Laurel told herself firmly, was something that would be ignored.

CADE KNEW LAUREL WAS in for a shock when she saw the animals. However, he hadn't expected her to turn the color of parchment and sway unsteadily on her feet when they entered the cement floored holding area where all forty-seven rescued animals were currently being kept. They were purebred golden retrievers—you could clearly see that from the confirmation and the handsome heads. As for healthy… Cade figured all the dogs weighed less than half of what they should for their size. Their coats were dull, coarse and thin. A jubilant breed by nature, all of these dogs, from sire to dam to pup, had the listless, hopeless look of animals who had never known love or had much to hope for. They huddled together in their cages. No tails were wagging. No dogs were barking. They stared in mute defeat as Cade, Laurel and Frances Klenck, the head of the rescue group, walked up and down the aisle.

"You can see we've got our work cut out for us, trying to bring these animals back and get them ready to be adopted out," Frances said.

Her expression unbearably tender, Laurel knelt in front of the last cement-walled run with bars in front. "What's wrong with that one?" she asked, pointing to a three-month-old puppy that probably didn't weigh more than nine pounds. The pup was cowering in a corner, trembling visibly. Large patches of fur on its body appeared to have fallen out.

"We'll have to ask the vet," Frances replied.

"None of the other puppies here have lost hair like that," Laurel said, still kneeling in front of the cage.

Cade knew disaster was about to strike. The sooner they got down to business and he dragged Laurel out of here, the better. "DDF will supply a year's worth of food for each dog, as well as collars, leashes, food and water dishes."

Frances Klenck beamed. "Thank you very much, Mr. Dunnigan. Your generosity will not go unnoticed. I assure you I'll mention it in every press release or interview I do."

"Actually, I'd prefer you not do that," Cade said firmly.

Laurel stood, keeping one eye on the puppy trembling in the corner. "Why not?" she asked with a puzzled frown. "I'd think you'd want the publicity."

Cade recalled what his grandfather had taught him, years ago. "Charity isn't charity if someone else knows about it," he said.

"I don't understand." Laurel edged closer.

Seeing the strap of her pretty yellow sundress had fallen down, just as he had thought it would, Cade pushed it back up on her shoulder. Wishing her skin wasn't so silky-soft or warm, his reaction to her so potent, he turned his mind back to the conversation and explained practically, "Whenever a company or celebrity jumps in to help out in a situation like this, their motives are considered suspect by a great deal of the public. Is the person or company helping out of the goodness of their heart, or doing it for free publicity? If the latter is presumed, as it often is when it seems the donor has something to gain, public perception sinks like a stone in a river. I'd rather avoid that pitfall, with the opening of our flagship store in two weeks."

"I see your point," Frances murmured thoughtfully, siding with Cade.

"I don't," Laurel stated.

Of course you don't, Cade thought. *If you agreed with me, then it would be easy, and you and I aren't ever going to do anything easy.*

She stepped closer, the floral scent of her skin and hair inundating his senses. "I think you're in a position to really help these poor animals get back on their feet and find permanent homes."

That was what he was doing with his generous donation!

"We do need a pet store to sponsor the adoption fair," Frances Klenck said. "It would be wonderful if that could be the new DDF superstore and day spa."

"The new pet store is located in Highland Park," Cade explained as patiently as he could. "That area of town caters to a very upscale clientele." With lots and lots of money to spend. Cade needed those dog owners spending like crazy at the flagship store, to convince the DDF board to expand into other areas of the city, and eventually across the country, as well.

"Don't these dogs deserve the very best, too?" Laurel demanded indignantly.

"Of course they do," Cade countered in exasperation. "I'm just saying that some of our customers in Highland Park might be put off by these animals' less than stellar appearance right now."

Laurel glanced again at the trembling puppy in the corner. "Aren't there going to be grooming facilities at the new store?"

"Yes." Cade ignored the pitiful looks the puppy was giving Laurel. He could not afford to get emotionally involved here, and neither could she. They had enough to deal with already. Cade gave Laurel a look that usually had his business subordinates shaking in their shoes. "What's your point?"

"My point—" she flashed a defiant smile "—is this is the perfect opportunity for a 'before and after' event at the flagship store. I'm saying DDF should show people the difference a good bath and a haircut—not to mention a steady diet of high quality Dunnigan Dog Food—can make."

"It could be a win-win situation for everyone," Frances Klenck agreed.

Cade moved to block Laurel's view of the mangy-looking puppy. He stood, legs braced apart, arms folded in front of him. "Even if I wanted to coordinate such an event, I don't have the time or resources right now to manage such a task," he said.

Laurel beamed happily. "But I do," she insisted.

Cade had known she was going to be trouble. He just hadn't thought she'd be *this* much trouble. And he really hadn't expected to keep wanting to give in to her.

"Maybe I should let the two of you work this out alone," Frances said delicately. "I'll be out front, waiting for everyone else to show up to take the dogs out of here."

"Good idea," Cade said.

As soon as they were alone again, save for forty-seven dogs who were now staring at Cade as if they understood everything that was going on and were begging for his help, Laurel pivoted back to him. "The publicity generated from this mission of mercy could be exactly what you need to garner the kind of community awareness needed to make DDF's flagship store and doggie day spa a stunning success."

Determined to play it cool, Cade remained where he was, his back to the dogs in the cages. He shoved his hands in his pockets. "I told you I don't want to use the dogs for my gain."

"Then do it for their gain, and let them use you—and your access to the media—to help them find loving, caring homes," Laurel pleaded in a low, intimate tone. She splayed her hands across his chest and tipped her head up, tempting him with her big blue eyes. "You know you want to help them," she persisted softly.

Resisting the urge to take her all the way into his arms, Cade replied in a gruff, no-nonsense tone, "It's a big job." Too big, in his estimation.

"I am up to the task. Besides, I'll have Frances Klenck's help. All I have to do is coordinate things at DDF. Please, Cade."

Cade could not deny the animals had been through a rough time and needed a lot of support. The effort would also keep Laurel very busy. The busier she was, the less chance she would have to distract him with her sexy presence, or remind him of how difficult it was going to be stay married without embarking on any kind of intimate relationship.

"All right." He finally relented, knowing even as he spoke the words that it was probably a mistake.

He studied her soberly, then warned, "But if I see even a hint of what appears to be grandstanding or publicity seeking on DDF's behalf—"

Laurel lifted both hands, stepped back. "You won't," she hastily assured him.

"I'll call a halt to everything but the aforementioned donations," Cade finished.

She flashed him a dazzling smile. "You won't be sorry you're doing this."

Cade had heard that before, never to good result.

But not one to tempt fate, any more than it had already been tempted, he remained silent.

While Laurel stayed behind to help transport the animals to people who had offered their homes as temporary refuge, or to vets who had donated their services, Cade went on to the flagship store to finalize the finishing touches for the grand opening.

He was the last one there, and about to go home for the day, when Laurel came through the door.

She wasn't alone.

When Cade saw who she had with her, he couldn't help but groan.

Chapter Seven

Laurel had known Cade wouldn't agree with what she had done. But she hadn't expected him to seem quite so...perturbed.

"Don't look at me like that," she said as she strode into the flagship store, a trembling puppy clasped to her chest. When she knelt to put it down on the floor, she noticed the front of her yellow sundress was covered with dirt smudges and hair. She literally looked like she had been rolling in mud. Smelly mud.

Cade leaned back and clamped his arms over his broad chest. "Tell me you didn't agree to take care of that dog temporarily," he growled.

Pointedly ignoring the exasperation in his low voice, Laurel stayed where she was while the puppy stood on shaking legs, and fearfully looked around. She touched the back of its head, saw the animal flinch, but continued gently stroking the little white-blond pup behind the ears until it calmed down a bit.

"I didn't agree to temporarily take care of this puppy," she said softly, smiling as the puppy looked up at her with dark, liquid eyes. Reluctantly, Laurel turned her glance up to Cade. He hadn't moved from his place against the metal shelving filled with bags of Dunnigan's Premium Dog Food. She flashed him the smile she used when trying to convince her parents the sacrifice she was currently making was really best for all concerned. "I agreed to take care of Patches permanently."

Cade's frown deepened, even as compassion and empathy

glimmered briefly in his gray eyes. For the life of her, Laurel couldn't figure out why he was so concerned about this. Or why he seemed to think this shy little puppy could be a threat to their happiness in any way. It wasn't as if Cade were averse to pets—he had a dog of his own he dearly loved!

An awkward silence fell.

Cade quirked a dissenting brow. "Patches?"

"That's what I named her." Deciding Patches was comfortable enough now to look around a bit, she stood gracefully again. Nerves jangling, she lifted her chin in quiet defiance. "It fits, don't you think?"

If anything, Cade's expression turned even grimmer. His gray eyes shone with a cynicism that stung as he gave her a thorough once-over. "I'm surprised Frances Klenck let you walk off with that dog," he said.

Laurel looked at Cade, letting him know with a glance she was not passing Patches off like a magazine she had flipped through and no longer wanted. Nor did she intend to allow Cade to influence her actions in this matter. Patches needed her, and Laurel knew, for reasons hard to explain, that she needed the little puppy in her life as well. Fate had led them toward each other and would keep them together. "Frances didn't want to, but they didn't have an emergency placement for this one, so she said I could care for Patches until her vet appointment tomorrow afternoon. Frances wanted me to really think about it before taking on such an enormous responsibility."

Cade straightened and sauntered forward. "Smart woman, that Frances Klenck," he drawled.

Laurel studied his handsome face and tall, muscled frame. There was nothing soft or easy about him. He was who he was, take it or leave it. Trying not to think how much they had in common that way, she continued matter-of-factly, "Speaking of Frances, she and the others will be by here in about five minutes to pick up the pet supplies you promised them on DDF's behalf."

Eyes narrowing, Cade continued to study Laurel relentlessly. "Are they all bringing dogs with them?"

Telling herself it was tension causing her heart to pound and her body to tingle—and not his proximity—Laurel lifted her face to his. She could feel the blood rushing to her cheeks even as she sought to get a handle on her soaring emotions. "No. Frances, her husband and two teenage sons are picking up the supplies. They'll distribute them to everyone else. She and her husband are both using their vans, so they think they can fit everything in them."

Cade inclined his head to the side. "Forty-seven bags of dog food is a lot."

He was right, Laurel noted a short while later, as the Klencks struggled to fit everything into their two minivans. But eventually they managed. "That was awfully generous of you to send bottles of dog shampoo, too," she said. She waved at the Klencks as they drove off.

Cade shrugged, nodding toward the puppy Laurel had chosen for her very own. "They're going to need them if all the dogs smell as bad as that one."

Laurel had put up with Cade's reluctance for a while now, but this was too much. Her temper kicked into full gear. "Her name is Patches. And I plan to bathe her as soon as we get her home," she stated indignantly, more than a little irked at the way Cade kept looking at the pup. She had expected Cade, a loving dog owner, to be a lot more receptive to what she was doing, once he got used to the idea of having two dogs instead of one in his home. Instead, he kept looking at Laurel as if she had lost her mind, and Patches as if she were something to be both pitied and avoided. With a sigh of frustration, Laurel moved away from him and tried not to imagine a life with a man so hell-bent on having his own way all the time.

"You want to bathe the pup here?" Cade asked gruffly.

Laurel looked behind the glass-walled partition to the state-of-the-art grooming facilities, complete with doggie bathtubs and handheld showerheads. Aware he was still eyeing her with a depth of male interest she found disturbing, she replied, "Are you serious?"

Cade jammed his hands on his hips and grumbled, "I'd rather not do it at all." He paused, looking her up and down, from the hem of her dirt-smeared dress to the breeze-mussed strands of her hair. "But if we take her home in that condition, my Porsche is going to smell like she does, and I'd prefer not to have that happen."

Laurel regarded him sweetly. "You're doing the right thing. I can't say your reasoning is the least bit charitable, but I guess I'll take the end result."

Cade harrumphed, muttered something under his breath about fools and their errands she was just as glad not to catch, and walked off to the shelves. He moved quickly up and down the aisles, returning with a bright orange water-absorbing towel, a bottle of No Tears puppy shampoo, an adjustable collar and a nylon training lead. As Laurel picked up the quivering retriever, Cade slipped the collar over the puppy's head, adjusted it and snapped the lead on to that. Obviously, Laurel realized, he had done this many times.

"Put her down here," Cade said, indicating the first three-sided, stainless steel shower stall. He secured the lead onto the wall hook, showed her how to turn on the water, and stepped back. "You're all set."

Frightened, Patches began to whine and shake uncontrollably. Ignoring the fact that she was close enough to see the speculation gleaming in Cade's eyes, Laurel asked, "You're not going to help?"

He braced his legs a little farther apart, his gaze skimming her deliberately. "Your dog, your responsibility."

He was sounding more and more like the rest of the men in her life. Insufferable. Overbearing. Worse, he was standing there, arms folded, leaning against the glass-walled partition as if he expected her to fail. "Fine," Laurel said, wishing she knew what to do first. She hated stumbling in front of an audience. But really, she reassured herself firmly, how different could this be from bathing any baby? And that was something she had done and done well!

She turned on the water, adjusted the temperature and directed the warm spray onto Patches's back. Laurel had expected the water to feel good to the little puppy. Instead, it scared the dickens out of her. Patches yelped as if Laurel were torturing her, and tried to escape the short leash by wiggling, shaking and pulling this way and that. The more the pup realized she couldn't escape, the louder her cries of distress grew. She pawed frantically at Laurel's forearms, scratching her sharply with her nails in the process. Crying out, Laurel jumped back and dropped the hose, which proceeded to lash about, spraying water everywhere.

Swearing, Cade jumped in to capture the elusive showerhead, and clamp a large, steadying hand beneath Patches's middle. "Come on, pup, you're fine," he said in a deep soothing voice. "Hold still and this will all be over before you know it." To Laurel, he instructed, "Get the bottle of shampoo and let's get this girl lathered up before she has a heart attack."

Laurel quickly complied, directing a stream of shampoo down the puppy's back. She reached over Cade to help work the shampoo in with both hands, while he held Patches with one hand and used the other to wash, too. The puppy continued to whimper inconsolably as the bath continued, but was definitely looking up at Cade worshipfully as the fragrant bubbles saturated her coat and the considerable smell and dirt washed away.

"Is that enough?" Laurel said after a minute.

Cade shook his head. "Keep rinsing."

"You're sure?"

He nodded. "The key to getting a dog clean and comfortable is making sure all the soap is thoroughly rinsed out of its hair. Whenever you think you're done, rinse again for the same amount of time, and you'll probably be good."

"She doesn't seem to be minding the water as much now," Laurel remarked.

He smiled down at the pup, tenderness flowing from him in waves, despite his avowed decision not to get involved. "She's probably just worn herself out."

Finally, Laurel was done. Again, Cade was quick to take charge. "Get the towel. Let's dry her off and wrap her up," he said.

Grateful for all his help with the difficult task, Laurel complied, getting as much water out of Patches's fur as she could with the super-absorbent cloth. When she had finished, Cade un-hooked the lead from the basin and hefted the shaking puppy into her waiting arms.

The floor in the grooming area was as damp as Cade and Laurel, and covered with hair and bubbles of fragrant-smelling dog shampoo. He shook his head at the mess, then reached for the cell phone in his pocket and punched in a number. "Have the janitorial supplies been delivered to the flagship store yet?" He frowned. "That's what I thought. Call our cleaning service and have them come over here and do a thorough mop-up in the grooming area of the store tonight. Thanks." He cut the connection, turned to Laurel and Patches. "Let's get some dog food, dishes and a training crate and head out of here," he said.

"WHY DO WE NEED a training crate?" Laurel asked as Cade loaded the unassembled pet den with curved plastic sides and steel-mesh door into the trunk of his Porsche. "And why did you get such a big one?" It was an extra large, which seemed ridiculously big for such a little dog.

"This is the size required for retrievers." Cade held the door for Laurel. He took Patches in his arms while she eased into the seat and put her belt on, then handed the cuddly puppy back to her and circled the rear of the car. "Patches will grow into it, once she gets healthy," he added when he'd opened the driver's side door.

"Why not just get her a small one now and a big one later?" Laurel watched him slide behind the wheel and slip the key in the ignition.

Cade started the car and backed out of the parking space. "Because once she breaks in this crate and gets her smell on it, it will be her own safe little place, her shelter against all things big and scary, and she is not going to want to have to break in another. She will be emotionally attached to this one."

So you do care, Laurel thought smugly, *even if it would slay you to admit it....*

"Plus—" Cade frowned, continuing in an introspective voice rife with exasperation "—this crate is compliant with regulations for domestic and international travel, so if you do decide to keep Patches and you ever need to take her somewhere by plane or vehicle, she can use it for that, as well. If you don't keep her, then the crate can go with her when she moves to her permanent home."

Okay. He had just lost all the brownie points he had gained by helping her, Laurel thought.

"Either way, Patches will appreciate the security of her own room, so to speak."

Knowing it was impolitic to bite the hand that was feeding her puppy, Laurel murmured, "Good to know."

Ignoring the slight sarcastic undertone in her voice, Cade gave Laurel, and the puppy snuggled against her chest, an assessing glance. "You really don't know anything about caring for a dog, do you?"

Laurel stroked the head of the exhausted animal snoozing against her breasts. She knew now why people went so gaga over their canine pets. This was just as fulfilling as holding a baby. "Obviously, you do."

His expression guarded, he promised, "I'll get you a book."

Knowing she would never understand him unless he started telling her what was on his mind and in his heart, she ignored his hint to back off. "I'd rather have you show me."

"Like I said—" Cade kept both hands on the wheel and his emotions firmly in check "—I'm not going to have time for this."

Laurel watched him adjust the electronic controls to allow slightly cooler air into the car. "How much time can it take?"

He snorted in derision. "Out of the mouths of babes…"

"You'll see," Laurel predicted optimistically. "She's not going to be a problem at all."

"That remains to be seen," he remarked as he drove the short distance from the flagship store to his home in Highland Park. "I don't know how Beast is going to react to having a puppy around, even momentarily."

Laurel arched her brow as they sailed through a green light, then another. "You don't think Beast would try and eat her for breakfast, do you?"

Cade hit the brakes. They cruised around a corner into a residential area. "Probably not, as long as we remember to feed him."

"Ha, ha. Very funny." The Dunnigan mansion loomed. "How is Beast going to react?" she asked as they turned into the driveway.

Cade shook his head noncommittally. "I guess we'll find out," he predicted, shooting her a wry look. He parked the car and got out. Laurel stayed where she was, the still-snoozing Patches clasped to her chest. Cade opened her door. She didn't move. "Now what are you doing?" he asked her in exasperation.

"Thinking maybe I should take Patches and go back to my apartment," Laurel said, frowning right back at him.

Cade sighed and sent his glance skyward. "Does your building allow pets?" he asked her bluntly.

"Well, no…" Laurel was loath to admit she really hadn't thought this through. Yet, anyway.

Cade motioned her out of the vehicle. "Then you had better bring that puppy inside."

CADE DIDN'T KNOW WHY he was giving Laurel such a hard time, except maybe, like Frances Klenck, he wanted her to really consider what she was volunteering to do here. Given how green she was, how little she knew about the effort involved in caring for a puppy, never mind one with needs like Patches, he figured she would change her mind about adopting the retriever in no time. And if she didn't, well, he had already developed a plan B.

Beast had already figured out they had a visitor by the time they reached the front door. Cade could see him running back and forth behind the wavy glass on either side of the door, and hear him barking his head off. In response, Patches—who had woken up when Laurel emerged from the car—trembled all the harder.

Cade gestured for Laurel to hand Patches over to him. "Allow me to make the introductions."

She bit her lip. "I'm not certain—"

"Trust me." He reassured her with a glance. "It will be fine.

Just be sure and keep Patches's lead on, even after we put her down. We don't want her running off into the street."

Cade opened the front door. Beast came barreling out, just as he had the night before. He galloped right past them into the front yard, where he quickly marked his territory, then came back— no longer barking—to stand in front of Cade, who cradled the pup in his big hands. "Beast, we have a temporary house guest," he announced firmly. "Her name is Patches and she's had a rough time, so I expect you to be nice to her."

Cade set the trembling Patches down on the grass. As Beast nosed closer, curious but calm now, Patches squatted on the grass and relieved herself. "See that, Beast?" Cade said quietly, as he knelt between the two inquisitive dogs, petting both of them. "She's already paying you respect."

Laurel knelt opposite Cade. She seemed amazed at how well the two dogs were already getting on.

"What are you talking about?" she asked.

"Submissive wetting," Cade explained. "When a female dog sees a bigger one, or even a male, she will squat and wet to show that she acknowledges their strength and ability to dominate her. That's why," he continued practically, aware he had Laurel's rapt attention, "if you own a female dog, it's best to have her greet any newcomers—especially male newcomers—outside, until she gets a little older, so you don't have wetting accidents inside the house. That goes for humans as well as other dogs."

Cade stood to give the dogs a little more room to nuzzle and get to know each other.

Her palm still cupped protectively over Patches, Laurel looked up at Cade. "Have you ever owned a female dog?"

"Once, a long time ago," Cade said, not sure how they had gotten onto this track, and wishing they hadn't. He didn't talk about his beloved Dixie to anyone.

Seeing more of his emotions than he would have wished, Laurel let go of Patches altogether and asked quietly, "Before Beast?"

Cade waited a moment before replying. "Yes."

Another pulse beat of silence passed. "How many dogs have

you owned?" she pressed, rising gracefully to her feet. She edged closer in a drift of perfume and sweet-smelling dog shampoo.

"Just two," Cade said.

A flush of color coming into her cheeks, Laurel studied Cade in frustration, obviously wishing he would be more forthcoming. "Have you ever had two dogs at once?"

"No." Cade frowned and gave her a look signaling this line of questioning was at an end, whether she wanted it to be or not. "I'm a one-dog-at-a-time kind of guy."

To his relief, she got the hint and backed off. "So what next?" she asked, beginning to look a little flushed in the late-day heat.

"I say we feed them—" Cade handed her Patches's lead "—and put the pup into her crate for a long nap. And then get back to the real business at hand."

"Which is?" Laurel watched as he strode back to the car, removed the unassembled crate, bag of puppy food and two dishes from his trunk. He carried them into the house, moving quickly through the foyer to the mudroom off the kitchen, where Beast's food and water dishes were kept. Cade filled those and left Beast in there alone to eat, then took Patches's belongings out to the sunporch overlooking the swimming pool. Laurel followed, Patches in her arms.

Cade sat cross-legged on the floor and began assembling the crate. "I want you and me to throw a dinner party for the members of the board tomorrow evening."

Laurel sat down on the end of a padded chaise. She put Patches on the floor, so the pup could walk around, and watched Cade push bolts through the predrilled holes and secure them with nuts. "That's a little short notice, isn't it?"

Finished, Cade tested the metal gate. It swung open and shut nicely. "I'm sure we can get a restaurant to accommodate us."

As Laurel leaned forward to keep watch over her puppy, the strap of her sundress fell over her arm. She paused to push it back up. "Why not do it here?"

Trying not to think how much he'd like to relieve her of both bothersome straps—and while he was at it, her dirt-stained, rumpled sundress—Cade pushed the portable kennel over next to an interior wall, opposite the door. Anything to keep himself from stealing another glance at Laurel's soft, full breasts, or imagining how the sweet weight of them would feel in his hands. "You can cook?"

Laurel made a face. "Not at that level," she admitted. "But we could have it catered."

And feel even more like a real couple than they already did? Cade thought. Too much more of this and he'd be thinking—and acting like—they were married in every sense, "It sounds like too much trouble," he told her curtly.

Laurel frowned, clearly disappointed. Hurt came and went in her deep blue eyes. "What's the purpose of this board meeting?"

Cade put half a cup of dog food in Patches's bowl, then stepped outside to get water from the faucet next to the porch. "To convince the members of the board that—despite the events of the weekend—I am still the right person to lead the company. I want to show them that my marrying you was not a foolish action."

Laurel looked at him through the screen. "You're not going to try and pretend we're in love, are you?"

Cade stepped back onto the porch. "Quite the contrary. I want to show them we have a workable business arrangement." Noting Patches still hadn't touched her food, Cade put some kibble in his palm and rubbed his scent into it.

"So there will be no kissing, no fake lovey-dovey stuff?" Laurel asked, her delicate brows arching inquisitively.

"None," Cade confirmed. Although he wouldn't mind kissing Laurel again. Not at all. Unfortunately, he knew he couldn't do that without risking becoming emotionally involved with her. And that was something he didn't want, not when he had a company to save from the greedy clutches of his cousin and uncle. Speaking of whom… "At the office today…" he began. He held his open palm beneath Patches's muzzle, watching as she thoroughly investigated the kibble and finally began to eat.

"Yes?" Laurel prompted.

He looked back at her. "When you were alone with George Jr. this morning, what did he say to you behind closed doors?"

LAUREL HADN'T EXPECTED CADE to ask her this. Nor did she know what to say. Should she tell him what George Jr. had said? It wasn't as if she could forget it. His words were haunting her even now.

You just need to be aware that Cade may seem a gentleman on the surface, but deep down, there's nothing but cynicism and calculation where his heart should be.... You want my advice? Get out while the getting is good.

"Laurel?" Cade persisted. "I can tell by the expression on your face that my cousin said something to you."

As Laurel tried to figure out how to handle this very tricky situation, she made a vague noncommittal sound in the back of her throat. She really didn't want to burden Cade with more trouble than he already had. Or pass on any trash talk about him. And yet this was the perfect opportunity to find out what she wanted to know. "He mentioned someone named Ariel," she said finally.

Cade swore beneath his breath and shook his head. "I figured he had done something like that."

Laurel slipped off the chaise and onto the floor, so they could talk more intimately. Her full skirt fanned out around her and she tucked it neatly over her legs. "You were engaged to her?"

"About five years ago, yes," Cade replied reluctantly. He picked up another three pieces of puppy kibble and warmed them in his palm.

"What happened?" Laurel couldn't help but smile as Patches ambled over and tasted what was in his casually outstretched hand. Maybe there was hope for Cade and Patches yet. Laurel looked back at his face determinedly. "Obviously, you two didn't get married. Why not?"

He grimaced. "She left me."

Honestly, Laurel thought, this was like trying to get blood out of a stone. She leaned forward urgently, her bent knee brushing his. "The question is why, Cade?" She had only to look at his face to know how much that hurt.

His shoulders tensed. "Because she was hopelessly romantic, and she could not accept how much DDF means to me."

"More than her?" The heartache Laurel felt for him echoed in her voice.

"She thought so." The expression on his face grim and unrelenting, Cade reached for more kibble.

Once again, Laurel suspected she was only getting a tiny bit of the story. She wanted it all. "Do you think Ariel was fair in her assessment of your priorities?"

"Probably."

Not good, Laurel thought. Not good at all.

Cade put the warmed kibble in Patches's food bowl. Patches considered it, then shuffled closer, and stuck her nose in the bowl to investigate.

"Do you have regrets about that?" Laurel studied Cade, wanting—needing—to know the kind of person he was at heart.

He made a disgruntled sound and rubbed the back of his neck. Abruptly, he sighed, as if weary to the core. A distant look came into his eyes. "It would never have worked in the end. Ariel was a hopeless romantic. Emotion dictated her every thought, decision and action."

"Whereas," Laurel quoted dryly, "you've got nothing but cynicism and calculation where your heart should be."

As she had suspected, it wasn't the first time Cade had heard his character described that way. "George Jr. told you that, too?"

She wanted to know his side of things. If goading him was the only way to get him talking… Laurel shrugged, assuming the role of devil's advocate. "Apparently it's no secret."

Cade's jaw clenched. He sighed again in exasperation. "Look, I want to be married. It's a two-by-two world. And let's face it. A lot of things in business—like this dinner party I want to have for the board of directors—are a lot easier if you have a spouse to support you and manage the details."

Which is where I come in, Laurel thought.

"But I'm also honest," Cade continued, the brooding look in his eyes replaced with quiet resolution. "My relationship with

Ariel taught me something about myself." He paused and regarded Laurel steadily. "I know now that my family company has always come first in my life, and it always will, and I'm not going to pretend otherwise. Which is why I now approach marriage with the same practical, clear-eyed vision I approach my business. Because that is the only way any relationship with me will ever work."

He was shortchanging himself and anyone who chose to become involved with him. Such as herself. "I disagree," Laurel countered quietly. "I think it takes a strong love to form a foundation for a relationship between a man and a woman."

He sighed, looking a little surly and a lot frustrated. "Love is not something that can be counted on, Laurel."

Aware of being more vulnerable now than she had in a very long time, she frowned and argued back, just as forcefully, "Love is the only commodity worth having in this life." She threw up her hands, aware her voice was rising emotionally, yet not caring. "My family drives me crazy, okay?" She struggled to her feet and began to pace the length of the sunporch. Her skirt swished against her legs as she moved. "It hurts like hell that they disapprove of me and my tendency to get involved helping others, often—admittedly—to the detriment of myself. But I know they love me, and I know my parents love and cherish each other, too. Their bond forms the foundation for our entire family. And that is what I want for myself." She wasn't going to settle for less.

Patches sat back on her haunches and looked up at Laurel. "If that's the case, then why aren't you already married?" Cade asked curiously.

Laurel flushed. "I was engaged. Once. A couple of years ago."

His eyes narrowed. "What happened?"

She swallowed. Her turn to be on the hot seat. "It's a long story."

Cade did not protest when Patches climbed up onto his lap and cuddled against his thigh. Nor did he encourage it. He looked down at the puppy, then back up at Laurel, and gestured carelessly. "I've got time."

Laurel knew she couldn't expect him to confide in her if she didn't also confide in him, and more than anything she wanted them to understand each other. She struggled to find the right words. "Marc worked for my dad's company." Aware Cade was listening intently, she pushed on. "We met at the company picnic and started dating right away. I thought he was The One." Laurel shook her head in bitterness and regret. "My parents weren't so sure."

"What put them off?" Cade asked.

She shrugged. "They both knew how ambitious Marc was, and felt he might be romancing me to accelerate his own career. So…" she inhaled shakily "…when he proposed, my dad sat us both down, offered his congratulations, and announced it would be best for all concerned if Marc look for a job elsewhere. He was as shocked as I was—neither of us saw that coming—but Marc accepted it like a gentleman and agreed to do so. But he also asked my father for high-level help, getting on the fast track at a comparable company so he could support me in the style to which I had become accustomed."

"I'm guessing your father didn't take that request well."

No kidding. Laurel forced a smile. "My dad politely suggested Marc would feel better about whatever success he achieved by doing it on his own. Again, Marc accepted my father's advice smoothly." In a flat, embarrassed voice, Laurel forced herself to go on and finish the rest of the story. "Not long after that, he accepted a job with another company and broke up with me."

"Because…?" Cade prompted in abject sympathy.

"Marc said he couldn't marry a woman whose father thought so little of him." Laurel knotted her hands together in regret. "I blamed my dad for that until Marc married the daughter of his new boss and became a company VP as part of the deal." Shame filled her. "When I realized my parents had been right about him all along, I vowed never to be unwittingly used like that again."

Cade regarded Laurel steadily. "And yet you agreed to marry me."

"Temporarily," Laurel acknowledged, with a lift of her head. "Because I owed you and knew the score. I won't stay on indefinitely, knowing I am just a means to an end." She paused and looked Cade straight in the eye, wanting to be absolutely clear about this much. "I have too much respect for myself to let anyone make a fool out of me again."

Chapter Eight

"I am not disrespecting her," Cade told Beast hours later, as the two of them hung out in his study, as far away as possible from Laurel and the now audibly unhappy Patches, who were upstairs in her bedroom. "I never pretended our marriage was going to be some big romantic deal." Even though when he was alone with Laurel, he sometimes felt it was turning out that way. "She offered to marry me. I took her up on it. End of story."

So why did he suddenly feel so guilty? As if he ought to be courting Laurel and seeing where this deep attraction of theirs might lead, given half a chance, instead of running from the desire as fast as he could?

In another part of the house, there was another howl, louder and lonelier than the last.

"Furthermore, it wasn't my idea to bring that homeless pup into the house. I already have the best dog in the whole world. Yes, you. If she doesn't know how to handle Patches, that's her problem."

Beast groaned and pushed his head farther under Cade's desk, as if that would shut out the sound. When the mournful wailing continued, Beast cast a hopeful look Cade's way.

He sighed. "You think I ought to go up there and help out, don't you?"

The Lab made a high-pitched sound and continued staring at him.

"Fine." Cade pushed back his chair. "I just hope she's not in her pajamas or something." He had enough trouble getting the image of her in that sexy yellow sundress out of his mind.

"You stay here," he told Beast, before exiting the room and shutting the door behind him.

Cade climbed the rear stairs and strode down the hall toward Laurel's room. By the time he reached the door, his ears were aching. He could only imagine how hers felt. He rapped hard. She swung open the door.

Immediately, he noticed two things. She was not in conventional pajamas. She'd just had a shower. Her maple-syrup-colored hair was sleek and wet and coiled on the back of her head, the heavy length held in place with a clip. Her face was scrubbed bare and she smelled like soap and shampoo and the perfume she liked to wear. A snug-fitting, pastel-pink T-shirt that said DANGER HERE fell just past her rib cage. Darker pink running shorts started just beneath her navel and stopped as they reached her upper thighs. She was definitely not wearing a bra. And her long legs were incredibly sleek and sexy, both above and below the knee.

"I imagine you're here to complain about the noise," Laurel said, giving him a pointed look. "And tell me what a terrible pet owner I am because I can't get Patches to quiet down."

Liking the tartness in her voice almost as much as the fiery indignation in her blue eyes, Cade drawled laconically, "That was the plan, yes." Yet now that he was here and confronted with the situation, all he wanted to do was help.

Holding her steady gaze with ever-escalating pleasure, he asked, "What set Patches off?" He inclined his head to the frantically wailing canine. Laurel's puppy had been quiet as could be when he'd carried the training crate upstairs and Laurel had set Patches in it, shortly after supper. Now, the little golden retriever was running around the room, howling as if the world had ended.

Her lips forming a soft, delectable pout, Laurel stepped forward contentiously until the two of them were standing toe to toe. She angled her chin up to better look into his face. "I have no idea," she retorted in a low voice rife with frustration. "She was quiet when I got in the shower, but halfway through she started carrying on like that. I hurried as fast as I could, and then let her out of the crate, but that only seemed to make her more agitated and upset."

Against his better judgment, because he did not plan to become emotionally involved with this animal who obviously needed much more than he—or even Laurel—could ever give, Cade knelt down to get a better look at the pup. As the half-bald ball of yellow fur flew by, he caught the distressed look on the pup's face. "Maybe she needs to—"

Before he could finish the sentence, Patches stopped and squatted where she was.

Laurel clapped a hand over her mouth. "Oh. No… Patches! You're supposed to do that in the yard!"

She shot a distressed look at Cade. "I am so sorry."

"Well, at least we know what the problem was," he remarked dryly. "Let's get her outside." He scooped the suddenly quiet puppy up in his arms, trying hard not to notice how cuddly she was. "She may not be finished."

Laurel looked at the puddle on the floor. "I don't see how she could have anything left."

Cade lifted a brow.

"Oh!" Laurel clapped a hand over her mouth, even more distressed. Some of the color left her cheeks. "I didn't even think about that!"

"Good thing I did then," Cade drawled, deadpan. Glad Beast had guilted him into coming to the rescue, he led the way to the stairs. "When was the last time Patches went out?" he asked practically, deciding to school Laurel about this much.

She grabbed her sandals and hurried along beside him, her breasts jiggling beneath her top as she struggled to keep up. "After supper. I thought she'd be okay until morning, so I put her in her crate to go to sleep."

Laurel paused at the back door to put on her shoes. As she bent over, the back of her sleep-shorts rode up, exposing even more of her slender thighs. Telling himself not to think about what was under those pajamas, or how good she smelled, Cade turned on the outside lights, illuminating the entire yard. Aware that the last thing the two of them needed was a tête-à-tête in the moonlight—it was hard enough staying oblivious to his sexy new wife's presence as it was—Cade walked with her past the pool area to a grassy section at the rear and let Patches down. The puppy ran off immediately, sniffing hard as she went. Cade knew this was the kind of situation that could easily become a habit. To his surprise, he wasn't sure he minded. At least not nearly as much as he knew he should.

Cade turned back to Laurel, aware this was the first time he had ever seen her look completely out of her element. And he realized that he liked it when she turned to him for help, even if it was more or less by default. Cade relaxed beside her. Figuring it was to their mutual advantage to go over the dos and don'ts of housebreaking, he inclined his head toward hers and said, "First of all, a dog this age may not sleep all night. Second, she's going to have to go out every couple of hours to relieve herself. The best thing to do is let her be out for half an hour and do her stuff and give her some water, and food—if it's time for her to eat— which at this point she will need to do three times a day. Then you should put her back in the crate until it's time to do it again. If you want to let her romp around inside the house, off leash, I suggest you do that on the sunporch for up to thirty minutes at a time, if you are there to supervise her. The floor there is stone, so if there is an accident it will be easy to clean up. And if you are alert to the signs she's about to go there will be few of them, since from the porch you can quickly get her outside. And you should be sure she relieves herself before and after each 'play' session, because all the activity will quickly make her want to do just that. Otherwise, she should be in her crate. Period."

Laurel's eyes widened. "You mean leave her in her crate all the time?"

Cade recalled having the exact same conversation with Beast's breeder. He took her hand reassuringly and gave her the wise advice he had been given. "It's not cruel, Laurel. Crate training is a good thing. Dogs are den animals. Her crate serves as her room.

She will grow to like it and feel safe in there, and she won't soil her own quarters if she can help it, so that will help her start getting some control of her bladder and so on. And while she is this little, you can take the crate wherever you go, so she can be with you."

Laurel bit her lip. She looked over at the still-sniffing Patches, and then back down at their clasped hands. "What if she barks when I put her in it?"

Cade studied the color that had swept into her fair cheeks. "Ignore her until she quiets down and then praise her. And only take her out of the crate if she is quiet. Otherwise, Patches will get the idea all she has to do is bark and she will get her way. She needs to know her owner is in charge if she is ever going to feel secure. And a secure dog is a happy dog."

"Why didn't you tell me all this earlier?"

Because I didn't want to get attached to a dog that is only going to have to go back, Cade thought. But not sure Laurel was ready to hear that, he merely shrugged.

"You mean I'm going to have to get up every three to four hours all night?" Laurel asked, amazed.

Cade nodded, watching as Patches finally stopped running in circles, and squatted again to do what she mercifully had not done upstairs in the bedroom. "Unless you want to put up a pet gate and confine her in the laundry room and put some newspapers down, but I wouldn't recommend it. Patches is obviously suffering from separation anxiety, and being alone her first night away from the rest of the other dogs will only make her fearfulness worse. And that's a much slower way to house-train a dog."

Patches trotted toward them, panting hard. "She looks like she needs some water," Cade said.

Laurel went inside the back porch and returned with her water dish. Patches lapped at the liquid furiously, until she had drained it, then collapsed at Laurel's and Cade's feet. Laurel looked at him for advice. "You think she's ready to go back inside?"

Cade knew he was. The image of Laurel's breasts shifting freely beneath the skimpy T-shirt—and the fantasies such a vision engendered—were going to be with him all night. While she was sleeping—or tending to Patches—he would be lying alone in bed, thinking about the kisses they had shared, wishing there were more. And Cade knew himself well enough to realize those feelings, that growing starburst of desire, were not going away. The only blessing was that Laurel seemed to have no idea what he was considering, as, once again all practicality, she asked, "Do you have anything to clean the carpet with?"

Cade nodded. When they reached the sunporch, he held the door for them and escorted them through the hall to the kitchen. "Take Patches on up and put her in her crate. I'll meet you upstairs." He opened the cabinet beneath the kitchen sink. Next to the cleaning supplies was a spray bottle with enzyme cleaner specifically formulated for pet stains. He grabbed that and a roll of paper towels and went upstairs. By the time he got there, Patches was settled in her plastic crate, her face mashed up against the metal front. She was whimpering softly. Listening, Laurel seemed to be near tears. Cade understood why. The sound of a newly separated puppy calling futilely for its mother and the rest of its "pack" of siblings was heartrending. But Cade knew it wouldn't help to fall apart, the way Laurel was. Patches needed them to tell her—by their actions and attitude—that everything was indeed okay. The little puppy had no need to worry. She was not going back to a bad or scary situation. Her needs would be taken care of and she would find the love and devotion she craved.

Cade and Laurel both would see to that.

Ignoring the emotion brewing in the room, Cade handed the towels and spray cleaner to Laurel, then walked over to get the wastebasket. "Sop up the excess moisture with paper towels first. Then spray on the cleaner. Let it set for a good fifteen or twenty minutes, then sop that up with paper towels. If the stain or odor remains, repeat the process."

Laurel inclined her head at the whimpering Patches, even as she followed his directions. "This will get better, won't it, Cade?"

He hesitated. He knew what Laurel wanted to hear, but that was not the reality of the situation. "Training even a healthy, properly socialized puppy is a long process," he said finally. "A dog like this might be better off with someone like Frances Klenck."

Laurel shot him a drop-dead look. "In other words, you don't think I am capable of rearing a puppy," she stated coldly.

Cade hunkered down in front of her and lent a hand with the cleanup process. "I think it's a lot of work."

Laurel tossed her head, stubborn as ever. "Did you get Beast when he was a puppy?" Finished, she went into the bathroom to wash her hands.

Cade stood elbow to elbow with her and did the same. "Yes."

"Was he the only puppy you ever had?" Laurel asked, as they shared a hand towel.

Dangerous territory again. "No," he said carefully, avoiding her eyes. He hung the towel on the rack and led the way back into her bedroom. Patches had apparently given up on trying to cry her way out of her crate. Her face was still pressed against the wire door. She was breathing deeply and struggling to keep her eyes open. "I had another puppy, before him."

Patches continued to keep a watchful eye on Cade as he lounged against the bureau.

Laurel sank down on the edge of the bed. "Did you raise both puppies all on your own?"

Cade shrugged, aware he hadn't expected Laurel to be this curious, or this stubborn. Damn it, he liked spending time with her, even though he wasn't sure it was wise. And he liked kissing her even more. "The first one, I did. It was summertime and I was a kid. Because I was working when I got Beast, I had help from a dog walker. If you'd like, I'll call her and see if she can care for Patches tomorrow while we are both at work."

Laurel blinked. Her tongue snaked out to wet her lower lip. "I can't take Patches to work?"

"Trust me." Cade frowned, his exasperation beginning to get the better of him once again. He ran a hand across his jaw and realized that although he had shaved that morning, he needed to again. "That's not a good idea."

"You said you sometimes take Beast with you to work," she countered mulishly.

Admitting to himself all over again how good Laurel looked in the cropped sleep T-shirt and matching shorts, Cade told her with absolute honesty, "That, darlin', is because Beast is an obedience-trained, adult dog, not a confused, upset little puppy who hasn't been house-trained."

Laurel took the clip out of her hair. "I guess there is a difference," she mused, as she ran her fingers through the thick, wavy strands.

"Quite a difference." Aware he wanted her more than ever, Cade stepped as close to her as he dared. "So about the dog walker?"

Laurel pushed off the bed and stood. She tossed her still-damp mane of hair. "It won't be necessary tomorrow or even the next day. First thing tomorrow, Patches is going to one of the vets who volunteered to care for the rescued dogs—and she may have to stay for a day or two, depending on how long it takes to complete all the tests and do whatever is necessary to get her on the path to good health."

That was good, Cade thought. Laurel's time away from the homeless pup would hopefully enable her to gain some perspective, and decide if this was something she really wanted to undertake, long term.

"But when Patches does come back to me," she continued, oblivious to Cade's thoughts, "I'll hire a dog walker to look in on her during the days."

"It won't be a problem," Cade said. He could easily afford the expense. As long as he was CEO of Dunnigan Dog Food, anyway.

"You're right. It won't be your problem." Laurel scowled, her frustration with the situation apparent. "Because I'm paying for it."

Wondering why it was so hard for her to accept help, and so incredibly easy for her to give it, he shrugged. "Suit yourself."

"One more thing." Laurel put an arm across the portal and blocked the way out of her bedroom. Her perfume teased his senses. She tossed him a tight, humorless smile. "We never discussed salary." She paused, even more on edge. "I will be getting one for my work at DDF, won't I? I mean, at least minimum wage…"

There she went again, Cade thought in mounting irritation, putting the needs of others above her own. He didn't know why Laurel was so willing to go to the mat for everyone else, but couldn't seem to stop people from walking all over her to get what they wanted. All he knew was that it was time that stopped. And he had an idea how to accomplish just that.

For a long moment, Laurel did not think Cade was going to answer her. "Is that all you think you're worth?" he asked as he plucked her arm away from the door frame and strode past her into the hall. "Minimum wage?"

Laurel raced after him. It took two of her strides to keep up with his every one. "It's hard to gauge," she said, knowing as a college grad she should be making way more than that, even if she was just starting out at DDF. She also knew companies operated under set budgets that might or might not include adding extra staff midyear. "I don't know what everyone else there earns."

Cade walked into his bedroom. As if oblivious to her presence, he began to strip down. First his shirt, then his shoes, socks…and trousers! Laurel swallowed hard, reminding herself she had already seen him in racing trunks that left little to the imagination, when it came to his ultramasculine physique.

He turned to give her his full attention. His lips took on a cynical tilt. "What difference does that make?"

Laurel drew her eyes away from his slate-gray boxers. She definitely did not need to be thinking about size. "Well, some, I would think." She spoke in a strangled voice.

A peculiar glint came into his eyes. "So you aren't going to set a price for your services?"

Should she?

Cade stalked closer still. He quirked his brow in a way that seemed to indicate she had lost her mind. "You want *me* to do that for you?"

Laurel backed up until her legs hit the side of the bed. *What had gotten into him?* "Isn't that the way it usually works?" Her heart gave a nervous kick against her ribs. She angled her chin and smiled. "The person doing the hiring tells the person being hired what he or she is going to pay for the job."

Cade shrugged his broad shoulders and regarded her smugly, a sense of purpose glittering in his eyes. "Not always. And never in my case. But I suppose," he allowed, with a flash of humor, "that method will work out fine this time."

Fearing she knew exactly where this conversation was headed—a place they'd be wise not to go—Laurel flushed despite herself and tried to step past him.

Cade caught her before she could escape, and reeled her back to his side. "So," he asked her very, very softly, "does this mean I get to define your duties, too?"

Laurel could swear he had sex on his mind, which was ridiculous, since they had agreed this would be more business arrangement than marriage. "Don't bosses usually get to do that?" she asked, ignoring the sexual tension simmering between them.

Cade ran a hand up and down her arm, slipping his fingers beneath the hem of her cap sleeve to caress her shoulder. His gaze drifted over her like a warm breeze. "Employees can set limits, too."

Good point. And a prerogative she hadn't expected to need with Cade. Temper soaring because this was all a little too calculated for her, she moved his hand away. "Fine," she stated with all the steely determination of a Texas belle, born and bred. Defiantly, she met—then held—Cade's gaze, letting him know that some things about their attraction to each other were not meant to be run like a business. "Then I outlaw you touching me like that."

Cade paused to consider her words. Some of the laughter left his eyes, but none of the lazy male intention. He wrapped both his arms around her waist and tugged her close, so her lower half was pressed against his. Her heart raced as she felt the strength of his desire and the answering tingle deep inside her. Cade slowly tilted his head, lowered his lips to hers. "Suppose I want to kiss you then," he suggested playfully, his mouth hovering just above hers.

"Not as part of the job," Laurel warned, splaying both hands across the hard musculature of his chest, to hold him at bay.

Cade lifted a brow and smiled. "You wouldn't let me add wifely lovemaking duties to the salary grid?"

Laurel gulped as her thoughts turned unexpectedly amorous. Sure now that he was teasing her, she stated stiffly, "No, I would not!"

Releasing her, Cade grabbed a swimsuit from his dresser drawer and strolled into the adjacent bath. He shut the door most of the way and disappeared behind it. "How about as my assistant then?" he called out.

Trying not to think about the swish of his boxers hitting the floor, and the snap of the nylon racing suit being tugged up those rock-hard thighs and into place, Laurel closed her eyes. She wished she didn't know how good he looked practically naked. The sheer male excellence of what had already been revealed to her made her want to see the rest. "I think that would be illegal," she said dryly.

"I think," Cade mocked with exaggerated licentiousness, strolling right back out clad in nothing but skintight bright blue trunks, "you'd be right." He paused in front of her, folding his arms across his bare chest. A grin spreading across his face, he looked her up and down with a wistful sigh. "It doesn't stop me from wanting you, though."

Nor me you.

But wanting was not doing.

"It's going to have to," Laurel said firmly. She stood where she was, legs braced, hands planted on her hips, toes curling into the soft carpet. "Because there are limits to what I will or will not do for you, Cade." And she would not make love to him without it meaning something to them both on an emotional level.

"Good." Cade sobered, all business once again. "Now tell me again what salary you expect to make from DDF," he demanded.

Laurel stared at him, every bit as furious as she knew she had a right to be, considering the outrageous proposal he had just made. She stared at him in withering displeasure, then quoted the salary she had been making at her last job, plus twenty-five percent.

Cade paused to consider her demand. He seemed to know she

was reaching. "You won't accept minimum wage?" he asked after another painfully long moment.

"For this kind of harassment?" she responded in a voice dripping with sarcasm. "Not on your life!" She did not appreciate being jerked around like that, and it was time he knew it!

Cade grinned, clearly pleased. His expression became even more intent. "See how easy it was to stand up for yourself—even with someone like me pushing back at you, hard? You've got a deal." He plucked a towel off the rack in the bathroom, looped it around his neck and continued cheerfully, "I'll talk to human resources in the morning and get you on the DDF payroll as of yesterday."

Laurel regarded him in stunned disbelief. "Wait just one redhot minute. Are you trying to tell me you were hitting on me just now to teach me a lesson?"

Cade nodded. "I wanted to see if I could get you to stand up for yourself and put your needs above someone else's, namely mine." He clapped a congratulatory hand on her shoulder. "And you did."

THE MORE LAUREL THOUGHT about it, the angrier she got. Deciding she wasn't the only one who could be taught a very valuable lesson in the most dramatic way possible, she went down to the swimming pool, and perched on a deck chair, waiting for Cade to finish his workout.

When he had completed his last lap and emerged, dripping wet, out of the pool and into the April evening, she walked over to him. "We're not finished," she said.

Cade wiped his face with his towel, then began running it over his shoulders and neck. "I'm not giving you more money than what you asked for, so you can forget it," he said, apparently thinking he was cutting her off at the pass.

Laurel watched coyly as he rubbed his torso dry. "I don't want money."

Cade glanced up at her as he ran the terry cloth over his long, muscular legs. Finished, he tossed the towel onto a deck chair. "So then what do you want?" he asked.

Laurel smiled at him smugly, aware she wasn't the only one who could shock and tempt, and not mean one damn word of it. "Sex."

Cade blinked. "Excuse me?"

Laurel looked deep into his eyes, beginning to realize just how much fun this was going to be. "I'm your wife," she repeated in a low, deadpan voice. She shrugged, pretending she wasn't playing with fire here. "I want sex."

All the humor left his face, replaced by something much more complicated. And dangerous.

He strolled closer, all possessive, protective male. Aware he was watching her—a lot more grimly now—she waited for his response. "I thought you didn't want sex," Cade said finally.

Damn, but he was gorgeous, fresh from a workout. Laurel took his hand in hers and swung it lightly, playfully between them. She looked down at their clasped hands. His palm was so much larger and stronger. Yet her smaller, more delicate one fit into it perfectly. "Maybe I changed my mind," she purred in the sexiest voice she could manage.

Cade's fingers tightened on hers. The brooding look was back in his eyes. "What kind of game are you playing?" he demanded gruffly.

Laurel dropped his hand and stepped back. "The same one you were, you presumptuous know-it-all!" she declared.

"So you don't want sex?"

To her dismay he had the same look of utter concentration and ruthless determination in his eyes he had whenever he talked business.

"I don't want *you* pretending *you* want sex only to prove the point that I am weak and foolish!" Laurel corrected with a toss of her head.

"That little exercise I put you through earlier was not about sex, Laurel," Cade explained impatiently. "It was about self-respect and taking care of your own needs. I was proving how strong and sensible and self-protective you can be when motivated."

She lifted both her hands in the age-old signal to back off. "Well, I don't need you teaching me any lessons!" she said heatedly. Deciding this was one confrontation that was well over, she spun away.

Cade scoffed. "You're just ticked off because I didn't kiss you."

"Excuse me?" Laurel stomped right back.

Cade looked down at her, all damp, determined male. "You heard me," he repeated, even more complacently than before. His glance roved over her from head to toe before slowly and deliberately returning to her face. "You wanted me to kiss you and I didn't...and now you want to slug me for it."

Laurel gasped, unable to believe he had actually said such a thing. "I do not!"

He chuckled down at her. "Liar."

That was it. The last straw. Her hand flew up, seemingly of its own volition.

To Laurel's frustration, Cade caught it before it ever connected with his face. "Now who's conning whom?" he asked huskily.

Suddenly, Laurel was trembling. Not just because of the warmth of his fingers on her wrist, but because she feared he might be right. Not that she would let him know that. "I. Do. Not. Want. You. To. Kiss. Me," she said.

Cade's wicked smile widened. He clamped one arm around her waist, threaded the other hand through her hair and brought her against him, length to length. "Tell me that again in five minutes, and I'll believe you."

She barely had time to gasp before he fastened his lips on hers in a riveting, passionate kiss that robbed her of all will and reason. She moaned softly as he bent her backward and deepened the kiss until it was so hot and sensual it stole her breath away. The hardness of his chest pressed against her breasts. Lower still, she could feel the proof of his desire. She arched against him, needing, wanting, so much. He groaned, too, as their lips and tongues and mouths mated. A feeling of femininity swept through her, intensifying the liquid yearning she felt deep inside.

Laurel didn't want to give in to him, didn't want to surrender her heart and soul, didn't want to feel—never mind act—so married. Yet as Cade continued to kiss her deliberately and evocatively she found herself succumbing helplessly to the sweetness, the tenderness of his embrace. She loved the dark, male scent of him, and the feel of him, so warm and strong and hard, pressed up against her. She loved how he challenged her, the reckless, womanly way he made her feel. He wasn't afraid to push life to the limit, and for the first time in her life, he made her want to do the same. He was hard, relentless, irresistible in his pursuit of her. And for once that felt okay. It felt good to seek out what she required. And to go about finding it…in him.

With a groan of pleasure, he stole her breath. The passion in his hot, wet kiss fueled her own, his tongue sizzling along hers, circling and flicking across the edges of her teeth before dipping deep. Overwhelmed by the taste of him, she ran her hands over his cheekbones, the nape of his neck, his shoulders, chest. And still they kissed, again and again, until her heart pounded and her spirits soared, until she trembled and went weak in the knees.

Cade hadn't meant to kiss Laurel at all tonight. In fact, given how she was dressed, and how much he wanted her, he had warned himself against doing just that. He'd figured if they got started, even a little bit, well…something like this would happen. And he knew she didn't mean to kiss him back, which somehow made their coming together this way all the sweeter. Laurel in a temper was something glorious to behold. Laurel kissing him in a temper was even better. Her body was soft and warm as it molded to his, her lips acquiescent one minute, as if she had forgotten their argument, then impossibly fiesty and challenging the next. He could feel her fighting the want and need, just as he was. And he could feel her losing the battle. It was in the way her lips molded to his. In the depth and the torridness of their kiss, the fact it was going on and on and on, and getting hotter, more erotic by the minute.

Loving the way she responded to him, he swept his hand down her body, charting her dips and curves, then moved them back to her waist to slide beneath the hem of her sleep shirt. Her mouth was pliant beneath his, warm and sexy, her body supple, surrendering. She was wild in a way he had never imagined, every bit as giving as he could have wished. He forgot what he knew, and reveled in what they felt. She made a small, helpless sound of pleasure in the back of her throat when he found her breasts. Luxuriating in the silky feel of her bare skin, he palmed the weight of the full globes, rubbed the nipples with his thumbs, until they beaded, and the need to have her was a hot, incessant ache. Cade shifted his hands to her hips, guiding her closer still, fitting her against his arousal. Knowing, in a matter of seconds, the two of them could be stretched out on one of the chaises… discovering even more indescribable pleasure.

And she knew it, too, of course.

As well as all the reasons why they *shouldn't* give in to a momentary wish. Which was why, Cade figured, through the fog of his desire, and the even stronger mist of his deep, incessant need for her, that Laurel abruptly came to her senses and said, "No." She broke away from him, her breath coming hard and fast in her chest as sanity returned. Color lit her cheeks, emotion her eyes. "No."

The heat between them vanished as swiftly as it had appeared. Frustration welled up within him, along with a crushing disappointment. And the even more desperate need to retain his pride. Figuring if nothing else, he could sure as hell play it cool, Cade looked at her and drawled, "Exactly what you should have said all along."

THEY PARTED SOON AFTER, without another word. Sleep was elusive. Cade heard Laurel getting up with Patches all night long. He didn't go and help her, because he didn't want a replay of what had happened out by the pool. His gut sense told him something similar would occur if they were anywhere near each other in anything resembling an intimate setting. "It's not that we don't want each other," Cade told Beast, as the first light of dawn came whispering into his bedroom and sliced across his big, empty-feeling bed. "It's that we're both too smart to go down that particular road."

Beast lifted his head and regarded Cade with a mournful, empathetic gaze.

"Like it or not, want it or not, sex brings up all sorts of feelings," Cade continued, filling his canine friend in on the situation. He rolled to his side and reached down to pet Beast's silky black head, aware that even his best friend couldn't ease the loneliness he felt right now. "And the emotions aren't always the ones a person wants or would even expect to have. Sometimes," as had often happened to him, "when it's over, one of the parties involved is just sort of numb or, I don't know, empty inside. I know that sounds corny." Cade looked into Beast's liquid black eyes, doing his best to explain. "But that's the only way to describe it. Anyway, whatever emotions are felt, it's usually a problem, because more often than not both parties involved in the lovemaking are not on the same page, and realizing that makes someone mad and the other person uncomfortable. Or just plain sad or disappointed." And, he admitted silently, he was usually the one who was uncomfortable because he wasn't returning the feelings and falling in love, and it always ended badly.

Cade sighed as Beast nuzzled his hand. "I'm not the kind of guy, it seems, who can have a sex buddy and get away with it."

Which was why Cade had abstained for quite a while, letting work eradicate his healthy, male desires. Until last night, when temptation had arisen, and he'd answered Laurel's challenge.

And now the truth was out. He wanted Laurel to the point that he wasn't going to rest until he had made her his. And she definitely wanted him, whether she admitted it or not. If they weren't careful, this marriage of theirs would be consummated before they knew it.

And then where would they be?

Chapter Nine

"We need to talk," Cade told George Jr. shortly after arriving at the office the next morning. And Cade wanted to do it before Laurel's "surprise" arrived around ten that morning.

"Sure thing, cuz," George Jr. said, regarding him with breezy arrogance.

Cade looked at the game of blackjack on George Jr.'s monitor. Deciding the other employees did not need to hear this, he shut the door behind him. "How are you doing on the marketing plan for the opening of the Dunnigan Dog Care Center?"

George Jr. barely looked up. "I'm working on it," he lied amiably.

Cade's temper flared. It was one thing to dis him—he could take it. To disrespect the company entrusted to them was something else.

George Jr. pushed away from his desk and leaned back in his chair, hands clasped behind his head. "But it's like trying to make a hopelessly tarnished penny shine." He flashed a condescending smile. "A bad idea is a bad idea."

Frustration roiled in Cade's gut. "In other words, you're no more behind this venture than you were at the outset," he surmised calmly.

"That about sums it up, yeah," George Jr. agreed in a low, disinterested tone. "I plan to tell the other board members at the dinner party that you and your new bride are throwing this evening."

Cade had figured as much. He welcomed the discussion. He

also had an idea how he would handle his ne'er-do-well cousin's mutiny. In the meantime, he had a warning to deliver. "I heard what you said to Laurel yesterday." His jaw tightened. "Stay away from my wife."

George Jr. propped his shoes on his desk and regarded him with an expression of smug derision. "She didn't seem to know anything about Ariel."

Cade shrugged. "She does now."

That information seemed to take his cousin back, but soon George Jr. was as snide as ever. "Is she also aware that she, too, will never be anything more than a means to an end to you?"

Cade knew he had reason to feel guilty about the way he had treated Ariel. He'd thought he could protect his ex-fiancée's feelings by downplaying his career's importance to him. He knew now that did not work, and had vowed never to make the same mistake again. Hence, he had been totally honest with Laurel. Even when he knew it made him look bad in her view. "I'm not using Laurel," he said gruffly.

"Sure you are," George Jr. countered with an ugly smile. "And once the rest of the board realizes to what extent you would go to bankrupt this company and take it down a development and expansion path it never should have started on, they're going to realize what I already know—that you have no business being the CEO. So strap on the flak jacket, cuz. Tonight is going to be one wild ride."

Perhaps more than you know, Cade agreed wordlessly.

"IS EVERYTHING OKAY?" Laurel asked, sticking her head in Cade's office an hour later. "You look a little ticked off."

I am. "Nothing I can't handle," Cade said.

She studied him. "Or want to talk about, apparently."

He inclined his head in tacit admission. "You got that right."

"Okay, chief." Laurel walked all the way into the room. To-day she was wearing a knee-length pink-and-black paisley skirt more in line with the business-casual attire of the company, and a pink knit top with cutaway sleeves that made the most of her beautiful arms. She had a lacy pink cardigan tied around her waist. It only partly covered the pawprints along one hip that Patches had left as Laurel said goodbye to the pup before turning her over to Frances Klenck for her stay at the vet's.

Laurel smiled, the model of efficiency. You could hardly tell that she had been so upset to have to say goodbye to Patches that morning that she had cried for a good five minutes. Another indication, Cade thought, that Laurel was getting way too attached to a dog she wasn't up to caring for.

"I wanted to ask you to look at menus for the dinner party this evening." Laurel's perfume teased his senses as she put several down on the desk in front of him. "I found three restaurants that could cater it on such short notice—but I didn't know if any of the board members have dietary restrictions, so I thought I better check before I nailed down the final arrangements."

"No seafood—Dotty is allergic—but everyone likes Tex-Mex featuring either poultry or beef." He handed her the menu that looked best to him.

"Any preferences on actual dishes?"

"You decide."

Laurel made notes as they talked. "Buffet or sit-down?"

"Buffet." Cade let his glance rove over her upswept hair before turning to her lovely blue eyes. "And make sure there's plenty for seconds—Lance Ayers always likes to go back, as does Uncle George."

She ran her fingertip absently across her lower lip. "Dessert?"

"And several appetizers," Cade said, aware her action was reminding him of other, more intimate things. "Plus Mexican coffee, decaf and herbal tea."

Laurel licked her lip as she wrote. "Does the caterer need to bring dishes?"

Cade shook his head, wishing he still didn't want to kiss and hold her so much. Hadn't they proved last night what a bad idea that was? Hell, he was still feeling the effects of the unconsummated passion. Just being around her like again like this made him ache.

Oblivious to the ardent nature of his thoughts, Laurel glanced up at him, waiting for his reply.

"My mother's china and crystal are at the house," Cade replied curtly. "We'll use those."

Laurel put that down, too, then looked up. "I called the vet's office to check on Patches. Apparently she is doing well so far, although they still think I won't get her back for at least twenty-four hours." She sighed, her disappointment obvious.

"I'm sure she will be fine."

"I know that. I just miss her."

Not exactly the sentiment he wanted to hear. But certainly the opening he yearned for. "Listen," Cade said casually, "there's something I've been wanting to talk to you about." He frowned as the phone on his desk buzzed. He picked up and listened. "Send him in." Cade set the receiver down and looked at Laurel, hoping like heck this effort on his part went the way he hoped it would. "There's someone I want you to meet," he told her seriously.

She arched a brow, curious, as he got up and walked toward her.

Seconds later, a tall, distinguished-looking man with thinning gray hair walked in. He was dressed in a Stetson, western shirt, jeans and boots. He was carrying a small pet crate. Cade greeted him with a smile. "Laurel, I'd like you to meet Toby Saelinger. Toby, my wife, Laurel. Toby is the breeder who bred Beast. He owns Saelinger Kennels."

Toby set the crate on the floor, then walked back to shut the door to the office. He returned to the crate and pulled out the four-month-old yellow Labrador retriever Cade and Toby had talked about on the phone. "Meet Meadow," he told Laurel.

Meadow went down into a "play bow"—hindquarters hunched close to the floor, front legs stretched all the way out in front of her. Her intentions made known, she bounced back up with her tail wagging and pranced around the room in a proud "show dog" gait, greeting them all by turn.

"She's beautiful." Laurel smiled, admiring the soft, fluffy puppy with the short silky white-blond coat and velvety black nose and eyes. She knelt and petted Meadow gently.

Cade had hoped the two would get along. He knelt beside Laurel and Meadow. "She could be yours. Just say the word," he told Laurel cheerfully.

Laurel's eyes went from happy to wary in an instant. Her delectable lower lip slid out into a pout as she stood. "What do you mean? I already have a dog."

Now this, Cade thought, was the reaction he had braced himself for. "Not officially, not yet," he told her practically. Able to see this was not going well thus far, he rushed on. "I know you want a puppy of your very own, Laurel. I want you to have one that is healthy. And better yet, housebroken. Meadow is crate- and house-trained. She sleeps through the night. She's also hip, eye and heart certified."

Laurel blinked, bewildered. "What does that mean?"

"She's been examined by a vet and has no physical defects in those areas. And," Toby Saelinger explained, "she has started her obedience classes." He snapped his fingers for a demonstration. "Meadow, sit!"

Meadow stopped what she was doing and sat down, all serious.

"You can pet her again if you like," Toby told Laurel. "She loves affection. She really is the sweetest dog."

Laurel knelt down in front of the puppy, all welcoming warmth as she stroked the pup's silky blond head. "You're right," she murmured adoringly. "Meadow is gorgeous. I don't know when I've seen a more beautiful—or beautifully behaved—puppy. But," Laurel sighed, standing up, "I can't take her. I already have a dog. But thank you, anyway."

Toby looked at Cade, clearly confused. As he had every right to be, Cade thought. He had told Toby on the phone it was a done deal. "I'll call you later and we'll talk," he promised the older man.

Nodding in understanding, Toby collected Meadow and left.

Unfortunately, Cade noted, Laurel was not nearly as cooperative as she turned back to him, temper flashing in her eyes. "How could you?" she demanded, incredulous.

How could I not? Cade thought. *When this impulsive decision of yours has calamity written all over it?* He had figured Laurel would have realized that after just one sleepless night. Apparently not. So once again he tried his best to talk sense into her. "Look, I understand you wanting a dog for yourself. But it would be a mistake for you to take on a puppy like Patches, who needs so much," he said.

Laurel's brow arched. She folded her arms in front of her militantly. "Maybe for you. Not for me."

Cade closed the distance between them. "Need I remind you that your choice in this matter does affect me, since we are living together?" He wanted to make her life easier and happier. Not more difficult.

Laurel tilted her head to one side. "Are you asking me to make a choice between you and my puppy?" she demanded with Southern belle sweetness. "Because if you are…"

Cade studied her, not sure whether he wanted to talk some sense into her or simply kiss her. One thing was certain. He'd never met a more maddening woman in his life. "You'd really renege on your promise and leave me over a dog," he drawled sarcastically.

"You bet your arrogant soul I would!" Laurel declared. And on that note, she picked up her clipboard and stormed out.

"How long are you going to stay angry with me?" Cade asked, when he returned home hours later and found Laurel getting ready for their dinner party.

"That depends." She flashed him a bright, humorless smile. "How long do you have?"

Baffled by her obvious pique with him, Cade watched as she withdrew damask linens from the mahogany buffet. He edged closer. "I wasn't trying to tick you off."

Laurel dumped the linens in the center of the table and whirled to face him. "Right," she agreed sarcastically. "You were just trying to dump my puppy!"

Put that way, Cade had to concede his actions did sound bad. "You don't know what you're getting into with that dog," he retorted hotly. He was just trying to do what was best for everyone and still give her the puppy of her very own that she so obviously craved.

"Don't I?" She fixed him with a withering glare.

Cade bit down on a string of swear words. It was too late to take back what he had done. The most he could manage was a save. And judging by the disparaging looks she was continuing to give him, that was going to be one hell of a task. "Patches could have hip dysplasia," he said, trying again to approach her, his hands outstretched.

"She doesn't," Laurel stated flatly. "The vet already called. Her heart, hips and eyes all checked out. Not that you're interested," she continued loftily, with a toss of her glorious hair, "but her patchy fur loss has been caused by stress and malnutrition. The vet is sure that with proper food and a lot of tender loving care, she is going to be just fine, and will one day soon grow a coat every bit as glossy and beautiful as Meadow's. I've already signed up for puppy obedience classes with Patches. He said to continue with the crate training, when I get her back tomorrow. So, if that's all—"

"It's not all." Cade moved back slightly, and for want of anything better to do with them, shoved his hands deep in the pockets of his trousers. "Why won't you at least *consider* adopting Meadow instead of Patches?"

"Because a dog like Meadow is not going to have one bit of trouble finding a home." Laurel scowled as she put the pad on the table. "A puppy like Patches is." She looked up at him, moisture shimmering in her eyes. "She needs me, Cade."

And I need you, he thought, almost as surprised by the notion as he was by Laurel's reaction to the perfectly healthy purebred puppy he had tried to give her. He leaned in to lend a hand with the tablecloth. "You don't know anything about her sire and dam's medical history."

"So?" Laurel smoothed out the wrinkled fabric with the flat of her palm.

Cade straightened the edge. "You could get your heart broken if it doesn't work out."

Laurel picked up the stack of napkins and began putting one at each place setting. "I could get my heart broken taking a chance on you and this marriage, too, but it didn't stop you from advising me to do so."

"Listen to me." Cade caught her by the shoulders and made her face him. "Patches was not bred by responsible breeders. I doubt the owners of the puppy mill even looked at the genetic history of the dogs involved before they mated them, or considered the probability of the littermates developing cancer or some other physical abnormality or disease."

Laurel broke free of his grasp and paced away from him. "I think you're exaggerating the risks."

Cade brought out the silver chest. "I don't," he argued back.

"Okay, then." She sent him an exasperated look, as even more fire came into her eyes, making her look simultaneously sexy and unapproachable as hell. With her chin set stubbornly, she went back to pulling out the appropriate number of forks, spoons and knives. "Give me one example. Just who do you know that this has happened to—when they adopted a dog with an unfortunate beginning?"

"Me," Cade said quietly stepping forward to assist her with that, too. "It happened to me."

She turned pale as their fingers brushed.

Cade pulled out a chair and sat down. He drew Laurel onto his lap. "The first dog I adopted—Dixie—was a stray I found on our doorstep. She was a golden retriever-yellow Lab-beagle mix." Suddenly, he found there were tears in his eyes and a lump in his throat the size of walnut. Because he didn't want Laurel to suffer the same, he pushed on in a rusty sounding voice, "And I loved her so much."

Laurel's slender body relaxed in his arms. Compassion filled her blue eyes. "What happened?"

"Dixie got cancer when she was only two."

"And she died," Laurel guessed.

Cade nodded, aware his cheeks were wet, but not caring. "After six months of grueling chemotherapy and endless pain."

He gulped, recalling that awful time. It had killed him to see his beloved pet in so much pain, to not be able to explain to Dixie why she was having to suffer so much. And in the end, it hadn't made any difference, anyway. All Cade had done by searching out every possible cure was prolong his pet's agony. "Had I known that was in store for me…" Cade's voice caught as he passed a hand over his face. "Needless to say, I would have waited and gotten a dog with a better prognosis in the first place."

"One who wasn't likely to get cancer," Laurel stated.

"Right."

She wreathed her arms around Cade's shoulders. "And what if you hadn't taken Dixie in? Then what, Cade? Don't you see?" she murmured softly, looking deep into his eyes. "Dixie needed you the same way Patches needs me."

Cade knew Laurel thought so. He released a long breath and shoved his fingers through his hair.

Laurel drew her palms down his arms, soothing, reassuring. She wrapped her hands around his biceps. "What you did was a good thing, Cade." She kissed his cheek, the curve of his jaw, his ear.

"You have no idea how much it hurts to lose a dog that way," he warned.

"Loving is always a risk," she said gently. "But it's one I'm willing to take." She laid one palm across his heart, the other stayed at his waist. "The question is, why aren't you willing, too?"

Guilt flooded Cade, along with the more familiar hesitation. "I have Beast," he reminded her. His faithful friend and companion meant the world to him.

Laurel sat back and settled her bottom more firmly on his lap. "But no one else I can see."

How was it possible she had known him only a few short days and zeroed in on that fact of life?

"Why are you so afraid to get close to someone, Cade?" she whispered.

Because, he thought, *every time I've been happy—even briefly—that happiness has been snatched away from me.* So he had stopped risking his heart and became content to just be. His new motto had been Work on Business, Forget the Rest. That had seemed like a good and workable plan until Laurel came into his life. Now, thanks to her, he realized just how lonely he had become.

Cade gave in to impulse and covered her hand with his own. He paused, delighting in the warm feeling of her skin and the pulse throbbing in her wrist. "I'm not afraid." In fact he was curious to see where this fast-growing intimacy between them would lead.

Laurel drew a deep, energizing breath. "Then prove it," she dared softly, her eyes glimmering with emotion.

Cade knew she meant by adopting Patches into his heart, too. In order to change the subject, he chose to deliberately misunderstand. "Like this?" He took Laurel's chin in hand. Before she could do more than offer a token protest, he captured her lips with his. Heat fused with need. His arms wrapped around her and everything else fell away as he crushed her against him in a long, hot, possessive kiss. She gave him back everything he expected, everything he wanted. Her lips pressed against his, whisper-soft at first, then more bold and adventurous. With a groan of pleasure, she tangled her fingers in his hair and brought him closer still. Cade gloried in her trembling response, even as he grew impatient for more. Physical passion was nothing new to him; these feelings were. When he was with Laurel, especially like this, it melted something inside him. He found himself reaching out to her, and felt her giving of herself in return. The more she gave, the more *he* wanted to give. If they didn't have guests coming…

Telling himself this was definitely something that would be continued, Cade reined in his desire and reluctantly ended the kiss. They drew apart, breathless. Still wanting so much more.

Laurel was the first to collect herself. "You better be careful," she teased, in an obvious effort to hold him at bay. "Or you might find yourself really married—at least in the sexual sense."

Suddenly, Cade realized, that did not seem like such a bad thing.

"ALMOST READY?" CADE asked two hours later, strolling into her bedroom with Beast loping along behind him.

Laurel smiled at Cade's steady companion. She had never

realized how much company a dog could be. Pets definitely added a new dimension to your life. As did husbands…

"I just need to get this necklace on," she murmured.

Cade stepped behind her to assist with the clasp. The feel of his hands brushing her skin sent a shimmer of awareness through her. His head was so close to hers she could feel the heat of his breath on the nape of her neck. "You look beautiful tonight," he murmured.

"You look pretty fine yourself, chief," Laurel teased, meeting his eyes in the mirror, aware all over again how handsome he looked in a suit and tie.

Her use of the teasing endearment brought a sexy gleam to his eyes. He chuckled, the sound of his husky male laughter warming her heart. And that in turn made her think about the kiss they had shared earlier, and how much she wanted him. She hadn't come into this union expecting to do anything but bide her time until she could gracefully ease her way out of this very tricky situation. But something indefinable had changed between them. Slowly but surely, Cade had opened his heart to the potential of their marriage just as she had. The knowledge thrilled her as much as it scared her. If he kept looking at her like that, touching her like that, she knew excitement would inevitably trump fear. She would fall all the way in love with him. He might even fall for her. And they would end up in bed together, making love. Hot, wild, passionate love.

Laurel put her earrings in, trying not to think how right the two of them looked when they stood together like this. "The caterers are setting up in the kitchen."

He turned her around to face him, bringing her flush against him. "I know. I just went down to talk to them." Cade tucked the hair behind her ear. "Everything looks great, as does the dining room. You did a wonderful job setting this up."

They gazed at each other and smiled. "I want everything to go well for you tonight."

Cade frowned. "Easier said than done," he stated gruffly.

She tensed. "What do you mean?"

He released a long breath and propped his hands on his hips.

The action pushed back the edges of his dove-gray suit jacket, revealing the flatness of his abdomen beneath the starched shirt and tie. "George Jr. is spoiling for a fight."

And, as it turned out, it wasn't long in coming.

As soon as everyone had settled down with a drink and a plate of appetizers in the living room, Cade's cousin took center stage at the mantel. "Let's get down to business, shall we?"

Laurel lifted a brow. George Jr. was not the host, yet was acting as if he was. Cade appeared ready to give his cousin enough leeway to make him look like a horse's rear end.

"I have grave reservations about the potential of the flagship store," George Jr. continued haughtily.

Cade took a small sip of his drink. "Which is why, perhaps, you've been doing such a lousy job marketing it," he replied.

The tension among the board members rose exponentially.

George Jr. shrugged without apology. "I think there are much more efficient ways to raise company profits. The best way would be to lower the cost of producing Dunnigan Dog Food."

"You mean by using cheaper ingredients," Cade surmised.

George Jr. nodded. "As well as taking production south of the border, where it could be done much more economically. If we were to close our manufacturing plants here and move those jobs to a place where we would not have to supply medical and retirement benefits, we'd save a bundle."

"You'd also be costing thousands of people their jobs," Cade argued back.

George Jr. could have cared less. "Their livelihood isn't our concern."

"It should be," Cade said firmly.

The penny-pinching board member, Harvey Lemmon, said, "I'm all for saving money."

Dotty Yost added, "I worry about former employees suing us for the loss of their benefits and jobs."

"I don't think that's possible if we move the company to another country," George Sr. said, backing up his son.

"Maybe not, but there are moral considerations here," Cade

objected deliberately, making eye contact with every person in the room. "I for one am not comfortable with turning loyal employees who have worked for us for years out on the street, just so all of us can line our pockets."

Silence fell.

Laurel felt like cheering—Cade was doing such a good job.

Finally, Lance Ayers spoke up. "What about cheapening the dog food?" the retired oilman asked, as always, concerned about the bottom line. "How much more profit *would* that bring in?"

"If we lowered the meat content in all the food or did away with it altogether and substituted vegetable protein, we could increase profits by fifty percent," George Jr. said.

"Until," Cade countered, "the dog owners realize we've cheapened the product, and quit buying it altogether. Then our company could be forced into bankruptcy. I think the only way we can increase profits is to expand into the services area. Our flagship store will demonstrate that."

"And we're supposed to take your word on that?" George Jr. huffed. "Just as we take your word on the premise that switching one bride for another was a good idea? Face it, cuz, your personal life is a mess!"

Laurel had been quiet until now. The only non-DDF board member in the room, she hadn't felt that she had the right to put her two cents in; she was simply there to support and assist Cade, the way any good wife would. But now that the specter of her marriage had been introduced, she definitely had something to say. "First of all, George Jr., what goes on in a marriage is strictly between the two people involved." She stepped to the center of the room. "Do I look unhappy to anyone here?"

Wordlessly, everyone agreed that she did not.

Laurel positioned herself next to Cade and took his hand. "Second, there is nothing to say that an arranged marriage will not work out as nicely as a marriage entered into via passion and romance. In fact, a marriage like Cade's and mine probably stands a better chance of success in many respects because we are able to be so practical in our approach to just about everything. Obviously, Mr. Ayers agrees with this premise, or he would not have suggested his daughter marry Cade under similar circumstances."

"But that's just it," George Jr. pointed out, seemingly oblivious to the way Cade's hand had tightened possessively over hers. "Cade did not marry Mary Elena. He married you."

"So?" Laurel countered, doing her best to appear as unflappable as possible as she continued her argument to the board on Cade's behalf. "The end result is the same. Cade gained his inheritance and an accomplished wife who will support him. Not much to object to there."

Cade wrapped his arm around her shoulders. "Laurel has been wonderful to me. We're determined to make our marriage a success."

"Bull," George Jr. exclaimed. "Their relationship is a fraud from beginning to end, and every bit as destined to fail as his cockamamie plan for the flagship store!"

"Given that's the way you feel," Cade retorted. "I can't possibly ask you to keep working on the marketing campaign of a project of which you so strongly disapprove. Therefore, as acting CEO, I am relieving you of duty. You will no longer be in charge of marketing as long as I am in charge of the company."

George Jr.'s jaw dropped. His smile dimmed just a bit. "You can't fire me."

"Actually," Dotty Yost interjected delicately, "according to the company bylaws, he can."

"I'll sue you for unlawful dismissal if you try," George Jr. threatened.

"I'm not firing you from the company—yet," Cade said smoothly. "I am merely reassigning you."

"To what?" he demanded angrily.

Cade paused a beat and then lowered his voice, "Game development. You spend so much time at the office on your computer playing blackjack, in full view of the staff, I figure you would be the ideal choice to come up with a software game featuring Dunnigan Premium Dog Food."

"That's ridiculous!" George Jr. fumed.

"Feel free to quit anytime." The gleam in Cade's eyes was diamond-hard. "Because I can't justify paying an executive salary to someone who never seems to do any work. Unless…" Cade looked at the other board members, one by one "…you-all think I should?"

George Sr. cleared his throat and gazed at his son, no longer quite as proud of him as he had been. "Perhaps," he suggested politely, "we've discussed enough business for one night."

"I agree," Dotty Yost said, already rising and heading for the dining room, drink in hand. "The time to vote on a new CEO will come soon enough," she declared in an exhausted voice.

George Jr. regarded Cade grimly. "Right after I prove that your plans for the company expansion are as ultimately unworkable— and fraudulent—as your marriage."

Chapter Ten

"Thanks for helping me host the party tonight," Cade told Laurel hours later, after all their guests had left, and they were alone once again.

"I was happy to do it," she murmured.

"That's good to hear." A hint of a grateful smile touched Cade's lips. He trapped Laurel against the kitchen counter and braced an arm on either side of her. Looking down at her, he continued in a husky, emotional tone, "Because your support means a lot to me." As if to prove it, he stole a kiss, which started out erotic and turned into a tender expression of their growing feelings for each other. Laurel's arms wreathed his neck and her body curved helplessly into the strong, warm shelter of his. Cade was proving more and more impossible to resist. Especially when he kissed her like this. As if he meant it. When the sultry caress ended, Laurel looked up at him. Then, giving in to impulse, she stood on tiptoe and pressed her lips against his for what she promised herself was the very last time. Before bed, anyway. Who knew what tomorrow would bring?

Except, she thought with a sigh as the kiss ended, more trouble from Cade's cagey cousin.

"I understand why you're fighting so hard to keep control of your family company." After this evening's turmoil, she was more aware than ever now just how high the stakes were. "George Jr. would ruin DDF in no time," she predicted anxiously, looking deep into Cade's eyes.

Just that quickly, the expression on his face altered. "I can't let him do that, which is why I have got to make the grand opening of the flagship store a resounding success."

Her heart going out to him, she asked, "Who are you going to put in charge of marketing, in lieu of George Jr.?"

Cade's lips pressed together. He looked as calm as she was upset. "I'm going to handle it myself for the next two weeks."

"Are you going to have time for that?"

Cade reached out and took both her hands in his. "With your help, you bet. It's going to mean some awfully long hours, though," he warned softly, twining their fingers together intimately and searching her face.

"I'm up for the task," she told him confidently.

He smiled. "I thought you would be."

In the foyer, Beast let out a loud bark, then came racing back to the kitchen to sound an alarm. "Is that a car in the drive?" Laurel asked, cocking her head. She reached down to pet the top of Beast's head. The large black Lab reveled in the gentle way she scratched him behind his ears, even as he tried—tail thumping urgently—to get her to accompany him back to the front door.

Cade consulted his watch. "Right on time."

"Who's right on time?" Laurel asked, wincing as Beast let out another loud, warning bark.

Cade smiled at Laurel. "You'll see," he promised mysteriously, following Beast's path and leading the way outside. Frances Klenck's minivan sat in the drive. Laurel watched, puzzled, as the woman waved at Cade, climbed out of the driver's side and opened the back. Laurel gasped in delight as the rescue-group president emerged again, pet carrier in hand.

A familiar face peered out the wire mesh door. "Patches!" Laurel said.

Frances beamed. "Your husband didn't think you would be able to wait until morning to see her, so I called the vet and scheduled an early release for her."

Laurel sent Cade a grateful glance.

"We still on for tomorrow morning?" Cade asked the older woman.

Frances nodded. She spoke over her shoulder as she headed back to her minivan. "I'll be here at nine, sharp."

"What's going on tomorrow?" Laurel asked curiously. Cade put the carrier on the ground. She knelt and opened the crate door. Patches shot jubilantly out into her waiting arms.

"Frances and I are going to pull together plans for a rescue group Pet Adoption Day during the grand opening of the flagship store."

"Can I help?" Laurel asked, buoyed by his change of attitude on the matter.

"Actually, I'd like to increase your responsibilities and put you in total charge of the DDF end of things," he said.

"Sounds good to me," Laurel said, enthused. She wanted to be as much help to Cade—and the company— as possible.

Frances looked at Laurel. "We also need to publicize the event now and start taking applications. The rescue group has to interview potential dog owners, to make sure they are up for the task. It's important to make sure the dogs go to people who have the time, energy and commitment to care for them."

"I can get started on an advertising campaign tomorrow by sending out a press release," Laurel said.

Frances smiled. "Until then. Have a nice evening, folks! What's left of it."

"You, too," Laurel and Cade said in unison. They stood together, watching Frances drive away. Beast sat cuddled against Cade's leg.

Watching as Patches licked Laurel beneath her chin, Cade petted the pup with one hand and Beast with the other. "Your puppy seems to have missed you."

Laurel's heart swelled with love. "I missed her, too." She leaned over and kissed Cade on the lips. "Thank you, Cade."

He kissed her back. "You're welcome."

Contentment flowed through Laurel as they took the dogs out to the backyard, past the pool area, to the grassy landscaped lawn. Laurel set Patches down, and the puppy raced off to stretch her legs. Beast was right behind her nosing the grass and watching the smaller dog curiously.

Laurel studied Cade. "Does this mean you approve of my adopting her?"

He frowned. "I won't lie to you—I wish we had some guarantee that Patches's health would hold up over the long haul. But…" He shrugged. "I can also see that she needs you as much as you seem to need her, so what the heck, we'll work it out."

We, Laurel thought. Not *you*… She couldn't deny she was beginning to think that way, too. As if they were a team instead of two people trapped in a situation neither really wanted. It was funny what a marriage license and a ceremony could do to a woman. She'd only been married to Cade a short time and already she could see them both changing, for the better.

"Why are you smiling?" Cade asked, lightly stroking her hair.

Because your cousin was wrong. You do have a heart, Cade, Laurel thought. *A great big, hopelessly generous one.* But not sure he would want to hear that from her, at least at this point, she only said, "Because I'm happy." *In a way I never expected.*

"I am, too," Cade said softly. "You make me happy." He took her into his arms. His kiss was sweetly tender. She kissed him back, aware there was so much more than desire involved now. Their hearts and minds were becoming engaged, too. Who knew what would have happened if they hadn't heard a great big bark, just as they felt something whiz by their legs? Laurel and Cade drew apart just in time to see a frog leaping across the patio, toward the pool, Patches in hot pursuit. The frog hit the water with a splash. Patches tumbled in right after her.

Laurel gasped in dismay. "Can she swim?"

"She should be able to," Cade said. But already, Laurel noted in alarm, Patches was sinking toward the bottom of the deep end.

Laurel kicked off her shoes and, without even thinking, dived in after Patches. Beast hit the water, too, followed swiftly by Cade. As Laurel swam down toward the bottom, her skirt billowing out around her legs, she saw the frog swimming toward the drain. Patches was still following along after it.

Laurel grabbed her around the middle.

The puppy squirmed free.

Then Cade was beside them, grabbing hold, forcing the squirming, struggling puppy up for air. He broke through the surface at the same time as Laurel. Beast paddled to the top, too. Laurel looked at Cade. Cade looked at Laurel. "Oh, man," he said, and they both began to laugh.

"PUPPY ASLEEP?" CADE asked, half an hour later.

Laurel nodded. She strolled into the family room and joined Cade at the bar. Loving how intimate and cozy it felt to be here with him like this, she stated softly, "Patches was out five minutes after I toweled her off and put her in her crate." Her stomach fluttering with a thousand butterflies at the knowledge their evening together wasn't over yet, she looked around for Cade's big black Lab. "Where's Beast?"

"Sunporch," Cade reported, his grin widening. "He insists on hanging out there, making sure that frog doesn't come back." He shook his head in bemused recollection and poured them each a snifter of brandy. "What a way to end an evening," he drawled affectionately.

"No kidding," Laurel agreed wryly. Her heart pumping with elation, she studied Cade. His dark gold hair was still damp, the impossibly thick, short strands standing on end. He had shaved again—and she knew he had done it just for her. He was wearing stone-colored shorts and an apple-green T-shirt that although comfortably loose, still managed to mold the masculine contours of his shoulders and chest in a way that drew her glance again and again. As she neared him, she caught the brisk outdoorsy fragrance of his cologne. She caught his glance and deliberately did not look away. Nor did he. Her pulse kicking up another notch, Laurel smiled and sauntered even closer. Who knew marriage could be this much fun? She certainly hadn't! "You don't look too much the worse for wear," she noted playfully, brushing her fingertips across his chest. In fact, he looked damn good.

Cade caught her hand and lifted it to his lips for a brief but smoldering kiss. His glance slid over the inviting curves of her breasts, her flat abdomen and long slender legs, before returning to her tousled hair, soft lips and deep blue eyes. "A hot shower cures just about everything," he teased, taking her all the way into his arms.

Trying not to notice how warm, strong and solid he felt, Laurel sighed in contentment. "It certainly worked for me." She felt good all over. Sexy. Warm. Relaxed. Ready for just about anything, in her green-and-blue striped pajama pants and yellow camisole top.

Cade ran a hand lightly down her spine to the small of her back. His grip tightened possessively as he shifted her even closer to his chest. He buried his face in the just-washed waves of her hair. "You smell all flowery," he murmured with a sensual appreciation that kindled her senses.

A wave of longing swept through Laurel, followed by a peculiar lassitude in her whole body. Her limbs were heavy and weak, her insides tingling with excitement, and all he had done thus far was hold her and kiss the back of her hand! "I had to wash the chlorine out of my hair," she said softly. "As, obviously, did you."

Suddenly, his hands were framing her face and he was lifting it to his. He looked down at her, his thoughts seeming to travel the same enticing path as her own. "How can you tell?" His smile flashed, wicked and mesmerizing.

"Because you smell like your soap and shampoo."

He continued to hold her gaze. She could see the desire in his eyes, feel the heat from his body. Wordlessly, Laurel set her snifter down, her mind already made up. Why pretend this wasn't happening between them when it so clearly was? "I want to kiss you again," she admitted, cupping his face in turn.

Cade released a ragged breath, looking ready to take the high road at the first sign of indecision on her part. "I'm not so sure that's wise," he warned her gruffly.

"Who cares?" Laurel challenged, knowing this was no time for him to be gallant, when passion was compelling them together. "When something feels this right, Cade…"

Throwing caution to the wind, she pressed her lips to his. They were hot and soft, sensual and possessive, and she didn't even try to hide how she felt as she went up on tiptoe, drawing him closer yet. Cade's body tautened and then his arms were around her, guiding her deep into his embrace. His tongue explored her mouth, laying claim, again and again, until passion swept through her.

As Cade continued a kiss that was every bit as demanding as it was tender, Laurel moaned softly, knowing and welcoming the change that was coming. She had never thought about herself, her own desires, her own needs. Being married to Cade made her want to change all that. He made her want to take care of herself and do something for herself, not just everyone else. He made her want to experience life—and pleasure—to the absolute fullest. Before he had come into her life doing so would have somehow seemed wrong. Not tonight. Not here. Not now. Because, Laurel sensed, pleasing herself would also be pleasing her husband. And she wanted to do that more than anything.

Cade hadn't expected Laurel to kiss him. He hadn't expected their marriage to be anything but a sham and a means to his inheritance. But as he felt the soft surrender of her body pressed against the rock-hard demand of his, their union felt all too real. Something happened when they were together. It didn't matter if they were talking or taking care of their pets or working on DDF business. Whenever Cade was with Laurel, something magical sparked between them. Maybe it was chemistry. Maybe it was love. Cade only knew he had never felt so connected to a woman, so fast. Never wanted so very much to please. Never realized he could delight so in the feel of a mouth merged with his.

And yet, he thought as the sweet urgency of desire swept through him in undulating waves, making love was no simple thing…especially with a woman as complicated—and impetuous—as Laurel. By her own admission, she had been keeping herself under tight wraps, allowing her own lust for life, her own ambition, her need for passion and the physical side of love, to be overshadowed by the needs of others. And that gave the gentleman in Cade pause. He had been taught never to take advantage. To lay all his cards on the table and let the chips fall where they may.

He hadn't lied to her about the parameters of their marriage, the night they'd said, "I do." He wouldn't mislead her now. Determined to do the right thing, to let her make this decision with a clear head, he tightened his grip on her and tore his lips away. He knew if he made her his, even once, he was going to keep wanting her. Just as she would keep wanting him. And if that happened, he knew they would begin to really feel married. More than they already did. The thought didn't disturb him nearly as much as he knew it should. Yet his conscience forced him to slow down, be practical, matter-of-fact, even. "Are you sure?" he demanded.

Cade half expected Laurel to be ticked off at him for putting on the brakes. Instead, her sky-blue eyes glittered with a mixture of excitement and ardor. Her breasts rose and fell with each breath she took. Beneath the soft cotton, he could see her nipples budding….

Laurel's lips curved in an eager smile. "That I want to be with you?" She regarded him seductively, "To paraphrase you, dear husband, you bet."

She wrapped her arms around him, holding him so close they were almost one. The kiss that followed was a tempest so full of emotion and yearning he couldn't turn away. The blood thundered through him, pooling low. His lower half was rigid with arousal.

"Even knowing…if we start this…" he warned huskily, struggling between his desire to protect her and his desire to make mad, passionate love to her, here and now, damn the consequences. "There'll be no turning back, for either of us." *No pretending,* he thought silently, *that we are not husband and wife.* No pretending that this marriage of theirs hadn't become real in nearly every way.

Laurel smiled again, as if he had just given her the best present in all the world. "I know what I'm doing here. I want to make love with you, Cade."

The happiness within her brimming up unchecked, she slipped her arms about his neck, studied him with eyes that were profoundly hopeful. "Take me upstairs to your bed, and I'll show you just how sure I am."

"I was hoping you'd say that." Cade swept her into his arms and carried her up the stairs and down the hall. Heart pounding, he set her down next to the bed. Lowering his head, he kissed her the way he had wanted to from the first.

Laurel moaned, a little helpless sound that sent his senses swimming. Aware he had never wanted a woman the way he wanted her, he deepened the kiss even more. Her mouth was pliant beneath his, warm and sexy, her body soft, supple, surrendering. He put everything he had into the kiss, determined this night would be every bit as memorable as it deserved to be. Because nothing had ever seemed as right as this, he thought as his hands slid beneath the hem of her camisole top to caress the rounded swells of her breasts. Then the top was coming off…and her pajama pants, too. She was gloriously naked, more beautiful than he had imagined. Cade dispensed with his own clothes and stretched out next to her on the bed.

Laurel reached out to claim him with her hand. "I'm supposed to be doing the showing here," she teased.

"No getting ahead of me," Cade warned, as he rolled her onto her back and set about exploring her body with his lips and tongue. Murmuring in pleasure, he kissed his way up her thighs, past her navel, to her breasts, the nape of her neck, then down again. He cradled her close, letting her know she could be aggressive, too. When she moved her hips, rubbing against him, into him, he was shuddering himself.

"Now," Laurel whispered, sliding her palms from the small of his back to his sides, until the fit of his body to hers, the friction of being skin to skin, swept through them and she opened herself up to him like a flower in the spring.

Cade caught her by the hips, and then they were one. Beautifully so. For the first time in his life, he knew what it felt like to be connected to someone, body and soul. "You feel so good." So right.

Her body shivered with need. "So do you." She moaned again, and this time it was an entreaty, even as she yielded to him one instant, took control the next.

His spread fingertips tantalized the pebble-hard tips of her breasts. He kissed her hard, then sweetly, feeling a little like a conqueror who had just captured the fair, fiesty maiden of his dreams. "Tell me what you need," he urged, looking into her eyes, ignoring her raspy intake of breath as he bent his head and kissed her again. "Tell me what you want," he urged as he possessed her an inch at a time with a slow deliberateness that was as tantalizing to him as it was to her.

She arched up to meet him, thrust for thrust, her response as honest and uncompromising and unashamed as he had hoped it would be. "Deeper…"

"Like this…?" Driven by the same frantic need, Cade plunged and withdrew and plunged again, until her heart was beating in urgent rhythm with his.

"Exactly…like…this…" Laurel murmured, taking everything he offered, giving him everything in return. Gasping in pleasure, she wrapped her arms and legs around him, holding him closer, drawing him deeper still. Until then, Cade hadn't known his own control could be so easily lost, but it was. He was aware of every soft, warm inch of her, inside and out. Every sigh of surrender, every moan of desire and pulsation of need. Over and over again, he moved, taking her, until both of them were lost in the pleasure and one another, until he was so deeply buried in her he barely knew where her body ended and his began. And then reason fled, and they were free-falling into a sweet, swirling oblivion that had been, Cade thought, far too long in coming.

LAUREL HEARD PATCHES whimper shortly after 4:00 a.m. She eased from the safety and comfort of Cade's arms, grabbed her robe and belted it around her. Patches was hunched all the way forward in her crate. Laurel had been around her puppy enough to recognize an urgent call of nature when she saw one.

"Hang on, girl. I'll get you outside," Laurel said softly. She opened the gate and scooped Patches up in her arms. When they came downstairs, Beast leaped up from his place on the sunporch and followed them out into the yard. As soon as Laurel reached grass, she set Patches down. The pup ran one circle, then squatted in relief. Beast moved behind her lazily, until he found his own patch of grass and marked his territory, too.

Laurel stood out there in the moonlight, shivering in the cool night air, wondering how her life had changed so drastically, so fast. She had come into this marriage thinking she could exit it the same way—with her heart intact. Now she knew that wasn't true. If her union with Cade ended, she was going to be more devastated than she had ever been in her life. And yet, even knowing that, she couldn't regret having made love with him. Cade had given her the confidence to go after what she wanted, instead of pursuing what others needed, and putting herself last. For the first time in her life, she felt beautiful inside and out. And that knowledge worried her as much as it pleased her. What if this didn't last? How hard would it be to go back to the way things were before Cade had stormed the citadels of her heart…?

Cade moved behind her. Laurel's heart skipped a beat as she saw him, gilded in moonlight, wrapped only in a robe. As if sensing her sudden uncertainty, he wrapped his arms around her waist and pressed a kiss in her hair. "I would have gotten up with Patches," he said.

"It's not your responsibility," she reminded him quietly, aware she had volunteered to adopt Patches and now had to prove she was equipped to live up to that responsibility. She turned her attention to the golden puppy romping in the grass, seemingly oblivious to the fact it was still the middle of the night and they should *all* be sleeping. "Patches is my dog."

Cade tensed and his grip on her loosened. Too late, Laurel realized how that had sounded. She pivoted to face him. "I just meant…"

His grip tightened around her waist once again. His gaze fastened on hers. "I know what you meant. And you're right," he told her gently, but firmly, a compassionate gleam in his dark gray eyes. "Patches isn't my dog. She's yours. But that doesn't mean you and I shouldn't help each other out with some of the backyard runs, especially if it means you can get a little extra sleep."

Realizing this was a man who was not going to back down

from anything—or anyone—he wanted, Laurel smiled. Then replied, just as considerately, "Speaking of sleep, you can go back to bed."

Cade's sexy grin widened. "I think I'll wait for you," he drawled.

Laurel had only to look at his face to know what he had in mind. Which, coincidentally, was the same thing she wanted. Ignoring the tingling of her nipples and, lower still, the butterflies of desire that began to build, she warned, "Given the way Patches is running around, it's going to be a bit before that happens."

"That's okay." Cade gently caressed her spine, shoulder to waist, and the joy he expressed seemed to radiate from deep inside his heart. He looked down at her, all possessive male. "As long as she doesn't go swimming again."

Laurel couldn't help but chuckle as she thought of that debacle. "I hear you."

He stepped behind her once again, tugged her back against his torso and leaned down to whisper in her ear. "She really is going to be a beautiful dog when she fills out and grows up," he said, the warmth of his body penetrating hers, through the cotton of their robes.

Laurel's flush deepened, despite her efforts to remain cool, calm and collected. She really could make love with him again, right here and now. "You think so?" she asked in a strangled voice.

Cade slid her hair away from one shoulder. "A few months of premium puppy food and tender loving care and she'll be a new dog."

Laurel forced her attention back to Patches and the quick progress she was making. "She already seems more secure."

Cade pressed kisses on the exposed nape of Laurel's neck. "Dogs have an innate sense of who they can trust and who they can't."

She rested her head against his shoulder. "That's something I've struggled with," she admitted reluctantly.

He took her hand and drew her beneath a nearby tree. Pinning her to the trunk with his body, he bent his head and kissed her so passionately she sizzled. His tongue flicked across the edges of her teeth before delving deep in a slow mating dance. The next thing she knew, he was pushing her robe off one shoulder. She trembled as he bent and kissed her breast, before returning with deliberation to her mouth. Her whole body was quaking as he kissed her with surprising tenderness. Lifting his head at long last, he asked in a voice that seemed wrenched from his very heart, "What does your intuition tell you about me?"

Laurel drew an uneven breath. She didn't care if she was letting them get ahead of themselves once again. She only knew what she wanted, needed. And that was Cade. "It's telling me I can trust you." And trust, she knew, was an essential foundation for any relationship.

"I feel like I can trust you, too." He kissed her again, hotly, voraciously. Taking his time. Desire swept through her in dizzying waves. He shifted her higher. Laurel could feel the strength of his arousal pressing against the apex of her thighs, and she knew he was as caught up in the magic as she was. She arched against him wantonly, no longer caring what common sense dictated, only caring that their time together—this love affair, if that's what it was—never end.

Nearby, big dog and puppy collapsed in an exhausted heap.

Cade and Laurel heard their dramatic sighs and grinned in unison. "Ready to put the dogs back down for the rest of the night?" he asked.

She nodded, liking the fact that he, too, was on the edge, fighting his desire. "I'll take Patches up to her crate."

He edged his hips away from her, so he was no longer touching her in quite so intimate a way. "And I'll settle Beast in the room with her."

Laurel drew her robe back over her shoulder and tightened the belt. She could tell by the way Cade looked at her he wanted her more than ever. "You're not going to let Beast sleep in your bedroom at all tonight?" She knew that was the norm. Had Beast not been so concerned about the frog coming back, he would have already been up there.

"Beast understands you and I need our private time. Besides..." Cade cast a look at the way Patches was taking refuge next to the surprisingly paternal black Lab "...I think the two of them want to bunk down together as much as you and I do."

Laurel couldn't disagree with that. The dogs looked very happy hanging out together. And even happier, she noted, minutes later, when they were settled together in the guest room—Patches in her training crate, Beast sprawled on the floor next to it.

"Now where were we?" Cade teased as he guided Laurel back down the hall to the master bedroom.

"Right about here," she said, untying the belt of her robe...and his. Helping both drop to the floor. Cade took her in his arms and kissed her again, until there was no question about what he wanted or what was coming next. He swept her mouth with his tongue, circling, dipping deep in a rhythm of penetration and retreat. Longing flooded through her in undulating waves. With her breasts crushed against the powerful muscles of his chest, she was throbbing inside and out. She wanted to yield to him and the need that drove them both. And she wanted him to surrender to her, too.

Naked, he held her against the wall, demanding and receiving a response that sent her tumbling over the edge. He moved between her legs, nudging her thighs wide, lifted her against him and surged inside. With an exultant sigh, Laurel closed around the hot, hard length of him, their hearts thundering together, the world spinning. When she urged him on, he followed, giving up control right along with her. And this time they were discovering more than just mutual pleasure. They were exploring the promise of their marriage and their life together.

"I FIGURED YOU'D BE a wreck, given the events of the past few days," Lewis McCabe told Laurel the next morning, when he stopped by the office to see her. "I was wrong. I've never seen you look better."

And Laurel knew why. The lovemaking last night had put a glow in her cheeks and a smile on her face that wouldn't quit. Deciding this was a discussion that should not be had within earshot of anyone else, Laurel ushered her brother into the small private office she had been assigned at DDF corporate headquarters. She shut the door and offered him a chair. "Mom and Dad sent you, didn't they?"

Lewis sat down and pushed his eyeglasses farther up the bridge of his nose. As usual, he was dressed in funky clothes—striped canvas slacks, a bright orange T-shirt and a beaded necklace that seemed to come right out of the eighties. Looking at Lewis, you would never know he was CEO of his own computer game company, and something of a technical genius in his own right. Which was, Laurel knew, the way her brother wanted it. Too many people thought his hard-earned wealth and success gave them license to try and take advantage—monetarily or otherwise—of him. Lewis fought back by dressing like an eclectic idiot. He said it chased away fortune-hunting women. Laurel thought her brother was just protecting his heart, the same way she had before meeting up with Cade. Like Laurel, Lewis had a failed engagement behind him.

"Let's just say they didn't veto the idea when I suggested I stop by your new workplace to say hello, while I was in Dallas," Lewis admitted dryly.

Laurel wrinkled her nose. "I'm doing fine. So you and everyone else in the family should just quit worrying."

He shrugged and gave her a brotherly once-over. "You can't blame us for being concerned. Marriages of convenience are not exactly de rigeur in our family."

Given the way hers was turning out, Laurel thought maybe they should be. She leaned forward urgently, not about to let this stellar opportunity pass her by. "Listen, Lewis, as long as you're here…exactly how long does it take to get a computer game designed?"

"I HEARD ONE OF your brothers was here," Cade said several hours later, when he returned from the flagship store and found her in the tiny office she had been given since being asked to act as liaison between DDF and the golden retriever rescue group.

Laurel put down the press release she had been working on

for all radio, TV and newspapers in the area, and sat back in her chair. "Lewis gave me some ideas for a computer game involving Dunnigan Premium Dog Food."

Cade handed her the tall iced tea that he'd bought from the vendor on the first floor of the high-rise. He watched as Laurel took the paper off the straw and stuck it through the center of the plastic lid. "I wasn't serious about that."

"Maybe you should be." Laurel smiled as he sat down on the edge of her desk, facing her. "Think about it, Cade," she continued persuasively. "If Lewis's company were to design a fun— and educational—computer software game filled with interesting facts about dogs and their care, available only with proof of purchase, or purchase of services at a DDF dog care center, it could really boost sales."

Cade ripped the lid off his own paper cup and took a long drink. "How long would it take to put something like this together?"

Laurel swiveled toward him and crossed her legs at the knee. As her skirt hiked up slightly, exposing a slender expanse of thigh, it was all Cade could do not to forget they were at work and take her in his arms.

Laurel, however, was all business.

"Lewis said at minimum three months. But if you're willing to spend the development bucks—" her eyes lifted to his "— Lewis could probably have a prototype ready in time to show the DDF board by the time they vote for new CEO in ten days." Laurel handed Cade the notes, her fingers brushing his.

He studied the figures. "This just might work," he murmured, noting how fresh and pretty Laurel looked, her rich brown hair gleaming in the afternoon sunlight that flooded in through the windows.

She leaned her elbow on her desk and rested her chin on her fist. "Lewis's company is making some of the most popular games on the market today."

"I know." Cade reached out to untangle a strand of wavy hair from the small gold hoop in her ear. "I own a few."

She smiled. "So you want me to call him?"

Cade nodded. "Right away. But let's keep this to ourselves," he cautioned.

Laurel rubbed the back of her neck, her frustration obvious. "You think George Jr. would interfere if he knew?"

Cade moved around her to knead the tense muscles. "I know he would."

She closed her eyes and leaned into his touch. "He hasn't shown up at the office today."

Aware that her muscles had relaxed, and that both he and the skin beneath his hands were getting entirely too warm, Cade stepped back. "Which doesn't mean he isn't actively working to oust me as CEO."

Laurel stood, suddenly looking as restless as Cade felt. He didn't know whether it was the small size of her office, or just the greedy and unprincipled nature of the opposition facing them, but he suddenly felt as hemmed in as she looked. She sighed anxiously. "What could he be doing to undermine you?"

Cade shrugged. "I have no idea," he admitted grimly. "That's what bothers me." He did not want Laurel in the line of fire just because she was associated with him. "But we can't spend time worrying about it. We're due back at the house for a photo shoot."

Curious, Laurel lifted a delicate brow.

"The rescue group needs a place for a group photo of the forty-seven dogs up for adoption," he told her, then watched as she saved her work and shut the computer down. He held out a hand to her and helped her to her feet. "It's going to run in all the newspapers tomorrow. I told Frances Klenck they could use the backyard at the house. And they want both of us in the picture, as well as all the rescue workers."

Laurel stuffed the rough draft of her press release into her briefcase, then came out from behind her desk. "That's a lot of dogs and people," she murmured as she picked up her purse. "I wonder how Patches and Beast are going to respond to that."

Cade grinned. "Only one way to find out." And they'd do it together.

As CADE HAD FIGURED would be the case, Patches ended up on Laurel's lap as the picture was taken. Not one to be excluded, Beast settled himself next to Cade. The only sleek black Lab in a sea of yellow coats, and twice the size of any of the dogs looking for good homes and loving owners, Beast presented a comic—if kingly—presence, as he nestled against Cade's side and stared straight at the camera.

"Beautiful," the photographer who had volunteered her services declared. She showed the digital images on her camera monitor to everyone involved. "This is going to have people lining up to adopt the dogs."

Cade hoped so. The animals deserved a shot at a decent life. The pets in the various photos that had been taken certainly looked ready to be loved.

Beside Cade, Laurel uttered a soft, "Oh, no."

Following her turbulent gaze, he saw George Jr. strolling across the lawn toward them. His own mood sank like a stone in the river.

"What's going on here?" George Jr. inquired with false pleasantry as animals and temporary caretakers continued to spread out over the back lawn.

Frances Klenck was only too happy to explain what had happened thus far, adding, "All the local TV stations have agreed to cover the adoption fair during the grand opening of the Dunnigan Dog Care Center. Film of the event will go a long way toward covering the expenses our members are incurring to temporarily house and care for these dogs. Although I wish we could get them looking a little better, prior to their event. Their coats are so…"

"Scraggly?" George Jr. added helpfully.

Frances nodded. "A professional trim would go a long way toward making them more presentable—but at seventy-five dollars, minimum, per dog, we just don't have the funds."

That problem was easily solved. "We could do it at the dog care center, the day before it opens," Cade said.

Frances lit up like she had just won the lottery. "Are you serious?"

He nodded. "It'll give the groomers we're hiring a chance to break in the facilities and show off their work."

Laurel nodded, picking up on Cade's enthusiasm. "We could do before and after photos. There's bound to be a huge difference."

"In fact," the photographer ambled over and joined in, "we could take the before photos today."

She moved off to get dogs and handlers lined up so they could start. Frances Klenck went along to assist. George Jr., Cade and Laurel were left facing each other.

"I came over to apologize," George Jr. said. He paused to give Laurel a smug, considering look before turning his attention back to Cade. "I still think you are moving the company in the wrong direction, but I should have worked harder on the marketing plan, regardless of my feelings. So—" he shrugged "—I'm ready to get back to it, if it's okay with you."

Unable to shake the feeling that his rival would do anything to hurt and undermine him, including use Laurel against him, Cade countered just as smoothly, "Actually, it's not. I'd prefer to do it myself."

"There's no way you can manage everything your job as CEO entails plus that," his cousin said.

Cade shrugged and wrapped an arm around Laurel's waist. He pulled her close to his side. "I seem to be managing thus far." *With my lovely wife's help.*

George Jr. stared at him, undaunted. His expression relaxed into a charming smile. "All right, then. If that's the way you want it, cuz."

"It is," Cade said.

Laurel and he watched George Jr. stroll off, casual as could be. He slipped inside the house. A short time later, a car engine started with a purr. They heard him drive away.

"What do you think he's going to do now?" Laurel asked, looking only slightly less worried and upset.

Cade shook his head. "I wish I knew," he muttered. If he did, he would know how to protect Laurel from being caught in any crossfire. But he didn't. So he'd just have to keep watch and protect Laurel every way he could....

It took another hour, but finally the photo-taking was finished. Everyone in the rescue group left with their dogs. Only Cade, Laurel, Beast and Patches remained. It was just four-thirty, so they could head back to the office. Or... "How do you feel about working at home the rest of the day?" Cade asked.

Laurel smiled, looking as happy to be alone with him as he was to be with her. "Sounds good to me." She paused, turning along with Cade to see a flash of color appear at the gate in the wooden privacy fence. She sighed. "Don't look now, but we've got company—again."

Chapter Eleven

Laurel had known all along that the events that had prompted her marriage to Cade would eventually have to be dealt with. She had just hoped—foolishly, she saw now—it wouldn't be quite this soon.

Looking as beautiful and sophisticated as ever, Cade's ex-fiancée glided toward them, her high heels sinking into the thick carpet of grass. "So just how angry are you with me?" Mary Elena Ayers asked Cade.

I'd like to know that myself, Laurel thought, watching Cade welcome Mary Elena with a casual hug more indicative of their lifelong friendship than their failed engagement.

"Not at all." His mouth curved ruefully. "You were right to walk out on me the way you did. A marriage between us never would have worked even for a week, Mary Elena. We don't love each other."

Laurel let out the breath she had been holding. She hadn't been expecting this reaction from Cade any more than Mary Elena obviously had, but she would take it.

Her friend lifted a beautiful brow, clearly skeptical of the forgiveness on Cade's face. Like Laurel, she kept waiting for the other shoe to drop. "You didn't think love was a necessary component to a relationship when you proposed," she stated.

Cade rubbed his jaw. "Let's just say you walking out on me the way you did helped me wise up. Two people need more than a business deal and a shared wealthy background to forge a successful marriage."

"And yet," Mary Elena said, still struggling to understand, "from what I hear, your marriage to Laurel is thriving. There's no love involved between you... is there? I mean, how could there be?" Her glance cut to Laurel. "You two didn't even know each other when you said 'I do'!"

Cade hesitated.

Laurel didn't know what to say to that, either.

She knew she was falling head over heels in love with Cade—two hot and passionate lovemaking sessions had shown her that. But she had no idea if he even *believed* in the emotion.

"Let's just say that Laurel and I are on the same page the way you and I never were," Cade told Mary Elena after a brief pause.

Laurel did her best to contain her disappointment. She knew she had no right to feel even the tiniest bit disillusioned. Cade had never promised her anything more than a place to stay, a well-paying job at DDF and a sexual relationship that was wholly at her discretion.

"Do you have an end date to this arrangement?" Mary Elena asked.

Laurel could see—as well as feel—Cade's emotional shield going up. Never one to easily share his feelings with anyone, he was even less inclined to do so in this awkward situation. "Thirty-three years?" Cade quipped with a half-serious glance aimed Laurel's way.

Could they really stay married that long? Laurel wondered, realizing even as she asked it that she very well could....

"Seriously," Mary Elena pressed, her protectiveness toward Laurel apparent. "When are you two parting company?"

Knowing it was her turn to attempt an answer, Laurel shrugged, pretending a casual attitude she couldn't begin to really feel. "Cade and I agreed to stay together until things settle down at DDF and they name a permanent CEO." Beyond that, there was no agreement. They hadn't talked about it since the day the codicil to his father's will was read.

Mary Elena narrowed her eyes at Cade. "I hope he's paying you for this," she told Laurel.

"I'm getting a salary at DDF." *A very generous one.* Laurel had signed the papers the day before with the human resources people.

"I meant cash." Mary Elena looked at Cade. "I know you like to pour everything you earn right back into the company, but you should definitely be compensating Laurel for her help on such a personal level, aside from whatever she earns at work."

Laurel flushed, aware that taking money from Cade now would be akin to accepting cash from him for making love with him. "He doesn't need to do that, Mary Elena," she said, unable to keep the embarrassment from her voice. "I'm just helping him out as a friend."

"Time is money," Mary Elena replied briskly. "How often have I heard that from both you and my dad, Cade? And Laurel is certainly putting in her time, playing wife for you, throwing you a fabulous dinner party, helping you at work and at home. She deserves payment for that. Shame on you, Cade Dunnigan, for taking advantage of her that way!"

Guilt flashed in Cade's eyes, and just as promptly disappeared.

"He didn't take advantage of me," Laurel interjected wearily. That would imply she didn't know what she was doing. She had known exactly what she was doing from the get-go, and had signed on anyway. More damning still, even if she knew this would not have the fairy tale ending she was secretly beginning to want, Laurel knew she would do it all over again, to be able to feel and experience all she had since they'd married.

Mary Elena frowned. "I don't know how he ever got you to agree to marry him at the last minute, anyway. Actually," she mused thoughtfully, "I do. You have trouble saying no to anyone."

Laurel rolled her eyes. This was a disaster waiting to get worse. "I have no trouble saying no to this conversation," she said flatly.

Cade looked at Laurel, a mixture of regret and wariness in his gray eyes. "Maybe we should discuss this," he stated reluctantly. *Not here, not now.* "Later," Laurel said. *When we're alone.*

Mary Elena looked at Laurel, the complicity she felt for her predicament apparent. "At least tell me this. Is he treating you right?"

Laurel shrugged, not sure whether to laugh or cry at the bizarre turn the situation was taking. She had started out trying to protect Mary Elena. Now her friend was shielding her. "I can't complain," she said.

"Good." Mary Elena shot another irritated look at Cade. "Because if you take advantage or do her wrong in any way, never mind neglect to pay her handsomely for her time and trouble in helping you obtain permanent control of your company as well as your inheritance, you're going to find yourself dealing with me."

Laurel threw up her hands. "Why does everyone in Texas think I need protecting?" she asked, piqued.

"Maybe because you have one of the softest hearts I've ever been privileged to know," Mary Elena explained. "And speaking of favors...I need one from you, Cade. You know my father fired Manuel Garcia?"

Cade nodded. "Laurel mentioned it."

"Manuel has not been able to find another gardening position."

"I'm already under contract with a company for this place."

"I figured as much. I want you to hire him at the flagship store."

Cade paused. "Has he ever worked retail?"

"No. He's only been in the country about four years, but he brought his mother and two sisters over, and he's supporting them both. He really needs a job today. You've seen him. He's young and strong."

And impossibly virile and soulful, with eyes only for Mary Elena, Laurel thought.

"Not to mention incredibly smart and hardworking," Mary Elena continued.

"How is his English?"

"Getting better every day. I'm coaching him."

Cade's mouth firmed. "Has he ever run a cash register?"

"No, but like I said, he could learn. Please, Cade," Mary Elena begged. "I'd consider it a personal favor."

As Laurel expected, Cade's big heart won out over his wish

not to become involved in any more of Mary Elena's dramas. "Have him come by the flagship store first thing tomorrow morning," he said grudgingly. "I'll interview him personally. If I think I can use him, I'll give him a job."

"Thank you, Cade." Mary Elena leaned forward impulsively to kiss Cade's cheek in a Southern-style thank-you. "I'll be forever grateful. And now I need one more favor, this one from Laurel. Daddy still won't release any of my funds or take the freeze off my credit cards, so I need a place to stay, and I figured since your apartment is empty at the moment, Laurel, that you might consider subletting it to me."

Cade wrapped his arm around Laurel's shoulders. "To sublet something you have to pay money," he interjected dryly.

Laurel turned and shot an admonishing look at him. Mary Elena was her friend!

"Of course you can stay there, and you don't have to pay me anything," Laurel said.

"You're sure?" Mary Elena asked. "I haven't found a job yet, but I'm looking."

"I could hire you to work at the flagship store, too," Cade volunteered.

Mary Elena in a dog care center? Laurel thought. Wearing an apron and employee polo instead of her designer duds? Somehow Laurel couldn't imagine that. And neither could her friend.

"Uh, no," Mary Elena said. "Not really my speed, Cade. I'm looking for something in an art gallery or a design studio that would make use of my art history or interior design degrees."

Ignoring Cade's just-as-I-thought expression, Laurel asked helpfully, "Any chance you could get a paying position at one of the charities you've worked so hard for?"

"Not thus far." Mary Elena sighed. "But I'm trying." She hesitated. "About the rent…" she said seriously.

"Like I said, you don't need to pay me anything," Laurel assured her.

"Thank you. Thank you both." Mary Elena beamed. "You're the best."

THE PROBLEM WAS, Cade thought, as he rounded up the dogs while Laurel went to get their dinner, he didn't feel like the best. He felt as if he had taken advantage of Laurel, albeit unwittingly. He didn't like the feeling. He was accustomed to making his own way, without owing anyone anything. Whereas his wife was used to letting people take advantage of her sweet and giving nature. And that, Cade decided firmly, had to stop. No matter what he had to do. "You shouldn't let Mary Elena walk all over you like that." He carried Beast's food and water dishes out to the patio.

Laurel looked at him in surprise, then set Patches's dishes on the stone floor inside the sunporch. "Mary Elena would pay me rent if I wanted her to—but I don't."

Cade watched Laurel kneel beside the puppy. It wasn't an easy thing in the slender spring skirt she was wearing. The smooth cotton fabric slid midway up her thighs before she was able to stop its wayward progress.

Cade met Laurel's eyes calmly. "Maybe you should. Maybe," he continued, closing the distance between them, still viewing her through the floor-to-ceiling screen, "it's time someone held Mary Elena accountable for her actions."

Laurel rose to face him. "You think she's spoiled."

"Let's just say Lance Ayers's desire to protect his daughter from anything difficult or unpleasant has not reaped the results he wanted," he acknowledged dryly.

Laurel's eyes narrowed in silent reproof. "There's a lot more to Mary Elena than that."

"I'm not saying there isn't." He slipped inside the porch to stand beside her. "How did the two of you become friends, anyway?"

Laurel noticed Patches still wasn't eating, and bent down to encourage her, feeding her kibble from the palm of her hand. "We went to the University of Texas together. I met her my junior year. We volunteered for a lot of the same organizations. Mary Elena has a huge heart. She just doesn't let it show to anyone but her nearest and dearest friends, because she's afraid people will take advantage of her, the way she thinks people do me. And unlike me, Mary Elena works hard to see that doesn't happen."

"She may have been right about one thing," Cade admitted grudgingly. "I should be giving you some kind of financial remuneration for all the things you are doing for me, on a personal level. I'm not sure how best to go about it."

Laurel's face blushed a becoming pink. "How about we don't do it at all?" she murmured, head bent over her puppy.

"Then I'd be taking unfair advantage." Cade paused. He waited until she rose again before continuing. "I want to pay you for all you've done."

She took another step nearer, inundating him with the floral scent of her perfume. "Including sleeping with you?" she replied with a sweetness that set his teeth on edge.

Cade frowned. "You know that's not what I meant. I was talking about the wifely duties you've been doing."

"And sleeping with you isn't one of them, I gather."

Actually, to Cade, it sort of was. Sleeping with her gave them the kind of intimate, loving connection he had been wanting his whole life. Being with Laurel like that had given him a sort of peace he had not known existed, and would find himself hard-pressed, from this point forward, to do without. "I did not mean to offend you."

"Actually, you didn't," she said, as if her conclusion were blatantly obvious. "I put myself in this situation. I knew we had no business making love with each other if we weren't in love."

What was Laurel trying to tell him? Cade wondered uneasily. That she didn't love him now, and never would? Or that she was as confused about her feelings as he had been about his before he had taken her in his arms and made her his? The only thing he knew for certain was that everything was happening too fast for comfort. He liked to analyze a situation and mull over all his options before proceeding. With Laurel, more often than not, he found himself jumping in heart first. He wasn't used to that. She didn't appear as if she were, either.

"Going to bed just complicates our life together unnecessarily," Laurel continued crisply, picking Patches up and putting her in her crate for a much-needed rest period.

"Or makes it simpler," Cade argued, just as stubbornly. "Last night proved we wanted each other—"

The color in Laurel's cheeks deepened. "Physically, yes."

And emotionally, he thought. At least on his part. He struggled to keep the conversation as casual as she seemed to want. "I found being together that way very…um…relaxing."

"Well," she murmured with what he considered to be an unnecessarily self-righteous smile. "Bully for you."

He caught her arm before she could dash off. "I'm just trying to be honest."

She extricated herself from his grip and stomped away. "That, you are. And now I'm going to be honest with you." She turned and slayed him with a look. "I'm not a woman who has flings."

Cade scowled. "This isn't a fling," he told her gruffly. He resented her pretending it was!

Laurel clamped her hands across her waist in a way that drew his attention to the full curves of her breasts. "Well, it's certainly not a marriage!" she said hotly.

If there was one thing Cade understood, it was the ramifications of contractual agreements. He braced his hands on his hips, considering. Refusing to let her break their locked gazes. "It would seem that it is—now that we have consummated our relationship," he countered, unable to contain the satisfaction in his low tone.

"To consummate a marriage there would have to be intent," Laurel explained, as if he were particularly dense.

Cade moved in until there were mere inches between them. "If you're talking in a legal sense—"

She tossed her head. "I am."

"Then you're wrong." Cade studied her glossy, tousled hair and luminous face. He moved closer yet. "As far as the law is concerned, if you've said your vows and then make love, that's it—the marriage is consummated. It doesn't matter if you intended to legalize the union or were just fooling around for the heck of it during the, um…"

"Act?" Laurel supplied sarcastically.

Cade ignored her attempt at gallows humor. "What is done is done," he stated firmly. "The law makes no distinction." And neither, in this case, did he!

"Well, you don't have to look so happy about it!" she snapped.

Cade couldn't help it. Being with Laurel, even when they were matching wits and wills like this, made him more content than he had ever been. Was this what his mother and father had felt for each other? Why his parents couldn't seem to stay away from on another, even when their pride had them splitting up and divorcing, only to come back together again, more passionately and irrevocably than ever?

"And you," Cade stated genially, as long as they were telling each other how to act, "don't have to behave as if it's the worst thing in the world."

She looked upward, as if praying for strength, then gazed at him coolly. "It means we would have to get a divorce, not an annulment, once your struggle for control of your family company is at an end."

Not necessarily. "Or," Cade suggested pragmatically, "we could just stay married."

LAUREL STARED AT CADE, hardly able to believe what she was hearing. Worse than his happy smile was the look of smug satisfaction in his gray eyes. "To do that we would need to be in love." And although she was honest enough to admit love was exactly what she was feeling for her husband, she knew Cade and she were not on the same page in that regard. He was thinking practicality. She was thinking heart. She had to get out of here—fast—before she let her imagination run away with her.

"And maybe," Cade predicted, with a casualness that suddenly seemed very deceptive, "one day we'll get there."

Laurel's heart began to beat a little faster. "Because staying married is what we want," she guessed with a careful smile, wishing with all her heart that was the case.

"That's how most arranged marriages work." He shrugged nonchalantly, all sexy charm. "Ours is an arranged marriage."

Laurel took a deep breath and fought to keep her growing feelings in check. It wasn't the fact that he was a superb lover and a brilliant businessman who also saw the untapped potential in her. Or a man who understood what it was to love a pet. It was the way he made her feel whenever they were together. As if everything really was going to be okay, if only she would allow herself to trust him.

But how could she do that, Laurel wondered, given the way their "arrangement" had started, and the even more devastating way they had already agreed it would end?

"Or—possibly—shotgun marriage," Laurel corrected, squaring her shoulders and retaining her calm despite the sudden glimmer of mischief in his beautiful eyes. She left the sunporch and headed into the house, with Cade on her heels. She reached the laundry room, turned on the water and began washing the dog slobber off her hands. "Motivated by a broken promise, instead of a pregnancy," she continued, summing up the situation solemnly.

Cade added soap to his own palms and stuck his hands under the running water, too. His body nudged hers. Deciding this was how they'd gotten themselves in trouble in the first place—by touching!—Laurel shut off the water. The next thing she knew her back was to the washer and he was standing in front of her, an arm braced on either side of her.

He looked her square in the eye, considering. "Do you want to get pregnant?"

Apparently, Laurel noted, it wasn't such an outlandish idea to him. Her throat was so dry she could hardly swallow. She brought a hand up through the narrow space between their bodies and rubbed at her temples. "Could we please stay on task here?"

Cade gave her a wolfish grin that radiated sensuality. "What is the task?"

She refused to admit—in fantasy—how blissful the notion of having Cade's baby sounded to her. Almost as blissful as having her body caged in by the tall, strong, warm length of his. Her breath caught in her throat, her heart beat wildly in her chest and her head tipped back all the more. Aware she was already weakening and he hadn't even kissed her yet, Laurel spread her hands across his chest and hitched in a quick, bolstering breath. "The task, Cade, is me setting some boundaries with you."

He chuckled softly, surprising her with the tenderness and compassion in his gaze. A knowing smile curved his lips. He leaned down and dropped kisses along her temple. "I thought we had already done that."

Laurel arched against him. Her fingers curled in the starched fabric of his shirt, even as she struggled against the knowledge that she wanted to stay here with him forever. Aware hers was not a very practical attitude to have—Mary Elena had made her see that—Laurel gulped and tried to push past his braced arm. It was impossible to stay strong when he was looking at her like that. Impossible to rein in her emotions. To not feel so very wanted…and married. "Cade…"

His palms moved to her hips, bringing her flush against him. He looked impossibly handsome and determined in the soft light. She could feel his body pulsing with need. "I want you, Laurel. You want me. What's to negotiate there?" His gaze traveled over her, the desire in his eyes unmistakable as he slowly lowered his head to hers.

"Everything," she cautioned, but she was already melting, her eyes fluttering shut with a sigh.

"We've got chemistry," he whispered against her lips, his hands stroking her back persuasively, gathering her soft body against the harder length of his. "We're becoming very good friends."

Okay, she couldn't deny that, she thought as he paused to deliver a long, soulful kiss. "Friends don't sleep together, Cade."

He pushed the curtain of her hair aside and nuzzled his way down the nape of her neck. The next thing she knew their mouths were locked in a searing kiss. "We do."

Laurel groaned as his mouth moved inexorably over hers, tempting, teasing, persuading, claiming her. "You aren't playing fair," she whispered.

His eyes held a quiet steadiness that made her tremble. "I'm not playing anything." He gave her another kiss, more soulful and exciting than the last. "I'm showing you what I want."

Laurel knew if he kissed her again she really would be lost. It was hard enough not to give in to what he wanted. What they both wanted. "Which is what?" she demanded breathlessly.

"You—as my woman, from this moment forward." His eyes darkened soberly. "Tell me you'll let me be your man."

"Oh, Cade…" she whispered, knowing this was more of a commitment than she had ever expected to get.

As their gazes locked, held, she noted with satisfaction that he looked every bit as unsteady and ready for love as she felt. "Is that a yes?" he teased her wickedly.

"Yes." Laurel threw back her head joyfully. "Yes, yes…" And to prove it, she went up on tiptoe once more and kissed him as if the chance would never come again. Desire trembled inside her, making her insides go all fluid and warm. He tasted so good, so undeniably male, and she could feel his heart pounding and his erection pressing against her. All her life she had longed to be wanted the way he wanted her. The surprise was that she needed him, too. He hadn't mentioned love, nor had she, but she felt it just the same, in every touch, every kiss, every hug.

Cade began unbuttoning her blouse. "Want to go upstairs?"

"No," she said breathlessly, as he opened the front clasp of her bra, baring her to his rapacious view. She unbuttoned his shirt, too, loving the feel of the hard muscle and flat male nipples beneath her fingertips. She felt him quiver, and knew he was suffering the same flood of highly charged sensations as she.

"Here is just fine with me." She grinned at him mischievously, let her palms drift downward to his belt. He sucked in his breath and she opened the fly to his trousers, too.

He let her get only so far before he stopped her. "Hey." Laurel's brow furrowed. "I was just getting started."

"Haven't you heard? Ladies first." Aware he had been thinking about doing this all day, Cade shifted their attention to her. Hands on her waist, he lifted her up on the washer. For a second, he simply enjoyed the sight of her.

Blouse open to her waist. Her lips wet and swollen from his kisses; her hair tousled, cheeks pink. They'd hardly begun, and already her body was primed and ready for him. Just as he was ready for her. Trembling with a need—and a depth of feeling— he could no longer deny, knowing this was the surest way to make her feel the connection between them, he cupped her breasts with both hands, lifting the lush flesh to his mouth. Reveling in the quick response of her body, he caressed her with the pad of his thumb, his fingertips, his palms, then laved the tight buds with his tongue. She sighed in pleasure and his hands slipped beneath her skirt, pushing it upward, toward her waist. Needing the rest of her just as accessible, Cade lifted her slightly. He grinned at her quick intake of breath as he peeled off her panty hose and panties in one easy motion.

She sent him a look that was part temptation, part plea. "I think I'm getting ahead of you."

"Let's see." He parted her legs, then stepped between them, palms moving across slender thighs to her abdomen, her navel, and back again. "No," he decided playfully. He wanted her this way, all fire and passion. "Feels about right to me." Which was why, he thought, he could touch her like this forever, even if Laurel was clearly longing for more.

She arched as he found the sweetest, silkiest part of her. "You would say that," she gasped, opening up to him even more.

Cade smiled as their lips met in a torrid kiss. Perspiration beaded her body. Lower still, moisture bathed the insides of her thighs. Enjoying their sexy banter as much as their lengthy kisses and intimate touches, he teased, "And you would agree."

She whimpered low in her throat. Her hands curved around his shoulders. She gave him full rein. His fingers continued to stroke inside her. He suckled the silky nub gently, fluttering his tongue. She looked deliciously ravished. "Cade…"

Wanting that whisper of sensation to turn into a ravaging flood, he moved back to her breasts and continued with the same single-minded attention he applied to everything else. "I'm busy here."

Her back arched and her thighs fell even farther apart. "I can feel that, too."

"Can you?"

She quivered with unimaginable pleasure and nearly shot off her perch into his arms. "Oh… Yes…"

"How about this?" Cade stroked upward.

"Excellent," she gasped.

"And *this?*" He replaced his hand with the part of him she sought.

"Superior."

"And this?" He shifted her toward him.

"So good there is…no…rating for it," Laurel said, wrapping her legs around his waist.

"What about…?" He cupped her bottom with both hands.

"Oh, yes."

"And this?" He penetrated her slowly.

She closed around him like a wet, hot sheath. "Cade…"

And then they were one. Moving toward a single goal, seeking release, sweeping past obstacles, climbing ever higher. "That's it." Unable to help herself, she soared over the edge, taking her with him. He held her until the aftershocks passed, then kissed her rapaciously. "Better?"

She waited until the shuddering stopped, then drew back. "Not quite."

Cade lifted a brow, not sure how that could be improved. "I never got my turn," Laurel scolded with a teasing smile.

"And you want it."

"Oh, yes."

Interesting thought. Except… "I'm not sure I can…."

Then again, Cade thought, as she took him in hand, maybe he could….

"Your turn to sit." Laurel brought a chair in from the kitchen.

He studied her. "You really want to do this?"

When Laurel kissed him, it brimmed with a hunger and emotion she hadn't known she possessed. "I really do," she told him softly, knowing love was not just about taking, but giving. Blood rushed hot and needy through her veins. She guided him down onto the seat. "You make me feel so beautiful, Cade. So wanted." She straddled his lap and kissed him deeply, thoroughly.

"That's because you are." He kissed her back in the same intimate manner.

Laurel took off his shirt. "I want you to feel the same way."

Cade took off her blouse. "I do."

"Good to hear. Now." Laurel sighed with pleasure. "Where were we?"

Chapter Twelve

"Sure you don't mind us ducking out on you when we've got so much work to do here with the marketing plan?" Laurel asked, early the next evening.

Cade studied her upturned face. Despite the incredibly busy day they'd had at work, and the rushed take-out dinner after, she was as lovely and energetic as ever. While he had been swimming laps in the pool, she had changed out of her business clothes and into a pair of olive-green shorts and a cap-sleeved white T-shirt that made the most of her slender curves. Sneakers and socks adorned her feet. She had pinned her dark wavy hair on the back of her head in a way that had him wanting to take it down again or better yet, drag her back in the pool with him. The thought of making love to her there had testosterone flooding his system. But that would have to come later, Cade knew.

"We can burn the midnight oil when you get back," he told her with a smile. "Right now, you've got more important things to do."

"Such as taking Patches to her first crash course in puppy kindergarten," Laurel agreed, excitement dancing her in vivid blue eyes.

Cade ran a towel over his body, then pulled a T-shirt over his head. "Right." He headed for the laundry room, with Laurel—and the puppy in her arms—right beside him. Tail wagging, Beast brought up the left flank.

"I think it's going to be a lot of fun for both of us." Laurel accompanied Cade into the laundry room.

As he shucked his damp suit and replaced it with briefs and a pair of shorts, it was hard not to think about the way the two of them had made love in there the afternoon before. Or the way they had made love off and on all through the night. Laurel had proved to be every bit the fantastic lover he had hoped, and then some. Had that been all, it would have been enough to guarantee substantial happiness for both. And yet there was so much more to their union. The two of them were good companions. They shared the same values. She was interested in his business, understood how much it meant to him, and liked to work as hard—and play as hard—as he did. In fact, she seemed so perfect for him in every way it was hard to think of their marriage ever ending. Cade hadn't expected to feel that way, any more than he had expected to be falling in love with Laurel, but he was.

Oblivious to the direction of his thoughts, she continued curiously, "Did Beast attend puppy kindergarten?"

"He did—but it was before I got him." Cade watched her set Patches down on the tile laundry room floor. "We started with level-two obedience classes."

Beast and Patches looked at each other, then sat down side by side. "What do they teach in level one or puppy kindergarten?"

"The basic commands like Sit, Stay, Come, Quiet, Down, Chill." Cade tossed his swim trunks into the washing machine, along with a hamperful of dark cotton towels. He added detergent and fabric softener, then started the wash cycle.

"All in one lesson?" Laurel gaped, amazed.

Cade laughed, amused by her naiveté. "You'll be lucky if you get through Sit tonight."

Noting Patches begin to sniff and circle, Laurel snapped on a leash and led her—and Beast—back out to the yard behind the swimming pool. "I guess it's a good thing we're going to be doing these classes nightly, until Pet Adoption Day, then." Laurel bent and unsnapped the lead, watching as Patches got down to business. "Frances Klenck wants all the dogs to be as well trained as possible before they are exposed to TV news crews and crowds of people."

Cade smiled. "I'm sure she'll manage." When Patches was ready to go, he loaded the carrier into the car for Laurel. Then he caught her to him for a kiss. "Hurry home when you're done," he urged gruffly.

"I promise," she whispered back. She kissed him again, tenderly this time, and then reluctantly got in the car. Beast and Cade stood in the driveway, watching as she drove away, then they headed for Cade's study where a mountain of work awaited.

Beast nosed around the carpet, as if tracking a scent. He had done the same thing the previous evening, and this morning. Cade wasn't sure why. Patches hadn't been in this room. Laurel had, but Cade hadn't noticed Beast tracking her anywhere else.

Beast's "trail" took him over to the desk, where he sat looking up at Cade, whining softly. Guessing his dog was as bereft at the absence of Laurel and Patches as he was, Cade reached down and scratched him behind the ears. The dog continued to stare at him soulfully, as if trying to silently impart something vital.

Cade smiled at his pet affectionately and guessed at the reason for the black Lab's concern. "Lots of changes around here lately, right, buddy?"

Beast made a rumbling sound low in his throat.

"The ladies will be back soon, I promise," he said soothingly.

Beast groaned again and flopped down on the floor behind the desk. Cade rocked back in his chair, knowing he needed to get to work, but unable to focus on DDF business just yet. He kept thinking about his marriage to Laurel. How right it now felt. And yet how foolishly it had begun. Knowing he needed to bare his soul to someone, he looked at Beast and confided, "I really messed up with Laurel from the very beginning, when I made it clear that this situation was all about me getting my inheritance, no matter what the cost in personal terms to her, or to me." He paused, shook his head in regret. "I should have offered Laurel a much better deal, and would have had she demanded it. But she didn't, because she doesn't think that way."

Beast thumped his tail loudly.

"And I'll tell you something else." Cade continued thinking out loud as he explained the situation to his pet. "Mary Elena was right yesterday when she said that Laurel deserves to be rewarded for everything she is doing for me. Had she demanded fair compensation from the get-go, or had I thought of it, I certainly would have arranged to give it to her before things got so awkward in that regard. Of course, if I had actually paid her to act like my wife, then Laurel is right, I also would have been paying her for sex—at least in a roundabout way, and you and I both know that isn't right, either."

Cade sighed and shoved both his hands through his hair, not sure how something so simple had gotten so complicated. "Laurel wants love. I know that and so do you, so does everyone. Nothing less is going to satisfy her or make her stay with me for another month, never mind for the next thirty-three years. And the irony is, I have fallen in love with her. Hopelessly, crazy-in-love with her."

Beast eyed Cade skeptically.

Cade's mouth twisted ruefully. He knew exactly how his dog felt. A week ago, he wouldn't have believed it, either.

He drummed his fingers on the desktop. "And you know what is even more amazing? I wanted to tell Laurel how I felt that last night when we were making love, but I knew if I did, she would never accept it, not on the heels of our wifely sex for hire discussion. So I'm going to have to wait until the time is right, until I've laid the proper groundwork and I think she's fallen in love with me, too. And is ready to hear what I have to say. Ready to believe it."

Beast snuffled in disbelief.

"You think I'm approaching this too much like a business problem again, don't you?" Cade picked up his to-do list and pen. "Well, the truth is, I don't know any other way to operate. Even— or especially—when it comes to getting what I want on a personal level. I know, I know—" Cade held up a hand, as if Beast were going to interrupt "—it's going to take more than a few hot, passionate lovemaking sessions and sweet nothings whispered in

Laurel's ear to convince her that I'm speaking the truth, and that she and Patches should stay with the two of us forever. But she will believe me soon," he vowed determinedly. "I don't care what I have to do. I can romance a woman like nobody's business if I set my mind to it, and right now I want Laurel in my bed, and my life. And I know the only way that will happen on a permanent basis is if she believes I love her, heart and soul."

Beast whined in assent and settled his head back on his paws.

"So you just leave it to me. And watch and learn how a real master operates," Cade said with customary confidence.

Under "Damage Control—Marriage," Cade added two more items:

  5) Tell Laurel that I love her.
  6) Convince her to stay on permanently.

"How was class?" Cade asked Laurel several hours later, when she walked into his study, Patches snuggled in her arms.

Laurel perched on the edge of his desk, feeling remarkably happy to be "home" again. "It was great—until Frances Klenck's neighbor's cat decided to join us. You've never seen such pandemonium. All fourteen of the puppies in attendance tonight went absolutely crazy."

Cade slid a handwritten to-do list back in a manila file folder and put it in the in-basket on his desk. Then he took one of her hands in his and said dryly, "I gather there was a lot of barking?"

"Oh my word." Laurel rolled her eyes. "Not to mention running and squirming and straining at leashes. It's the first time I've ever seen Patches bark and carry on like that. You know how she's always trying to hide from things that frighten her? Well, not tonight. She dragged me halfway across the Klencks' backyard, trying to get to the interloper. It took a good fifteen minutes for us to settle them all down."

Cade grinned and reached over to pet Patches, too. "Well, I guess that explains the smudge of dirt on your cheek and the blade of grass in your hair."

Laurel blushed and shook her head. "So how did your work go?"

Cade frowned. "It's going to be a challenge to get a comprehensive marketing plan put together before the next board meeting."

"The one on May 3rd." Laurel put the tuckered out puppy down on the floor next to Beast, then gave them each a nylon chew bone.

"Right."

"Where the vote for new CEO takes place."

"Also correct."

"Are you worried about it?"

Cade hesitated. "I know my ideas for the company are good ones," he said finally.

"And yet...?" Laurel studied his face, guessing there was more.

His jaw set. "All the Dunnigans are known to be ruthless when it comes to getting what they want in their business and personal lives. That single-mindedness helped my grandfather create a company out of nothing, and my father grow it from a regional concern to a national maker of premium pet food."

He was so matter-of fact. A chill went down her spine. "Do you include yourself in that tally?"

Cade shrugged, the brooding look back on his face. "Let's just say I'm determined to do whatever is necessary in order to prevent George Jr. and George Sr. from ruining in a very short time what it took my father and grandfather fifty years to build. And I know, from watching the experience of other family-held corporations, just how quickly and easily that can happen when the motivating force behind the actions is greed."

Laurel let out a slow breath, aware she needed to be cautious here. "Surely the nonfamily members of the board of directors don't want to see DDF in ruin."

Cade winced. "They wouldn't consciously vote to put us out of business. On the contrary, they want the most return possible for their investment. You've probably already noticed that Harvey Lemmon pinches pennies to a ridiculous degree?"

Laurel nodded.

Cade pulled her onto his lap and wrapped both his arms around her. "I think Harvey could easily be persuaded to side with my uncle and cousin, if he believes they are more cost-conscious."

Laurel rested her head on his shoulder, loving the way he felt, so strong and warm and solid. "Even if their plans to cheapen the dog food drives people away from the product in the end?"

He massaged a hand down her spine. "There are ways George Jr. could alleviate that concern, at least in theory."

Laurel relaxed into his soothing touch. "Such as?"

Cade shrugged, his frustration with the situation evident. "By making a deal with one of the discount store chains to sell our product there, on the theory that the customers who are buying our dog food in premium pet stores would then purchase it in the discount store for a cheaper price."

"Until they realized it wasn't the same quality product and switched their allegiance to another premium brand."

"Right."

"I don't see how the board would vote for a business plan that is designed to lose customers for DDF," she pointed out.

Cade shrugged. "They might if George Jr. makes the argument that the sheer number of new and presumably loyal customers DDF would gain in discount stores would replace the premium-only customer base."

Laurel was impressed. Cade seemed to have thought of all the angles. But then, that was the kind of thorough, resolute businessperson he was. His willingness to persevere under even the most difficult and challenging conditions made him a great CEO. She bit her lip. "You think George Jr. could prove that?"

"It's possible to demonstrate any potential outcome with the right market-research and focus groups. It doesn't mean events will actually play out that way in reality. But that is the direction I expect him to go in the May 3rd board meeting, prior to the vote for CEO. And there's something else," he confided resolutely. "Lance Ayers isn't exactly happy with me, given the way things turned out with Mary Elena. It might not take much to persuade him to oust me as CEO, and the other two nonfamily board members often follow his lead and vote the same way Lance does."

"And if Dotty, Lance and Harvey vote with George Jr. and George Sr.," Laurel began, her voice clouded with turbulent emotion.

"The board will suffer a fifty-fifty split, which means that George Jr. and I would have to agree how to run things, a scenario that is not very likely, given our different views."

Goodness. He did have his hands full. Laurel furrowed her brow. "In light of that, should you even be considering giving Manuel Garcia a job at the flagship store?"

"Probably not, but it's the right thing to do," Cade stated. "Garcia should not be punished because Lance Ayers and I came up with a bad plan to insure I'd get my family inheritance. I should have known Mary Elena would never go through with it in the end."

Laurel appreciated Cade's principled behavior even as she felt chilled at his matter-of-fact description of his actions when it came to pursuing Mary Elena. The emotional side of her told her he had learned from his experience and knew better now. The less-willing-to-trust side of her said she would be wise not to let herself fall victim to the same type of win-at-all-costs plan to insure Cade's future. He had told her early on that love didn't insure a marriage—in his view, cool determination did.

An uncomfortable silence fell between them. Feeling increasingly vulnerable and on edge, Laurel stood and moved toward the windows. Darkness was falling, bathing the yard in a dusky light at odds with the turquoise glow of the lit swimming pool. "So what are you going to do?" she asked, leaning down to pet Patches and Beast simultaneously as they gnawed on their bones.

Cade turned his swivel chair toward her, but remained at his desk. She could sense his mind already shifting away from their intimate conversation, back into business mode. "I'm going to prove through my market research—and the success of the flagship store—that expansion into premium-level services is the best way to increase DDF profitability."

Laurel sat back on her heels, wondering what Cade would do if he had ever had to choose between her and the family company, then decided she didn't want to know. Not now. Maybe not ever.

She drew a deep, bolstering breath. "You think you can do that in the small amount of time remaining?"

Cade nodded and stated with an assured smile, "I've convinced all the board members to attend the grand opening. I think if they experience customer enthusiasm and the excitement of the event firsthand, they'll be inclined to at least vote me acting CEO for a two-year period. In that amount of time, I'll be able to demonstrate growth long term."

EARLY THE NEXT MORNING, AS Cade drove to the flagship store, to meet with the store manager, the fire marshal and the city inspectors to get final approvals so the business could open on schedule, he was still mulling over his conversation with Laurel the previous evening. He'd opened up more than he ever had before and bared his soul to her, yet she had seemed to resent his honesty in the end. Which just went to show, he thought with a brooding scowl, how people said they wanted to know the real you, but show them the rough edges and foibles and they were likely to run for the hills—or in Laurel's case, an early bedtime…alone.

Not that he could blame her for being asleep by the time he retired for the evening. It had been after one in the morning. It was the fact that she'd elected to sleep in the guest-room bed instead of his that had really bothered him. He'd thought they had established they were a couple now, and as such, she should have been sleeping in his bed with him.

But she hadn't. And after momentarily debating the wisdom of slipping in beside her, and most certainly waking Patches—who was sleeping in the crate nearby—he had decided to head for his own bed.

Accepting that maybe this was Laurel's way of gently letting him know he was pushing too hard too fast, he reluctantly decided he would have to give her the space she needed.

Fortunately, the beginning of his day went better than the evening before, and by eight-thirty that morning, Cade had garnered all the city approvals he needed for the grand opening.

The stocking of shelves had been completed. New employees were due to arrive any minute to begin their customer service education and training. And that was when Mary Elena Ayers walked in the double glass doors. She pushed her sunglasses to the top of her head and strode straight toward him. "Is there somewhere we can talk?" she asked without preamble.

Knowing it must be important if she were here at this hour—Mary Elena never had been much of a morning person—Cade led her to the manager's office and shut the door behind them. She opened her purse and extracted the engagement ring he had given her. "I can't keep this."

Cade held up a hand, palm out. "I don't want it."

She made a face. "Then return it and use the cash to pay Laurel's apartment rent for the next few months, or buy her some nice jewelry. She deserves at least that for bailing you out like she has."

Cade knew it had started out that way, but had swiftly turned into much more. The question was, how could he get Laurel to admit theirs was more than a temporary alliance designed to win him, control of his family company?

"And as far as Manuel goes," Mary Elena mused, "I know I twisted your arm to give him a job, but I hope you won't hold my behavior against him. He doesn't know that I asked this favor of you, and his pride would force him to refuse any offer of employment from you if he knew what I have done on his behalf."

Cade surveyed her wordlessly. "You really care about Manuel, don't you?"

Mary Elena blushed and ducked her head. "I just wish my father could see me with someone like him."

Cade shrugged. "Your father started out with pretty humble roots before he became a successful oilman and branched out into other areas of business. Maybe he and Manuel have more in common than they realize."

"I doubt Daddy would admit that." She sighed and shifted her sunglasses from her palm to the top of her head. "Daddy's so stubborn, Cade. He wants me with someone who already has money. He says that's the only way he'll know I'm not being married strictly for my inheritance. And without Daddy's permission, my friendship with Manuel is not likely to go any further. Manuel's sense of honor will not allow it. Family is everything to a man like him."

And to himself, too, Cade admitted. He suspected the same was true of Laurel, whether she wanted to admit it or not.

Was the disapproval of Laurel's family standing in their way, too?

"SO WHAT DO YOU think of the prototype?" Lewis McCabe asked Cade after he had completed the demonstration of the software game designed exclusively for DDF.

"I really like it." Cade rocked back in the chair behind his desk. He had asked Lewis to meet him at his home rather than the office, for two reasons. He didn't want his cousin catching wind of the promotional campaign Cade was planning to present to the board, prior to the CEO vote. Plus, he wanted a chance to talk to the extremely analytical Lewis about his baby sister. "The way you've incorporated the body language of dogs and their different types of barks as part of the game's sound package is really amazing."

"I think so, too." Laurel smiled as she swept into the room with three tall glasses of iced tea. She handed one to each of the men, and kept one for herself. She studied the graphics on the computer screen. "I also liked all the facts about dogs. For a new pet owner like me, it really teaches you a lot. Plus, it's fun to play, and the graphics are entertaining enough to delight both kids and adults."

Lewis winked at his sister. "Maybe I should have you on my marketing team," he said.

"No way," Cade countered, taking Laurel by the hand and reeling her in to his side. "Your sister has quickly proved indispensable to *me*."

"At work," Laurel amended with a self-conscious blush.

"And at home," Cade said, holding her eyes.

Lewis glanced from one to the other, then fixed them both with an intent look. "I had hoped to speak to Laurel about this alone, but now I'm thinking I should talk to you, too, Cade."

"Please do," he said.

Laurel scowled. "Please don't," she countered, just as urgently.

Lewis shrugged and fingered the eighties-style love beads around his neck. He looked at her decisively. "You've got to start taking Mom and Dad's calls."

Cade returned his attention to Laurel. "What is Lewis talking about?" he asked mildly.

She slipped away from him and didn't answer.

"She's been letting all their calls on her cell go straight to voice mail," Lewis explained. "She hasn't returned a one." He glared at his sister accusingly. "Not cool, Laurel."

Her cheeks turned a becoming pink. "I know what they're going to say," she muttered. She walked back to Cade and linked hands with him, as much for moral support, he figured, as for show. "I don't want to hear it."

His protective instincts rushing to the fore, Cade drew her close.

"It's only going to get harder as time goes by," Lewis predicted grimly before turning to Cade. "They've asked you both to join them on Saturday evening for dinner, at their home in Laramie. The rest of the family is going to be there. I advise you to show up. Doing so would go a long way toward easing Mom and Dad's minds, and reassuring them that Laurel hasn't gotten herself into another no-win situation that is only going to hurt her in the end."

"Thanks for putting it so nicely," she told Lewis sweetly. "But…no."

Cade looked at his wife. "I think we should go."

Laurel frowned. "You don't know what you're getting yourself into," she warned.

"Then maybe," Cade responded equably, "it's time I found out."

Chapter Thirteen

"I still think we're making a mistake," Laurel murmured, unable to shake her feeling of foreboding.

"We will be if you don't adjust your attitude," Cade admonished as he drove slowly through the charming West Texas town of Laramie and parked his Porsche on the street in front of the home where she had grown up. As always, the slate-gray paint, white trim and dark gray roof on the three-story Victorian were in perfect repair, the low-lying holly and juniper bushes neatly trimmed. Laurel surveyed the property with a mixture of nostalgia and dread. She and her friends had whiled away many an afternoon and evening on the porch that wrapped around the entire first floor, and with good reason. Her mother had worked hard to make it warm and welcoming, with its comfortable groupings of cushioned wicker furniture and hanging swing. Apparently her mother had been toiling away in her flower beds, as usual. They were filled with a profusion of Shasta daisies, scarlet sage and pink evening primrose.

Irked that Cade hadn't taken her advice and bypassed this McCabe family gauntlet altogether, Laurel frowned. "I suppose *your* attitude is perfect."

Cade shot her a quelling glance. "If you want to succeed in life, it's important to have a thorough, businesslike approach to every problem—including the personal."

Laurel hated the smug male confidence in his low tone. Attitudes like that always brought out the worst in her, and this was no exception. She slammed the car door and headed for the waist-high picket fence that edged the property. "So what's your plan?"

Cade caught up with her, took her elbow and steered her beneath one of the live oaks shading the front yard. Bracing an arm on the trunk beside her, he leaned in for an intimate word with her. "First, I'm going to listen to what your parents have to say to us, now that a little time has passed and they see that, despite all predictions to the contrary, you and I are still together. Second, I'm going to let them know in every way I can that my intentions toward you are honorable."

Laurel glared at him, her cheeks burning because he was hitting so close to home. "What in blue blazes is that supposed to mean?" she demanded. As if she needed her parents to protect her in this regard!

"It means I'm not planning to dump you as soon as I get the DDF board to vote me the new CEO. I want to stay married to you."

Laurel sucked in a quick breath. "So you'll retain your inheritance," she verified, knowing they needed to stay clear about the parameters of the situation, lest she succumb to temptation and fool herself into thinking this was a real marriage in every sense instead of simply an "arrangement" that had turned unexpectedly passionate, and surprisingly fulfilling on nearly every level—except one.

"So," Cade said, pulling her close and delivering a kiss that seemed every bit as heartfelt as it was passionate, "I'll retain you as my lover, my wife and a very, very important part of my life."

Looking into his eyes, Laurel couldn't help but believe everything was going to turn out all right, despite the unusual beginnings of their "partnership."

Unfortunately, just as she had predicted, her parents didn't seem to see it that way. As soon as Laurel and Cade had said hello to all of her brothers and their wives and children, who were gathered in the backyard, Kate asked Laurel to help her retrieve and fill the beverage tubs, so the men could carry them out.

"You're looking well," her mother remarked as soon as the two of them were alone.

"So are you," Laurel replied, aware the garage was cool and quiet, the perfect place to talk. "So, if that's all…" She wanted to table this discussion—permanently.

Kate put a hand on her shoulder and made no move to get started on their task. "Sweetheart, your father and I are worried about you."

The hell of it was, part of her was, too. Laurel stuck her hands in the pockets of her jeans. "You don't need to be."

Kate slid her a speculative glance. "You've fallen in love with him, haven't you?"

Laurel knew it would be futile to deny it. Her mother always had been able to read her like a book. Laurel lifted her hands and tried to pretend it was no big deal as she quipped, "How did you know?"

"I saw it on your face the moment you walked in." Kate paused, then continued gently, " I'm not so adept at reading Cade, however."

Unfortunately, neither was Laurel.

"Is he in love with you?" her mom asked as she got out the two large, galvanized steel washtubs the McCabes used at every backyard party.

Laurel shrugged as she opened the freezer and lifted out several bags of ice. "Sometimes I think so," she admitted reluctantly.

"And at other times?"

She took a deep breath and avoided her mother's probing gaze. "I'm reminded that our hasty marriage was just a means to an end."

Kate took a pair of utility scissors off the pegboard wall and snipped the tops off the plastic bags. "How long are you planning to stay married to him?"

Laurel helped upend the open bags of ice into the tubs. "Initially, it was just for a few weeks," she allowed uncomfortably.

"And now?" her mom pressed, bringing out several cardboard beverage packs of soft drinks.

Laurel went to get the beer and wine coolers from the garage refrigerator. "He doesn't want to split up, even then."

Kate prepared the tub of nonalcoholic drinks, Laurel the other. "How do you feel about that?"

Happy. Sad. Elated. Scared. She shrugged and took the empty cardboard over to the recycling station along the wall. She kept her voice as even as she could. "I don't know."

"Then let me ask you this." Kate wadded up the discarded plastic and carried it to the garbage can. "Are you serious about trying to make this marriage work?"

Maybe. If I had some sort of guarantee I wouldn't get my heart stomped all to pieces.

She paused, then, realizing it might help to confide in someone, said, "You're a psychologist and a grief counselor. You've seen a lot of heartache in your life…as well as a lot of happiness."

"Yes, honey," Kate replied, "I have."

Laurel searched her mother's face. "Do you think it's necessary to have both people in love with each other, for a marriage to work? Or is the love of one person, if it's powerful enough, all that's required to get a marriage off the ground and make a couple happy?" Even before her mother paused, Laurel knew she was grasping at straws here. She couldn't help it. She wanted Cade to be part of her life, forever…so very badly. Regardless of how it looked to anyone else.

Kate regarded her thoughtfully. "You're trying to decide whether you want to love Cade or not, is that it?"

Laurel nodded, too distraught to speak.

"Oh, honey." Her mom draped a reassuring arm around her shoulders. "Love doesn't work that way. You can't decide to feel love for someone or not, based on the probable outcome of any relationship."

The way Cade would, Laurel realized.

"You either do or don't love that person," Kate continued firmly but gently. "And love—true love—is all about giving of yourself, without regard to what you may or may not get in return."

The question was this, then, Laurel thought, as she accepted the comfort only her mother could give. Was she selfless and strong enough to love Cade even if she didn't ever get actual love back from him? Or, if that were ultimately the situation, would she end up feeling as disillusioned and used as she had in the past when she realized she had done all the giving in a relationship, the other person all the taking?

CADE SUSPECTED IT WOULDN'T be long before Laurel's father called him out, and he was correct in his assumption. As soon as she went off with Kate, Sam asked Cade to accompany him to his book-lined study at the front of the house. Once the double doors were shut, Sam McCabe wasted no time getting straight to the point. "A marriage in name only is not what Kate and I had planned for our only daughter."

Cade figured this was not the time to admit that his marriage had become a real one in nearly every way, so he merely said, "I'm not out to hurt Laurel, sir."

Sam eased behind his desk, searching Cade's face. "But you are using her to get what you want."

Guilt flooded him. Wishing he could deny that, he took a chair. "It started out that way, yes."

Sam propped his fingers together in front of him. "If you really care about her, the best thing would be for you to let her go so that she can have the kind of fulfilling romantic relationship she deserves."

Cade agreed that Laurel needed and deserved more, but he also knew he could give it to her. He tried his best to assure Sam that he now had only the truest motives where Laurel was concerned, but knew that words would get him only so far in earning her father's respect. He had to prove his devotion—and the first person he had to convince of this was his wife. So that evening, when she was curiously quiet on the drive back to Dallas, he made up his mind to be the best husband he could be to Laurel.

"I'm really tired," she said, as soon as they had settled the dogs for the night. "I think I'll head on up to bed."

Cade pressed a kiss to her temple. "Can I get you anything?" he asked gently. "Nightcap? Glass of lemonade? Milk and cookies?"

"No, thanks." She brushed off every suggestion with the same tense smile. "I'm really full from dinner."

Too upset by whatever her mother had said when they were alone, was more like it, Cade thought. He had seen Laurel pushing her food around on her plate during the meal with her family, and he was pretty sure everyone else had noticed her artificial cheer and lack of appetite, too.

"See you tomorrow then," he said, deciding if it was space his wife needed, he would give it to her. Meanwhile, he thought as he headed for his study, he had an appointment to make via e-mail. Hopefully, Trisha Teal would be able to get back to him soon. Because if anyone would know exactly what was appropriate in this situation, it would be her.

LAUREL GOT UP TWICE that night to take Patches out to the yard. The first time was shortly after midnight, the next was 4:00 a.m. When she woke again, Patches was whimpering excitedly and sunshine was streaming in through her bedroom windows. Cade was standing next to the bed, a tray in hand. He had showered and shaved. Brisk masculine cologne scented his jaw. The short-sleeved white polo shirt molded to his broad shoulders and powerful chest. Loose-fitting olive-green cargo shorts showcased long, muscular legs dusted with dark gold hair.

Recalling all too well how that swimmer's body felt clasped to hers, Laurel struggled to sit up. Not sure whether to feel grateful or suspicious of the sudden shift in his behavior—from all business to lazy weekend-morning mode—she pushed the hair from her eyes and fought for control. Given the fact she had slept solo, she had expected him to be resentful this morning, not nicer than ever. "Since when do you bring me breakfast in bed?"

Cade flashed her a dashing smile at odds with her wary reception. "Since today." He set it across her lap and brushed his lips across her temple. "You enjoy while I take Patches outside."

Five minutes later, he returned. "I left Beast and Patches on the sunporch. I think they'll be okay."

Laurel knew Beast—who had quickly become the father figure in the canine relationship—had a remarkably calming affect on her puppy. Still… "Patches might chew the wicker furniture."

Her effort to get rid of Cade quickly, before the situation became any more intimate, failed. "Then I'll have a talk with her," he drawled facetiously. He sat on the edge of the bed, next to Laurel. "How was your breakfast?"

Laurel gave him a thumbs-up. "I didn't know you could cook."

Cade filched a crumb of Danish from her plate. His gaze moved from her eyes to her lips and back again. "I'm not sure I'd call fruit, pastry and coffee cooking," he allowed with a slow, sexy smile that did funny things to her insides. "I went to the café a couple blocks over and ordered what I thought you'd like, then came home and put it on the china and brought it up."

"It's delicious."

His eyes scanned her face, searching for what she couldn't say. "Thanks."

She became aware that her pulse had picked up marginally. He looked so natural, hanging out in her bedroom with her this way. Laurel licked suddenly dry lips. "I'm curious why you thought this was necessary."

Cade shrugged with lazy male insistence. "It occurred to me I haven't treated you as well as I might, given all you have done for me this last week."

Knowing how easy it would be to find herself making love with him again, but determined not to be sensually distracted, Laurel sat back and crossed her arms in front of her. "It occurred to you or was pointed out to you by my father?" she queried dryly.

A mixture of guilt and regret flashed across Cade's face.

Her temper flared. "I should have known better than to take you home to Laramie!"

He leaned close enough to kiss her—but didn't. "You're angry with me?"

"You bet!"

His expression guarded, Cade studied her, taking in her tousled hair and strawberry-and-white-striped cotton pajamas. "Why?"

She glared at him, wishing she had a little more coverage than the button-front, vest-style pajama top as he gazed at her in a way that made her feel all hot and bothered. "I don't need you bringing me breakfast in bed because my father told you to do it." That was no different than her ex-fiancé courting her as a way to fast-track his career at her dad's company.

Cade leaned closer still, the look he gave her honest, implacable and self-assured. "He didn't tell me to bring you a tray this morning. That was my idea."

She flattened her palms against his chest, holding him at bay. "What exactly did my dad say to you last night?"

"Bottom line?" Cade lifted the tray off her lap and moved it aside, so nothing stood between them but the sheets—and their clothing. "Your father thinks I don't deserve a woman like you and that I should cut you free."

Achingly aware of just how bad that idea sounded to her, Laurel arched a delicate brow. "And you said to him?"

Cade shrugged. "I had a hard time convincing him otherwise. After all, I haven't treated you as well as I should."

"Bull." Laurel vaulted from the bed and shrugged on her robe. Her hands trembled as she knotted the belt tightly. "You've been nothing but forthright with me." She paced back and forth. Hot, embarrassed color filled her cheeks. Thanks to her father's meddling, she felt like an imbecile! "I know exactly where we stand."

Cade followed her. "Which is why you returned to the guest room."

She whirled so suddenly she almost slammed into his chest. "I told you I was tired!"

Cade towered over her, regarding her stonily. "Now who is full of bull? You're avoiding even the possibility of sleeping with me again, and I want to know why!"

Laurel planted her hands on her hips and glared up at him. "No, you don't."

He kept his eyes fixed on hers. "Yes, I do."

"If we sleep together…we're likely to make love."

Cade took her hand in his, letting her know with a look and a touch they had nothing to be ashamed about. He tightened his fingers reassuringly over hers. "Sounds good to me so far."

It would sound good to Laurel, too, if he had told her he loved her, but he hadn't done that yet. She pushed his hand away and tried again. Her chest rose and fell with each furious breath. "The fact we've been having sex with each other while I'm living here is complicating things unnecessarily, Cade."

He tilted his head. "I don't know about that," he said very, very softly. "Making love with you feels very necessary to me."

She refused to be swayed by his much more romantic description of events. With a haughty toss of her head, she stalked by him once again. "I'm not talking about physical release."

Cade caught her by the waist and whirled her around to face him. The next thing she knew she was wrapped in the warmth and strength of his arms. "Neither am I," he murmured. After lowering his head to hers, he traced a fiery, erotic path down the slope of her neck, across her jaw, behind her ear with his lips. Hot tingles swept through Laurel. It was all she could do to stay on her feet.

"I'm talking about feeling as close to you as possible, about holding you in my arms and kissing you," he whispered seductively.

Laurel glowered at him stubbornly, forcing herself to be as cool and logical as the situation demanded, when all she wanted was to be wild and passionate, completely swept away. "Cade..."

He captured her lips with his. There was no time to think, no time to resist as their mouths locked together in a searing kiss. She could only feel, and what she felt was a mixture of hot temper and physical passion, and a deeper, searing need to possess. Her arms clasped his waist, her body surged against his. Cade kissed her as if they had been apart forever, instead of a single night. As if he meant to make her his not just now, but for all time. Satisfaction rushed through Laurel, along with raw, aching need. One stolen kiss followed another and another and another. And as his lips and tongue continued to work their magic, she felt herself succumbing, the way she always did, to the dazzling seduction of her husband's embrace. She found herself falling even deeper in love with him. She knew if they didn't stop soon they would end up right back in bed together, with nothing established but their physical need for each other. Her heart—and their future happiness—would still be at risk.

With effort, she pulled herself together and pushed him away. Ignoring the flicker of hurt and frustration in his eyes, she forced herself to admonish sternly, for both their sakes. "I don't want you doing things like this just because of something my dad said to you." It made it impossible for her to keep their original bargain, which had been to make their marriage a very business-like—and temporary—arrangement that was simply a means to an end, instead of the mingling of hearts and souls she secretly wanted it to be.

The heated denial she had half expected—and secretly wanted—never came. Instead, a long, emotion-packed silence fell between them.

Ignoring the catch in her breath, she moved away. Only when they were a safe distance apart did she meet Cade's probing glance. "I think we should just concentrate on business and not worry about our marriage or our relationship." She took his slight nod and grim silence as tacit approval of her matter-of-fact proposal. "Once you are CEO and the future of DDF is secure, then we can worry about what to do next."

Maybe by then, Laurel added silently, *you will have realized you love me.* Because she knew if he didn't love her by then, there was no way she could stay on as either his lover or his wife. It would be just too painful.

"IT MUST BE IMPORTANT IF you call me over here on a Monday evening," Trisha Teal told Cade.

He ushered her inside and escorted her back to his study. "It is. And we don't have a lot of time—Laurel will be back from the puppy kindergarten training session in less than an hour." Cade needed his plan to work. "Did you bring the rings?"

"A whole case of them." Trisha opened it up on his desk. "I've got everything from emeralds to diamonds, platinum to gold."

Cade studied the glittering array of jewelry. "It's an engagement ring, so it should be a diamond. And platinum, since our wedding bands are platinum. Unless you think I should replace those, too?"

Trisha shrugged. "It might not be a bad idea, given the fact that you and Mary Elena picked them out for the two of you."

Cade winced. "Don't remind me."

Trisha's lip curved ruefully. "It's not as if anyone in Dallas can forget. It's not every day that a man exchanges one bride for another the hour before the ceremony is to begin."

Cade frowned as he studied a marquis diamond. "The circumstances were extenuating."

"I know," Trisha repeated drolly. "You needed to marry someone to collect your inheritance. I just didn't think you'd stay hitched, Cade, since you were never one to show any interest in marriage."

The hell of it was, he knew he probably wouldn't have if his bride had been anyone else. Not about to reveal his feelings to Trisha before he confided in Laurel, he stated mildly, "Let's just say I've changed my mind about that."

Trisha cocked a curious brow. "Of your own volition or because, money-and-inheritance-wise, you don't have a choice?"

Because I love her, Cade thought. Not that Laurel was anywhere near ready to believe that just yet. Which was where the rings came in…. He was hoping the gift would give them a fresh start. He looked up at Trisha once again. "Back to business…."

"Of course."

"I want to purchase a wedding and engagement ring set for Laurel."

Trisha slipped into professional mode. "Tell me about her. Does your wife like flamboyant demonstration of wealth? Or is she more comfortable with something simpler and understated?"

Cade didn't even have to think about it. "Understated," he said.

"Simple does not mean cheap. Every woman wants to be pampered, deep down…." She picked out several rings for him to examine. "Every woman wants to know that she's loved, and a good way to demonstrate it is with a magnificent ring." Zeroing in on the one Cade held in his palm, Trisha smiled and said, "I promise you, Cade, if you give Laurel this ring you'll have her eating out of your hand in no time…."

"I'm not trying to manipulate her, Trisha," Cade said gruffly.

I just want Laurel to see that although we may have started out all wrong, we still have time and opportunity to make things right.

Hopefully, the rings he picked out today would do the trick.

LAUREL WAS SURPRISED TO see George Jr. waiting for her when she and Patches walked out of Frances Klenck's back gate—where class had been held—to the street where her car was parked. Of all the people she did not want to see, Cade's snotty cousin topped the list. Bad enough he was doing everything he could to sabotage Cade at work; now he was out to destroy her relationship with Cade, too.

"Ever get the feeling you've joined the wrong team?" He fell into step beside her.

"No." Laurel picked up her pace. "I haven't."

He smirked. "Maybe you should."

Her limited patience at an end, Laurel sent him a withering look. "Don't you ever get tired of playing these little games of yours?"

George Jr. shrugged and slid his hands in the pockets of his elegant pants. "You may have heard, when it comes to business and money we Dunnigans are a ruthless bunch."

Hearing him include himself and Cade in the same nefarious category made her ill. She clenched her teeth. George Jr. was spoiling for a nasty exchange. She decided she would give him one. She smiled back at him, just as snidely. "What is your point, Junior?"

He frowned at her sarcasm, but did not back off. "Do you know where your husband is tonight?"

"Yes."

"Do you know who he is spending time with?"

Cade was alone, with Beast. At least he had been when she had left the house. A trickle of uneasiness slid down her spine. "I really have to go." She moved to step past him, not easy since the leashed Patches was intent on going wherever her sensitive nose led her.

George Jr. moved to block her way. "Ever met Trisha Teal?"

Laurel paused. Cade had never struck her as a womanizer, but then neither had her ex-fiancé.

"She's gorgeous. Successful. She's got a beautiful smile and an even more beautiful laugh. He's with her right now."

Okay. Just for the hell of it, she'd bite. "And you know this because…?"

George Jr. grinned smugly. "I drove over to the house to talk to him, and saw her car in the drive. Yours was nowhere in sight. I knew the puppy training classes were this evening. So here I am to warn you that circumstances—and husbands—are not always what they seem."

Like my marriage to Cade, for instance, Laurel thought. No one but she and Cade had any idea how complicated that had become. She watched Patches circle and sniff more intently. "I think I know Cade," she said eventually.

"Do you?" George Jr. taunted.

Laurel waited for Patches to relieve herself in the grass next to the curb, then picked up the puppy and secured her in the carrying case on the car seat.

"Do you know he's playing you for the biggest fool ever by romancing you to your face and carrying on with Trisha behind your back?"

Laurel whirled, struggling to keep her temper in check, and responded crisply, "First of all, whatever Cade and my arrangement is, it's none of your business. Second, you know as well as everyone else that Cade and I got married with our eyes wide open."

"The DDF board would love to hear about that."

Laurel ignored his goading. "It's none of their business, either."

Seeming to realize he had struck a nerve, George Jr. leaned in with a speculative glance. "If you join with my father and me, Laurel, I'll see you not only keep your job at DDF I'll make sure you're promoted to vice president."

Laurel opened her car door. "What about Cade?"

"He won't stay if he's not chief executive officer."

Laurel wasn't so sure that was true, given how Cade felt about the company his father and grandfather had started. "Will you stay if the situation is reversed?" she asked, curious.

"It's not going to be," George Jr. vowed furiously.

Laurel shrugged. "Says you."

"Look." Impatience tinged his low tone. "All you have to do is get a copy of his marketing pitch and give it to me ahead of time. I'll see you are rewarded handsomely."

Laurel gave Cade's nemesis an icy smile. "And if I don't?" she questioned bluntly.

"Then I'm taking you down, right along with Cade."

Chapter Fourteen

When Laurel got home, she headed straight for Cade's study. He was exactly where she had left him, sitting at his desk, working on the marketing plan. Unlike her, he hadn't changed out of his work clothes. The only thing he had done was unfasten another button on his starched blue shirt and roll up his sleeves. His hair was more rumpled than usual, his eyes rimmed with fatigue.

Spying her in the doorway, he stopped typing, leaned back and smiled. "I was beginning to worry about you." He crossed to her side and kissed her cheek. "Class run late tonight?"

Aware they were getting used to touching each other this way, to behaving very much like a couple, even though they hadn't made love or slept together for several days, Laurel gazed into his eyes and tried not to think how comforting it was to have someone waiting at home for her. "No, I was delayed, leaving." Laurel set her puppy down on the study rug. Patches made straight for Beast, who lay there patiently, watching, while Patches romped around him.

Laurel turned her attention back to Cade. "George Jr. was waiting for me when Patches and I walked out." Although she hated to be the bearer of bad news, she figured Cade had a right to know what his cousin was up to behind his back. "He asked me for a copy of your marketing plan."

Cade frowned. Weary lines bracketed his lips. "Doesn't surprise me. I figured he'd do something underhanded."

Laurel fastened her gaze on the computer screen. It was dominated by colorful graphs. "He also offered me a vice presidency if I help him gain the CEO position."

Lifting a brow, Cade scanned her from head to toe. "And you said...?"

Laurel blushed at the attention and the obvious desire underlying it. "That I know where my loyalties lie."

"Right here, I hope." Cade wrapped her in a warm hug. Laurel had promised herself she wasn't going to pursue the sexual aspects of their relationship any more until they had worked out everything else. She took a deep breath, drew on some of the energy arcing between them, and used it to fortify herself. She splayed her hands across his chest. "So how was your evening tonight?" She forced herself to sound casual.

"Oh, you know." Cade shrugged and let her go. "The usual. Work, work, work." He turned away and headed back to his desk.

She followed, keeping a discreet distance. "How is the marketing plan coming?"

Cade picked up the pages he had been working on, as well as the memory key from his computer, and carried them over to the wall safe. "I think it's going to be excellent. It's a pain not to be able to pull it together in the office, but I feel better keeping the work locked up here."

Ever met Trisha Teal? She's gorgeous. Cade's with her right now....

Laurel pushed aside the memory of George Jr.'s taunt. She smiled and sauntered closer, to better study Cade's face. The quickest way to get to the bottom of this mystery was to simply ask. "You didn't do anything else besides work?"

Cade looked down at her, perplexed. "Like what?"

"I don't know." Laurel discovered her heart was pounding as she embarked on what was essentially an unprecedented third degree. "Go for a swim. Or go out for dinner. See someone. Talk on the phone. Take Beast for a walk." *Find someone else to sleep with, since you haven't been making love with me....*

Deliberately, she pushed the jealous thought away.

Hadn't she told herself on the drive home she was not going to let George Jr. goad her into accusing Cade of anything? Especially since Laurel knew that was exactly what his cousin wanted?

Oblivious to the dark nature of her thoughts, Cade tucked a strand of hair behind her ear. "I would still like to go for a swim. I haven't had dinner yet or talked on the phone, and I didn't take Beast for a walk, since he is now getting plenty of exercise romping around the backyard with Patches. Speaking of which," he said, as Beast finally lumbered to his feet and went into a deep play bow at Patches's tiny feet, "I think that would be a good place to take them right now, before one of them gets excited and decorates the rug."

As they set about doing that, Laurel realized in frustration that Cade had just deftly avoided her most important question. Because he had something to hide, or because she had couched it among too many other items?

When they reached the grass where the two dogs could romp, Laurel let her puppy run free once again.

"I am hungry, though," Cade admitted amiably at length. He smiled, watching Laurel straighten once again. "You?"

She shook her head. In an effort to curtail the time spent with Cade, she had already eaten. "I stopped for a salad on the way home from work tonight."

"That was hours ago."

Laurel swallowed around the sudden lump of emotion in her throat. "I'm fine, really."

"Then why don't you look fine?" he asked her softly, deliberately holding her eyes.

Because if George Jr. wasn't lying—and you were with another woman tonight in my absence—why haven't you just come out and told me about it? "I guess it's just been a long day and the fatigue is catching up with me," Laurel answered. She hated the mistrustful way she felt.

"If you want, I could get up with Patches tonight," Cade offered.

"She'd have to sleep in the room with you."

"Beast and I wouldn't mind."

"Then I'd be alone."

Cade's lips curved in a mischievous grin. He waggled his eyebrows at her. "So sleep in the room with us. My bed is plenty big enough."

Laurel paced back and forth, her sneakers sinking into the soft grass. "I don't think I'd get much rest if I did that."

There was a flicker of concern in his eyes, as if for a moment he weighed passion against friendship and wondered if he would have to choose between them. "Sure you would," he teased, his voice relaxing into a deeper baritone, "if rest is really what you want. I can be a gentleman, Laurel."

She had only to look at the sudden seriousness of his expression to know that. "I'm not questioning your chivalrous nature."

Cade's eyes narrowed in obvious displeasure. "Then what are you questioning?" he demanded impatiently.

Laurel sighed. "Exactly what is right for me."

IN THE END, TO CADE'S disappointment, Laurel decided to sleep with Patches in the guest room. As she had the previous two nights, she took her puppy with her and went to bed early. Too wired to even consider going to sleep, Cade made himself a sandwich from the groceries that Laurel had stocked in the fridge over the weekend. Figuring he would work out first, eat later, he slid the meal back in the fridge, changed into his swim trunks and hit the pool. He was so frustrated with the way Laurel kept backing away from him that he did double his normal workout, and he was still strung tight as a bow when he emerged from the water and toweled off.

Cade looked over at Beast. His big black Lab had been lying on the concrete, head on his paws, watching, the whole time. Now, he lifted his head and gazed at Cade in mournful silence.

That was the good thing about dogs, Cade thought. They felt what you felt. If you wanted to play, so did they. If you were sad, they were sad. Beast was steady, predictable, loyal. He loved Cade as much as Cade loved him.

So why wasn't it that easy with women? he mused. And why

couldn't he seem to figure out what Laurel had been wrestling with tonight? Clearly, she'd had something troubling on her mind when she returned from class, other than his cousin's attempted bribe. She had been edgy, ill-at-ease, but whatever the reason, she hadn't wanted to discuss it with him.

So, against his better instincts, he had let it go for now, figuring if she needed room to figure things out on her own he would somehow find the patience to give it to her. And that, too, was different. Cade had grown up knowing he could have just about anything he wanted—in a material sense, anyway. After being constantly disappointed by his parents, he hadn't allowed himself to lust after anything emotional or intangible. It had seemed simple. You couldn't lose what you didn't want. So he hadn't allowed himself to yearn for the kind of familial happiness he had lacked as a child. And that approach had worked great until Laurel came into his life. Just that swiftly, everything had changed.

Now he wanted.

And what he wanted wasn't anything he could buy.

It was Laurel. Her love, her devotion, her heart.

He wasn't used to biding his time or putting off until tomorrow what could be accomplished today. Aware that the strain was beginning to tell on him, Cade sank down on the chaise next to Beast. He buried his face in the towel, then looked up at the starlit sky. Funny, how differently he had hoped the end to this day would go. He'd purchased a beautiful engagement ring and a new wedding ring for Laurel this evening. But he had no idea when or how he was going to give the rings to her, or the slightest hope she would accept either from him. Clearly, the mood had not been right tonight. The closer he wanted to be to Laurel, the more she seemed to run away from him. That had to change. The question, he ruminated silently, was when. And how. He had the feeling waiting too long to make his next move would be as dangerous to their relationship as not waiting long enough.

"WHO WAS THAT?" CADE asked two days later as Laurel hung up the kitchen phone. In the week and a half she had been working at DDF headquarters, she had adjusted her work clothing to better fit in with the rest of the staff. Today she was dressed in a trim black skirt and a white sleeveless blouse. A deep rose cardigan was tied around her shoulders. She looked pretty and professional. More pulled-together working woman than pampered Southern belle. And she was all his except for one thing. She no longer wanted him to make love to her.

No, Cade thought, that wasn't exactly true. She did want him to make love to her. He saw it in her eyes every time she looked at him, and especially when she urged him—however surreptitiously—to walk away. It was almost as if this self-imposed moratorium on the physical aspects of their relationship was a test to see if they had anything between them but sex. And much to Laurel's surprise—and his satisfaction—they did. They both loved the challenge of business, their dogs and most of all, though she would be damned if she would admit it, each other....

The only thing that comforted him was the knowledge that their inability to take their emotional intimacy to the next level was beginning to wear her down. Just as it was him.

Laurel tossed Cade a quick smile and went back to pouring two glasses of juice. She reached for a third tumbler and filled that, too. "That was Lance Ayers. He said he will be here in two minutes to talk to you."

Cade was still buttoning his shirt. His shoes were upstairs on the bedroom closet floor. He was hardly ready for company and he knew he didn't want any. This time of morning was for him and Laurel. Period. "We haven't even had breakfast."

Laurel shrugged as she glanced out at the sunporch, where Beast and Patches were busy getting reacquainted after a night spent apart. "Lance doesn't care. He says it's important."

Which probably meant, Cade thought, that he was here about Mary Elena....

As if on cue, the doorbell rang. Looking only slightly less tense than Cade felt, Laurel said, "I'll get it."

Seconds later, she was walking back into the kitchen with

Lance Ayers right behind her. He seemed loaded for bear, Cade noted. Not a good sign at just seven-thirty in the morning.

Lance grimaced and got straight to the point. "I understand you gave Manuel Garcia a job at the flagship store."

Cade continued making coffee. "That's correct."

"Fire him," Lance ordered.

Cade pushed the button, watched the red light come on, then looked up. "No," he said, just as flatly.

Lance Ayers frowned. "If you don't, I may not be able to support you for CEO."

Not good news. But then, Cade thought, he hadn't really expected any. "I'm sorry to hear that," he replied evenly, looking the man who had nearly been his father-in-law in the eye, "but I refuse to fire any employee who is doing a damn fine job."

Lance scowled. "I want him out of Dallas."

Cade sipped his juice. "What happened between me and Mary Elena is not Manuel's fault."

"The hell it's not." Lance pushed away the juice Laurel offered him, and turned practically purple with rage. "If Mary Elena hadn't been making goo-goo eyes at Manuel, she would have walked down the aisle with you!" Abruptly recalling who was in the room with them, Lance cut Laurel an apologetic glance. "Sorry, Laurel. No offense, but it's true."

To Cade's relief, she took the older man's ranting in stride. "You're right," she said, her attitude one of maturity and candor. "It is true. Mary Elena is attracted to Manuel in a way she was never attracted to Cade."

Cade stared at Laurel, not sure whether to be offended or relieved by that matter-of-fact statement.

She shrugged. "Mary Elena told me that she couldn't imagine going to bed with Cade, never mind making babies with him, and she has always wanted lots and lots of babies, Mr. Ayers. Which means grandbabies for you. Mary Elena found the idea of trying to do that with Cade…distasteful. That's why she got so sick the day of the rehearsal dinner," Laurel continued, her cheeks flushing slightly. "She knew she couldn't go through with it. And the thought of telling either of you the real reason why practically gave her a nervous breakdown."

"Well, now that you've made that clear, I think we should stay out of this," Cade stated bluntly, glad someone had finally stopped Lance Ayers in his tracks.

"I don't," Laurel countered, ignoring Cade's order to cease and desist. She stepped forward, hands outstretched. "Mr. Ayers, someone has to be straight with you. You need to stop trying to control Mary Elena's life, and let her live it however she sees fit, in whatever way makes her happy."

Lance frowned and shook his head. He fingered the rim of his Stetson. "That's just it. Mary Elena never will be happy with that young stud. He is six years younger than she is. He doesn't have a college education."

Laurel made a soft, dissenting sound. "It seems to me that could be remedied, especially by someone of your financial means."

You go, girl, Cade thought.

"He doesn't understand the kind of life she has led," Lance countered.

On the contrary, Cade thought. "Manuel understands that he can't see Mary Elena in a romantic sense without your approval," he interjected quietly.

"He told you that?" Lance said.

"No, Mary Elena did. She's pretty upset about it. But Manuel is standing firm. Family is very important to him. He won't deliberately get between you and your daughter. He knows that would lead to unhappiness on all sides."

"You have misjudged him," Laurel stated quietly, backing Cade up. "As for what happened regarding the wedding—you want to blame someone for that debacle? Blame me. I was the maid of honor. I knew Mary Elena was having grave doubts. I should have encouraged her to tell both of you how she was feeling, and helped her back out before it got to the point of no return for Cade. Instead, I told her it was just prewedding jitters and would pass. And the two of you should have noticed how unhappy and nervous Mary Elena was about everything and insisted she talk to you about her feelings. But you didn't and I didn't. During all of this, the only person in Dallas who encouraged her to follow her heart and do what was right for her was Manuel. Not because he had anything to gain, but because he truly cared for her." Laurel paused a moment to let her words sink in. "You ought to give him a chance. I know he doesn't have money, but from what Mary Elena has told me, neither did you when you started out in the oil business, years ago."

For the first time, Lance Ayers looked uncertain.

"Maybe Manuel and Mary Elena will work out, maybe they won't," Laurel continued empathetically. "But if you don't support her, Mr. Ayers, you'll lose your daughter."

And it was clear, Cade noted, Lance Ayers did not want that.

"SO, I'M THAT UNDESIRABLE a potential lover," Cade concluded with comically exaggerated gravity after showing Lance Ayers out. He grinned at Laurel as he sauntered back into the kitchen. "Do I come across that way to you, too? Is that why you've been sleeping in the other room?"

Laurel blushed at Cade's deliberate misconstruction. She knew he was teasing her. She also knew—in retrospect—how her matter-of-fact appraisal of the situation must have sounded to him. She winced. "I'm sorry. I didn't mean to blurt that out." And she certainly hadn't meant to wound his male pride.

"To tell you the truth," Cade admitted, suddenly serious again, "I'm not surprised to hear that was a big part of her motivation for running off."

Laurel looked at him.

Cade poured them each a mug of coffee. "Mary Elena is a beautiful woman, but she was not attractive in that particular way to me, either. And since I do want kids…lots of them…it was going to pose a problem someday down the road."

Trying not to get her hopes up, because she wanted lots of kids, too, Laurel stirred cream and sugar into her coffee. "And yet you would have married Mary Elena anyway, despite the lack of sizzle between you."

Nodding, he lifted his mug to his lips. "In retrospect, I can see how blind I was to the reality of the situation. But at the time, I thought if I married someone who understood we don't always find the love of our life, it would all eventually work out. Mary Elena thought so, too. And on paper, anyway, we were a good match."

Laurel couldn't help but note how handsome Cade looked, standing in the morning sunlight streaming through the windows. "Are you sorry she didn't marry you?"

Cade put down his mug, took hers and set it down, too. He wrapped his arms about her waist and, taking full advantage of the ribbon of desire spreading through her, kissed her full on the mouth until her toes curled and a hot flush swept through her entire body. "What do you think?" he murmured, bringing Laurel close for yet another long, thorough kiss. "Still don't know?" he teased, and kissed her again.

Unable to help herself, Laurel began to yield, and then caught herself and moaned low in her throat. "Cade…the office…"

"To hell with the office," he murmured, then slipped his hand inside her blouse and bra to cup the soft curve of her breast. "This morning we're going in late."

Laurel moaned as his fingertips closed over her nipple, massaging it into a point. The pleasure was almost unbearable as everything went fuzzy around her except for the hot, hard pressure of his mouth. She knew all the reasons why they shouldn't continue to consummate this marriage, yet she had the urge to surrender completely to his tender touch and sensuous kisses as he carried her up the stairs, deposited her on the still rumpled covers of his bed, and dropped down beside her. "We shouldn't…"

Cade stroked his hand down her side, his caressing touch every bit as sure and sensual and somehow comforting as his kiss. "What we shouldn't do is sleep apart or stay apart." His lips moved to her breast as he inched her skirt up. His thigh moved between hers, urging her legs apart. Her back arched off the bed as he found her with his hands and lips and tongue. "I miss you when you're not with me, Laurel," he murmured as he moved to

arouse her again and again and again. "I want you with me."
Tendrils of white heat swept through her as his mouth moved sensually to the hollow between her breasts, then returned with devastating slowness to her mouth. "So I can kiss you here." He spoke as his tongue moved across her lips. "And here." He trailed kisses across her abdomen. Moved lower still. "And here…"

"Oh, Cade…" Laurel gave up to the tension building inside her. New waves of sensation and longing washed over her. He was generating flames of heat, tremors of desire.

"Tell me you want me as much as I want you," he urged, cupping a hand around the most delicate part of her, another beneath her.

Gaze locked on his as he caressed her, she admitted, "I do."

"Promise me you'll sleep in my bed tonight," he said intently.

"I promise," Laurel whispered, watching his eyes gleam with distinctly male satisfaction.

"And every other night," he commanded gruffly, stripping down.

"From here on out, I promise." With trembling fingers, she stripped, too. They came together again. Twining her arms around his neck, she accepted the thrust and parry of his tongue. She arched her body closer, reveling in the feel of hard muscle and warm silken skin. "Cade…"

Holding her fast with one strong arm clamped around her waist, he kissed her rapaciously. "Hmm?"

Able to bear no more, Laurel shuddered. "I want you. Now."

Eyes dark, he shifted over her. As impatient as she, he lifted her against him. She wanted him…needed him…so much. He seemed to want her, too, just as desperately. And then she was opening herself up to him, accepting him all the way inside, as deep as he could go. He whispered her name with an intensity she did not know he possessed, and then they were moving as one, kissing until he took her breath away. Needing Cade as she had never needed anyone before, Laurel surrendered her heart, her soul, as they moved together, reaching for some lofty distant point. Suddenly, there was no more thinking, only feeling—only this kiss, this moment, each other. They shuddered together in release, and then, still clinging, slowly back down to earth.

FOR CADE, ONCE LAUREL WAS back in his arms and his bed, everything else seemed to fall into place, too. For the first time ever he felt whole, as if he had a full life. Not just work and more work—although he and Laurel both did enough of that as they hurriedly prepared for the grand opening of the first Dunnigan Dog Care Center. But because his happiness didn't end the moment he left the office, for the first time, he felt fulfillment in his personal life as well. And it was all due to Laurel, and the light and joy she brought to him. Now all he had to do, he thought as the weekend approached, was convince her that they should not only stay hitched, but make their marriage a real and lasting one in every way.

"Do you realize this is the first complete evening we will spend together since the weekend we got married?" Cade remarked early Friday evening as he set up the gas grill.

"As a matter of fact…" Laurel brought out a platter of steaks and two foil-wrapped baked potatoes. She sent him a flirtatious glance. "I was just thinking that myself."

"Normally at this time you and Patches are in Frances Klenck's version of puppy boot camp." Cade smiled.

Laurel sat down to shuck two ears of corn. "Class was cancelled because all the dogs are exhausted from their grooming appointments at the store today."

"How did that go?" Cade set the potatoes on to bake, then came over to lend a hand. He would have liked to attend but had been in a meeting with the accountants, going over the numbers for the marketing plans he would present to the board prior to the CEO vote Sunday afternoon. Not that he'd had to worry. Laurel had been happy to manage the baths and haircuts of all forty-seven recently rescued dogs, as well as act as public relations liaison for DDF and the media. Everyone in the company was talking about what a good job she was doing.

"It went amazingly well." Her hair tumbling over her shoulders, Laurel bent her head. With care, she removed several strands of corn silk still clinging to the yellow kernels. "You can't believe how good the dogs are starting to look."

Cade tore off foil. "That's because they've all been on diets of Dunnigan Premium Dog Food for the last ten days."

Laurel wrapped both ears. "I think even Patches's coat is beginning to even out."

Cade cast a glance at the corner of the yard, where Beast and Patches were romping around in the grass. "The bald spots are filling in," he agreed.

Laurel smiled. "It's amazing what a little tender loving care can do."

"A lot of tender loving care," Cade corrected, opening a long-necked bottle of Lone Star beer for each of them. "You've taken a puppy who appeared to have never known so much as a kind word, and made her feel loved and secure."

The way Cade had made *her* feel loved and secure, Laurel thought. Since they had come together Wednesday morning, they had spent every night making love, and slept wrapped in each other's arms, only to awaken the next morning and make love again.

As a result of that and a million other little things, she was beginning to feel really and truly married.

Laurel glided closer, loving the casual intimacy of the evening as much as the perfect April weather. The temperature was in the low eighties. Both humidity and breeze were minimal. A cloudless sky indicated there would be great stargazing that night, too. "Mary Elena moved back in with her dad. Did I tell you?" Laurel asked.

Cade took her wrist and kissed the inside of it.

"She said they're really talking for the first time in their lives."

"That's good."

"Mr. Ayers isn't angry with you anymore, either."

"I'm glad to hear it."

So was Laurel. "I also learned from my landlord that my rent had been paid up for next month, and that my husband had been inquiring about what it would take to break my lease."

Cade paused, the beer bottle halfway to his lips. He lowered it slowly to his side. "I meant to tell you about that."

Laurel perched on the edge of the chaise. "Did you now?"

Cade sat down beside her. "I figured paying your rent for you might be a better surprise than flowers or breakfast in bed." He shifted toward her, studied her wordlessly. "I gather it wasn't?"

Yes and no, Laurel thought, aware his unexpected action reminded her of her ex-fiancé's need to impress her in a financial sense, and her father's need to control and protect her. "Why do you think you have to do anything like that to be with me?" she asked curiously.

Shrugging, Cade stood and began to pace. "Most women demand that sort of attention."

Laurel rose gracefully and crossed to his side. "I'm not most women, Cade. I don't need the mundane responsibilities taken care of for me or financial remuneration in exchange for my affections. I thought you had figured that out already."

"Well, then, maybe I need to do that for you," Cade allowed slowly, a brooding expression coming into his eyes.

"Why?" Laurel set her drink aside.

Cade did the same. "Because I've got so much to make up for," he said softly.

Laurel bit her lip. "I don't understand."

He exhaled roughly. "I started our connection with each other all wrong. First, I bullied you into marrying me in Mary Elena's place. Then I brought you here, instead of taking you on a honeymoon, and was so busy noticing what a beautiful bride you were, that I forgot all about Beast, and let him come charging out and knock you into the bushes."

Laurel grinned, recalling that surprising moment. "What would you have done differently?"

Cade whistled for the dogs. Beast came running, Patches hard on the big Lab's heels. Cade opened the door and let them into the sunroom, which had been gated off for safety's sake. He turned back to Laurel. "I'd have proposed instead of coercing you into marriage, then taken you on an extended, incredibly luxurious honeymoon. And then—" he walked over to turn down the temperature on the gas grill "—I would have brought you back here." Cade closed the distance between them, determination on his face. "Swept you up in my arms." He demonstrated admirably. "And carried you over the threshold—like this."

"Only one thing, Cade. We just went through the kitchen door," Laurel teased. "We were at the front door the night of our wedding."

He braced a hand on either side of her, caging her between his hard body and the counter. "You get my drift." He paused to kiss her slowly, thoroughly. "Then," he continued languidly, "I would have opened up a bottle of champagne and given you the wedding night of your dreams." He traced the side of her face with his thumb. His eyes were darker, sexier than she had ever seen them. "A night we would always remember."

Laurel gripped his shoulders possessively, knowing she would never find love this tender or powerful again. She pressed her lips to the underside of his jaw, his chin, his lips. "You've already given me many days and nights I'll never forget."

Cade grasped her hips, urging her closer yet. He kissed her deeply. "Not enough to satisfy me," he murmured, kissing her again and again.

Laurel knew they would be comfortable upstairs in his bed. She also knew they would never make it. Excitement pounded through her as his hands eased beneath the hem of her T-shirt. She had dispensed with her bra at the same time she had shed her work clothes, and he found her breasts with his hands. Her response to his fevered touch was instantaneous.

Yearning, passion and need spilled into their kiss. Cade slipped his hands inside the elastic of her shorts, caressed her warmly, intimately, at the same time she found him. Still kissing, touching her all the while, he pushed her shorts down her legs to the floor. She divested him of his. Whimpering, she shuddered against him as the liquid heat inside her began to implode. And still he made her tremble, again and again, until they could take it no longer, their breath coming in quick, shallow spurts.

"I want you. Now. Here," he whispered against her mouth.

"Oh, Cade, I want you, too," Laurel murmured back throatily. "So much."

She let him lift her to exactly where she needed to be, and opened her thighs. She trembled with a fierce unquenchable ache as their bodies melted into each other, powerfully, lovingly. He cupped her buttocks in his hands, pushing her harder, faster, making her tremble, making her cry out, and then he, too, was past the point of no return.

Afterward, Laurel cuddled close to him, filled with serenity unlike anything she had ever felt. She wished she could stay this way forever. Unable to contain the joy bubbling up inside her, she whispered, "I love you."

Cade squeezed her tightly, all the tenderness she had ever hoped to see evident in his dark gray eyes. "I love you, too."

Chapter Fifteen

"Nervous?" Cade asked Laurel Saturday morning. In no hurry, he draped the tie around his neck and lounged against the bureau.

"Honestly?" Laurel rummaged through the clothes hanging in the guest room closet. She paused to flash Cade an edgy smile. "Yes." She bypassed a pretty sundress and sleek black pantsuit and brought out a slim navy skirt and tailored, pale blue blouse more suited to the occasion.

"Why?" Cade tucked his shirt into the waistband of his trousers.

Trying not to think how right it felt to be doing something this intimate with him, she slipped off her robe and into her business clothes, while he tied his necktie. "A lot is riding on today's success." Indeed, she had spent the last two weeks making sure every single detail was in place. DDF's credibility and hers were on the line. She turned so Cade could help her with the clasp on her gold necklace, then swung back around to face him. "Every newspaper and television station in the area has promised to have reporters and cameramen there to document the rescued pet event."

Cade smiled, already looking as proud of her as he was pleased with her performance at work. "Maybe this will help, then," he told her gently. Pulling a velvet box from his pocket, he opened the lid.

Laurel looked down at the shimmering diamond engagement ring and matching wedding band nestled on the satin lining. Her breath caught in her throat as she struggled to get a handle on her soaring emotions. "When did you do this?" She searched his face, trying to ascertain the meaning of his gesture.

"A few days ago." Cade lifted her left hand and slipped on the rings, which fit perfectly. And more importantly, made her feel really and truly married to him. "An old friend of mine helped me out," he told her softly.

Laurel flushed self-consciously. The seeds of doubt she had been struggling against sprang to life once again. She turned her back to Cade and felt her shoulder brush the hardness of his chest. "Do I know this old friend?"

Cade turned her around to face him. His eyes softened as they searched her upturned face. "Do you know Trisha Teal?"

The woman George Jr. had mentioned. Laurel pushed aside a flare of jealousy. Her throat and chest were so congested with emotion she could barely breathe. "I don't think I've ever met her," she said cautiously, searching Cade's face. Her heart skipped several beats and her nerves frayed all the more.

Cade kept his eyes on hers. "Her family owns a jewelry store in the Galleria Mall. We've known each other since high school."

Laurel relaxed. That explained why Trisha Teal had been at the house, and why he hadn't mentioned it.

Cade's gaze narrowed. "You look relieved," he noted.

"I am." She wanted—needed—to know how all these pieces fit together. "As well as curious," Laurel said, irritated by the telltale breathlessness of her voice as she turned away slightly and fastened on the earrings that matched her necklace. She knew they had today, this moment in their marriage, and absolutely no guarantees about the future. Yet the way Cade had made love to her the night before, and all the times leading up to it, seemed to indicate otherwise…. "Why are you giving these rings to me now?" she asked.

"Two reasons." Cade leaned closer in a drift of masculine cologne. He threaded his hands through her hair, pushing it away from her ears. Sliding his thumbs beneath her chin, he lifted her face to his. "First, because I think they'll bring you luck at the news event this morning. And secondly—" he lowered his lips to hers and kissed her sweetly, solemnly "—because I want to demonstrate to you in a very concrete way how very much I want you to remain my wife." He backed her up against the wall, pressing his body against hers. "Not just until after tomorrow's vote, when I am named CEO, but from here on out."

Laurel's efforts to guard her heart failed. She was more open to love and vulnerable to Cade than ever before. As he lowered his mouth to hers, she whispered tenderly, "You mean that, don't you?"

He nodded, and added in a brusque, uneven voice, "With every fiber of my being." He kissed her again, languorously, implacably. "Tell me you'll do it, Laurel."

There was nothing impulsive or temporary about his kiss. Nothing fleeting about her feelings. Laurel snuggled into his warmth, aware that in Cade she had found everything she had ever wanted and needed in a man. "I will," she promised as he kissed her again.

Had it not been for the sound of Beast and Patches barking out on the sunporch, Laurel knew they might have been sidetracked into making love again. Reluctantly, they drew apart. Cade smiled. "I think they're trying to tell us something."

Nodding, Laurel squeezed his hand and went in search of shoes that matched her outfit. "We better hurry. We can't afford to be late today."

THE DIFFERENCE IN the animals they had picked up from the shelter in Denton, and the beautifully groomed dogs brought out to the roped off area of the parking lot in front of the DDF flagship store, was just amazing, Laurel thought. All forty-seven dogs were still too thin, but in the two weeks since they had been rescued, they had lost that hopeless, neglected look. Tails were wagging merrily and heads were up, even as they sat on the sidewalk in front of the store and waited to be paraded in.

As Laurel threaded her way through the crowd of spectators, potential adoptive pet owners, and media, she couldn't help but smile proudly. It had taken a lot of effort to get them here—daily obedience classes, lots of tender loving care, time and attention—

but that had been worth it, for everyone involved. She took a moment to gaze down adoringly at the leashed Patches in her arms.

Laurel nodded at all the DDF board members in the audience—except George Jr., who had not shown up yet—then stepped up to the microphone erected on the portable wooden stage brought in for the event. "Welcome," she said to one and all.

"Hey, Laurel, how does it feel to be married to Cade Dunnigan?" one of the reporters in the audience shouted. Laurel's earlier edginess immediately returned. She had been afraid she might be singled out like this. Especially since she and Cade had declined to comment publicly on their impulsive marriage to this point.

"Yeah," another called. "Are you glad you were his stand-in bride?"

"Are you planning to stay married to him?" a third demanded.

"Or are you just in it to help him get his inheritance?" a fourth asked.

Out of the corner of her eye, Laurel could see the board members frowning. She could hardly blame them. This occasion was supposed to be about the flagship store, not the CEO's public train wreck of a personal life. Thankfully, Cade had stopped waiting for his introduction and was moving toward her, across the stage. As he reached her, he took her hand and squeezed it tightly in a public show of solidarity.

Determined to demonstrate that his faith in her had not been misplaced, Laurel leaned toward the microphone and smiled into the cameras, letting the happiness and love she felt radiate from her in powerful waves. "It feels great," she told the crowd of interested spectators and reporters sincerely. "And not only am I very glad I married Cade Dunnigan, I am planning to remain Mrs. Cade Dunnigan." She and Cade exchanged pleasure-filled looks, then she turned back to the assembled guests. "But that isn't why we're here today," she continued seriously. "We're here to help these forty-seven rescued golden retrievers find loving homes." Laurel lifted her arm and gave the signal to start the parade of dogs into the roped off area. "And to open the very first Dunnigan Dog Care Center."

She glanced down at her notes, so she could begin the description of each individual dog in need of a home. Before she could get started, Patches whimpered unexpectedly and began to struggle in her arms. To her dismay, the other dogs marching into the area began to strain at their leashes as well, and turn in the direction Patches was looking. Following her puppy's gaze, Laurel saw three teenage boys pushing their way in. One seemed to have something large and gray and furry in his arms. Laurel gasped, and then all hell broke loose as the teen thrust his arms out and tossed a cat into the midst of the dogs.

Not unexpectedly, chaos erupted. Patches leaped from Laurel's arms to join the fray. Barks rose over the startled screams and shouts of spectators as the cat tried to run this way and that and was blocked at every turn by an excited retriever. The people holding the leashes were being yanked every which way. Laurel knew something had to be done, even as Cade raced down the steps to retrieve Patches.

"Stop!" she shouted into the microphone in her most commanding voice. Like magic, all the dogs stopped in their tracks. "Sit!" Laurel yelled, and all forty-seven rear ends connected automatically with the pavement, exactly as they had been taught. "Stay!"

A startled silence fell over the crowd. It was almost as if, Laurel noted, they were playing a game of Statue. The only one who paid no attention to her command was the cat, which raced off across the parking lot, following the direction the three teenagers had taken.

Knowing if ever a public relations save was required now was the time, Laurel leaned toward the microphone once again and said, "And that, ladies and gentleman, is the best demonstration ever as to why obedience-training your pets is a very good thing!"

Applause erupted as someone from the audience went after the cat.

The faces on the board members relaxed. Dotty Yost, Lance

Ayers and Harvey Lemmon joined in enthusiastically. "Now," Laurel continued, as if that near catastrophe had been part of the scheduled events, "I'd like to introduce each and every one of the pets who are up for adoption today."

"HERE'S TO A VERY successful first day of business," Cade said, clinking champagne glasses with Laurel later that evening.

She smiled as they completed their toast, and watched him sink down in the chair behind his desk. His study was fast becoming one of her favorite places in the whole house. "I can't believe they had to restock the shelves three times before close of business," she murmured, slipping onto his lap.

Cade emanated satisfaction as he put his glass aside and massaged her shoulders. "Combining the grand opening with the rescue event really helped generate both interest and sales."

Laurel dipped a strawberry in whipped cream and hand-fed it to him. "It helped that the television stations played the tape of the dogs going from chaotic to calm over and over all day long."

Cade fed her a strawberry, too. "It was on every news cycle and news break on every station."

Laurel sipped her champagne as worry slipped through her, unbidden. "George Jr. is still steamed about that."

"Yeah," Cade mused, "he wasn't very gracious when he finally showed up at the event, was he?"

Laurel paused thoughtfully as her attention went back to the near disaster. "I still don't get why those teenage boys threw the cat in the middle of the dogs."

Cade lifted her hand to his lips and pressed a kiss to the back of it. "It could have been a prank or a dare," he supposed.

Her body warming everywhere they touched, as well as everywhere they didn't, Laurel mused, "It certainly took attention away from the scandal surrounding our marriage."

Cade kissed his way up her wrist to the sensitive skin inside her elbow. "Have I mentioned how very proud I am of the way you handled those reporters' questions?"

Refusing to let the forces against them spoil their victory celebration, Laurel wrapped her arms about Cade's neck and snuggled close. "You have now."

He framed her face with his hands and kissed her with the same deep abiding hunger she felt for him. "Or how proud I am of the way you orchestrated everything about today's pet adoption event?" he continued huskily.

She had only to look into his eyes to see how much he respected and appreciated her. Laurel swallowed hard around the knot of emotion in her throat. "I told you it was going to be a very rewarding thing to do."

"And you were right." He paused to give her another sultry kiss. "Which is why," he continued soberly, "I'd like to offer you a job as the new director of community relations at DDF."

Not sure what to make of that, Laurel straightened his shirt collar. "I didn't know DDF had such a position."

Cade regarded her with his customary confidence. "They do now."

Leery of rocking the boat, when their life together seemed to be going so smoothly at long last, Laurel hesitated. "You don't have to do this, Cade. I'm happy to stay on the beginner track and work my way up in the company the way everyone else is required to do."

He sobered abruptly. "This promotion won't be nepotism, Laurel. You've earned it. You got DDF involved and helped coordinate the care and training of all forty-seven of those dogs so they could find permanent homes, and your masterful handling of publicity made the grand opening of our first flagship store a rousing success. And everyone knows it. If anything," Cade confessed ruefully, "I owe you an apology for bringing you in at such a low level to begin with. College grads with business degrees and five years experience *don't* start in the mailroom at DDF."

Laurel knew she and Cade had come a long way from the testy mood between them at the start of their marriage. As ready to move on as he, she dipped her head in gracious acknowledgment. "Then I accept the apology and the job."

"Good." Cade's handsome face took on a wide grin. "Because I can no longer imagine DDF without you."

They kissed again, in tenderness and celebration. Then, knowing that, like it or not, they still had work ahead of them, they put their drinks aside and went back to assembling the copies of Cade's marketing plan that would be passed out to board members prior to the CEO vote the next afternoon. As they continued to work in companionable silence, Laurel frowned.

"You're thinking about George Jr. again, aren't you?" Cade guessed.

Reluctantly, she admitted this was so. "He did everything he could to undermine you with the press this afternoon. You should have heard some of the things he said about you—just within earshot of me, of course. I think he was trying to get a rise out of me."

Cade studied her. "But you didn't give in to him."

"No. I don't like him."

"Neither do I," Cade admitted unhappily.

Laurel bit her lip indecisively. "I almost think…"

"What?" Cade prodded when she didn't go on.

She swallowed. "I almost think that George Jr. had something to do with that cat being thrown into the roped off area."

The muscles in Cade's shoulders relaxed. "I've been thinking the same thing," he admitted with a beleaguered sigh. "If the dogs hadn't been as well-trained as they were, that cat's appearance would have ruined the whole event."

"And possibly cost those pets their new homes," Laurel pointed out. She paused. "Do you think there might be some way to prove it?"

Cade frowned. "Possibly. If we could identify those boys."

Unfortunately, Laurel and Cade soon found out, none of the TV news stations had netted anything. The producers confirmed that the cameras had been trained on the scheduled events at the time the cat was thrown into the ring, so to speak, so no one had any film of the three teenage culprits Laurel and Cade had spotted from the stage.

"What about security cameras mounted outside the stores?" Laurel murmured. "Do you think it's possible one of those lenses caught something in the parking lot?"

"Only one way to find out," Cade said.

Unfortunately, to Laurel and Cade's mutual chagrin, tracking down store owners on the weekend turned out to be a very difficult thing to do. Gathering copies of the security tapes took even longer. It was midmorning of the next day by the time they had what they needed. "Here it is," Cade said, pointing to the videotape he had been reviewing on his home VCR. "George Jr. talking to those three teenage boys."

"But this alone doesn't really prove anything," Laurel stated worriedly. "We don't see a cat, or money changing hands. And without that…"

"You're right." Cade's jaw tightened resolutely. "I need the testimony of those three kids if I'm going to mention this to the board of directors before the vote."

Laurel peered at the TV screen. She could just make out the license plate of the car the boys had been driving. She reached for the phone and punched in her brother Kevin's number. As a detective with the Laramie County Sheriff's Department, he could probably get them the information they needed. "I know how we can do just that," she said.

"YOU'RE LOOKING GORGEOUS," George Jr. told Laurel the minute she opened the front door. He was wearing a double-breasted sharkskin business suit meant to disguise his soft middle. "I'm surprised Cade left you behind," he continued with a smirk, pushing past. He gave Laurel a sly look. "Or aren't you invited to the board of directors meeting this afternoon?"

"I'm going." Glad the copies of the marketing plan were already safely locked away in the trunk of the car, Laurel picked up her briefcase and purse. "In fact," she announced with a pointed smile, "I was just about to leave."

George Jr. plucked a miniature tape recorder from his coat pocket. "Not before you hear what's on this."

Laurel girded herself for battle. "I don't have time for that."

"Sure you do." George Jr. strolled confidently past her, toward Cade's study. "Although," he goaded nastily, "you probably want to sit down first."

Figuring it was the only way she would get rid of him, Laurel did.

George Jr. hit the play button and Cade's voice filled the room. "You think I'm approaching this too much like a business problem again, don't you?" Laurel heard her husband ask in a low pragmatic tone. "The truth is I don't know any other way to operate especially when it comes to getting what I want on a personal level…."

What was it Cade had said? Laurel mused, as a chill of recognition went through her. "*All Dunnigans are known to be ruthless when it comes to getting what they want in their business and personal lives, myself included. I'm determined to do whatever is necessary in order to prevent George Jr. and George Sr. from ruining in a very short time what it took my grandfather and father fifty years to build…*"

"So what's going on?" a woman's soft, melodious voice asked Cade in return.

"I really messed up with Laurel from the very beginning, when I made it clear that this situation is all about me getting my inheritance, no matter what the cost in personal terms to her," Cade's voice continued on the tape—blunt, matter-of-fact, slightly regretful.

For Laurel it was like a blow to the solar plexus.

"I should have offered her a much better deal," he continued with conviction.

The woman's voice concurred softly, "Every woman wants to be pampered, deep down."

Cade sighed. "Laurel wants love. Nothing less is going to satisfy her." Another pause chilled Laurel to her soul. "I don't care what I have to do," he continued in a low, resolute tone. "I can romance a woman like nobody's business and right now I want Laurel in my bed."

"The best way to demonstrate that is with this magnificent ring." The woman's persuasive laughter filled the room. "I promise you, Cade, you give her this diamond and tell her everything she wants to hear and you'll have her eating out of your hand…."

George Jr. clicked off the tape recorder. He regarded Laurel smugly. "Heard enough?"

"I don't believe a word of it."

"Then maybe," he said as he reached over, opened the center drawer of Cade's desk and took out the same manila file folder Laurel had seen Cade handle many times, "you'll believe this."

George Jr. opened it up. Laurel stared down at two lists and felt her world spin off its axis. "Damage Control—Business," she read, with a sinking feeling of dismay and dread. And "Damage Control—Marriage." There were six items in each category, written in what she sadly recognized as Cade's handwriting. All had neat little red checkmarks beside them.

"I told you there was nothing but cynicism and cold calculation where Cade's heart should be," his cousin said smugly.

Unable to bear looking at the traitorous lists a second longer, Laurel shut the file folder. Her hands were trembling, her thoughts in turmoil.

"He's a very thorough guy, my cousin," George Jr. observed nastily. "Unfortunately, not thorough enough. Or Cade would have realized his every conversation for the last week or so was being taped." Apparently unable to resist bragging, George Jr. knelt and reached beneath the desk. When he stood again he had a small metal disk in his hand and a complacent, arrogant look on his face. "I left this listening device here the day I stopped by the house. It was easy enough to do with all the people running in and out, helping to take the before photographs of the rescued dogs. I know how Cade likes to hang out in here when he's home, and I figured it wouldn't take long to get proof of his calculating nature."

Folding his arms across his chest, George Jr. continued to regard Laurel smugly. "So, Mrs. Dunnigan, now you know you're a means to an end, are you ready to take me up on my offer and tell the board of directors what an underhanded man you are married to?" When Laurel said nothing—she was too stunned to think, never mind formulate a reply—he sneered. "Can't decide? Well, I'll let you think about it, and if you want to look at Cade's revealing to-do list and or listen to your copy of this oh-so-revealing tape—" he tossed it to her "—a few more times before you show up at the board of director's meeting you can do that, too."

"WHAT'S WRONG?" LEWIS asked as Laurel met up with her brother outside DDF headquarters half an hour later.

"Nothing," Laurel fibbed. Her arms filled with the half-dozen notebooks emblazoned with the DDF logo, she fell into step beside her computer-genuis brother. Her life was falling apart at the seams, yet she had to keep moving, keep doing what had to be done. If she didn't, George Jr. would win. As much as Laurel loathed and mistrusted her "husband" right now, she was not going to let that happen. There would be time—and privacy—to thoroughly lose her temper and confront Cade later. Right now, she had a company to save from sure ruin. Which was what would certainly happen if George Jr. were ever to take charge.

"You don't look like it's nothing," Lewis remarked, as he carried his own presentation materials into the elevator.

That's because I'm shaken to the core, Laurel thought. She didn't want to believe what had been written on those two damage control lists, but she had no choice—they had definitely been written in Cade's own hand. It had clearly been his voice on the tape, and—if her guess was correct—Trisha Teal's as well. The thought Cade might have played her for a fool made Laurel physically ill. However, that didn't mean she intended to let George Jr. get away with his underhanded machinations.

"Is the video game prototype ready to demonstrate?" Laurel asked, steering her thoughts to business once again.

Lewis nodded. "I've added some more enhancements since I showed it to you and Cade. You're going to be very pleased. Where is he, by the way?"

"He had an errand to run. He's meeting me here," Laurel said, just as the elevator doors opened. And it was a good thing Cade hadn't been at the house when she had learned of the depth of his treachery. Otherwise she surely would have decked him.

George Jr. smiled at them from the other side of the portal. George Sr. was standing next to him, looking nervous and on edge. Laurel wondered how much the older man knew about his son's activities, and whether or not he condoned everything George Jr. had done.

Because it was Sunday afternoon, the floor was deserted, except for those attending the board meeting. Laurel led Lewis to the conference room, where the vote was going to be held. By the time she had helped him set up, and passed out the copies of the marketing report Cade had prepared, everyone was there but the current CEO himself.

She stepped outside to call him on his cell. "I'm about five minutes away from the parking garage," Cade told her.

Still reeling at the thought he might have betrayed her, Laurel struggled to keep her voice even. "Did you get what you needed?"

"And then some," Cade told her, confident as ever.

Laurel walked back inside. All eyes turned to her. It took every ounce of self-control she had to remain composed. "Cade will be here directly."

"I say we go ahead and get started without him," George Jr. suggested. He moved to stand beside her at the head of the table. "And first up on the agenda is Laurel's very recent realization that her marriage to Cade Dunnigan is as much a smoke-and-mirrors sham as his plans to successfully grow this company."

"Wait a minute," Dotty Yost interrupted. "Laurel told the media yesterday that she was very happily married and intended to stay married to Cade."

And she had meant it with all her heart at the time, Laurel thought miserably.

"Has that changed?" Harvey Lemmon asked.

Laurel wasn't quite sure how to answer that.

"Would you like to tell them about the tape you made of Cade and another woman or shall I?" George Jr. asked smoothly.

The bald-faced lie was exactly what Laurel needed to compel her to action. "Wait a minute." She turned to him in indignation. "I didn't plant that listening device in Cade's study!"

"She's right," George Jr. admitted, with obvious chagrin, as he turned to look at the board members. "I did it—at Laurel's request. You see, she's been suspicious of Cade's motives for first coercing her into the marriage—in Mary Elena Ayers's place— and then alternately pressuring and romancing her to stay in it, ever since. Cade pretended to love and desire her—and went all-out to convince her of that, even going so far as getting his old girlfriend, Trisha Teal, to help him select the perfect diamond engagement and brand-new wedding ring, to seal the deal. It would have worked, too, had Laurel not been one step ahead of him and commissioned the secret recording in the study at home. You see, she knew, as did I, that Cade conducts a lot of business in there."

They had even made love in there, Laurel realized, with a sinking feeling of disgust. Did George Jr. have a tape of that, too?

Lewis was suddenly at her side. "You don't look very good," her brother told her. He slid an arm around her waist. "Maybe you and I should just leave."

Laurel shook off his protective grip. "No," she said, marshaling her strength once again. "I have to set the record straight," she stated fiercely. She paused to look each and every board member in the eye. "Cade is not the person you-all should mistrust. He loves this company. He would do anything for it." *Including,* she thought to herself miserably, *use and romance me.* Laurel turned and pointed an accusing finger at the person standing beside her. "George Jr. is the person you cannot trust."

"Wait a minute, Laurel. If you feel that way, then why did you ask him to help you bug Cade's study?" George Sr. asked, looking confused.

"I didn't," she explained, exasperated. "George Jr. did that on his own. I didn't even know about it until he played that tape for me today."

George Jr. continued his Academy Award performance. Appearing stunned and confused, he laid a hand across his heart. "I don't understand why you are lying about this, Laurel. Unless…" he paused and looked even more wounded "…it's all part of a convoluted plan to discredit me?"

"That's a laugh," Laurel retorted furiously. She shook her head in disgust. "You are such a liar." And so damn good at it, too! She would have believed him herself had she not known better!

"What proof do you have of that?" Lance Ayers asked calmly.

"Plenty, as it turns out," Cade said as he walked in just in the nick of time, videotape in hand, three sheepish teenage boys straggling behind him.

"What are they doing here?" George Sr. demanded, looking more irritated and confused than ever. He pointed at the casually clad youths.

"On the premise that a picture is worth a thousand words…" Cade slid a tape in the VCR Laurel had already set up for him, and pushed Play. A picture of George Jr. talking to the three boys in the parking lot came on the TV screen. "These young men are going to explain to us exactly what happened at the grand opening of the flagship store yesterday," Cade said.

"We didn't mean to cause any trouble," the smallest one said.

"We were just there to go to the music store at the other end of the shopping center," the second added, as Harvey Lemmon, Dotty Yost and Lance Ayers all looked on in absolute fury.

"Then that guy—" the third teen pointed to George Jr. "—came up to us and offered us one hundred dollars each in cash if we would take this cat over and dump it in the middle of the dogs. He told us it would demonstrate how obedience-trained dogs could stay calm in situations that would drive other dogs nuts in the most dramatic way possible. And so we did it, just like he said to, and then when all the dogs went crazy, we got scared and took off. We never meant to cause any trouble."

Cade thanked the young men and escorted them from the room. He turned back to the board of directors, the picture of fierce male determination. "I think we can all agree we don't need someone at the helm of Dunnigan Dog Food who will sabotage the company for his own gain."

Chapter Sixteen

This should have been one of the happiest moments of his life, Cade thought, as he parked his Porsche in the driveway. It wasn't, and wouldn't be until he found out what was going on with his wife.

He found her in the backyard. Laurel was seated in a chaise longue she had pulled beneath the shade of a live oak that edged the lawn. She had a manila file folder in her lap, a small portable tape recorder in her hand. Beast and Patches were playing a game of chase in the grass, and though Laurel was watching over their spirited antics, there wasn't a hint of a smile on her face. Not a good sign, Cade thought.

He picked up a chair from the pool area and carried it over to where she was. He set it down in the grass, catty-corner to hers, and sank into it. They were sitting so close, his knee brushed her slender thigh.

She didn't react to that, either. "You left before the board voted," Cade remarked quietly. She had taken her hair down since returning home. The dark tousled waves gleamed in the sun. Her cheeks were unnaturally flushed, her lips bare. She was still wearing what she had worn to the board meeting. In a white silk blouse, trim khaki skirt and heels, she had never looked prettier, or more in need of a hug. It was all he could do not to take her in his arms. But knowing they had important things to discuss, he kept his hands to himself.

"I presume you're the new CEO," she said in a low, dull tone. Cade nodded. "On the condition I immediately fire George

Jr., which I did." He paused to unknot his tie and loosen the first two buttons of his shirt. "The company lawyers will be working out his severance package with him tomorrow."

She kept her face turned away from his. Her slender shoulders were rigid with tension. "Is your uncle upset about that?"

Cade watched as she wearily rested her head on the back of the chaise. "So much so he and George Jr. are selling the rest of their shares in the company to the other three board members."

She gave him a troubled smile that did not begin to reach her eyes. "I guess that's good news."

You *would never know that by your increasingly unhappy expression,* Cade thought to himself. Out loud, he continued doing everything he could to discover the reason behind her anger and save the situation. "It's very good news," he told her, "since I won't have someone on our team constantly sabotaging my efforts to grow the company."

Beast came up, nuzzled Cade's palm and then promptly ran off again.

Cade inclined his head toward Laurel's hand. "Is that the tape everyone is talking about?"

Her chin took on a defiant tilt. "Yes."

"Mind if I listen to it?" he asked, his mood remote and tense, the way it always was when a situation started to go sour.

She thrust the recorder at him. "Be my guest."

Cade turned it on and heard his own voice, ruminating thoughtfully, "You think I'm approaching this too much like a business problem again, don't you? The truth is I don't know any other way to operate, especially when it comes to getting what I want on a personal level."

Cade frowned, as he heard Trisha Teal respond to him in the same pleasantly analytical tone. "So what's going on?" she asked.

Cade couldn't believe what he was hearing. He and Trisha had never talked about the inner workings of his marriage to Laurel!

Before he could set the record straight, he heard his voice again. "I really messed up with Laurel from the very beginning when I made it clear that this situation is all about me getting my inheritance, no matter what the cost in personal terms to her. I should have offered her a much better deal."

"I guess you should have," Laurel murmured sarcastically.

And then, to his shock and dismay Cade heard Trisha's voice again, concurring softly, "Every woman wants to be pampered, deep down."

Cade clenched his hands as Laurel's look turned even more lethal and accusing.

Then he heard himself state firmly—purposefully—on the tape, "Laurel wants love. Nothing less is going to satisfy her. I don't care what I have to do…. I can romance a woman like nobody's business. And right now I want Laurel in my bed…."

"I promise you, Cade…" he winced at Trisha's soothing reply "…you give her this diamond and you'll have her eating out of your hand—"

Laurel plucked the recorder from Cade's hands and punched the off button. "I presume you have an explanation," she prompted coldly.

He shrugged, still struggling to make sense of all he had heard, even as his anger at being falsely accused rose. "I obviously said all that."

"To Trisha."

They had talked about the diamond ring. Which one to select. Why. Cade's jaw tautened. "I don't recall the conversation going quite that way." And frankly, he would have expected Laurel to have a lot more faith in him, given everything they had already been through.

"Then do you recall this?" She thrust the file at him.

Bracing himself for whatever lay ahead, Cade opened it up. Inside, he saw his two damage control lists.

Laurel snatched the damning pages right back. "'One,'" she read outloud, in a voice dripping with sarcasm. "'Move Laurel into the house. Two.'" She glared at him. "'Convince Laurel to assist with the dinner for board members. Three. Work out the sexual aspects of the relationship.' Boy—" she shook her head bitterly "—we really did that, didn't we?"

Cade had thought so. Now, he didn't think they had worked out much of anything, on any level.

"'Four, speak with Laurel's parents, Sam and Kate McCabe. Five, tell her that I love her.'" Laurel clenched her lips together. Tears of hurt shimmered in her eyes. "And 'Six, convince her to stay on permanently as my wife.'" She let the pages flutter back to her side. "Wow. Talk about CEO material there." She shook her head at him in silent censure. "You really had it all figured out."

Cade couldn't argue about the list's authenticity. Those, at least, were pretty much just what they seemed—written proof of his intent. "It's not like that," he protested argumentatively.

"It most certainly is," Laurel retorted, her voice rising emotionally. She thrust the file folder at him once again. "You've checked off every item on both lists, personal and business!"

Cade caught them and tossed them aside. She started to move away from him, but with a hand on her shoulder, he pulled her back. "I wrote those lists the first night we were married!"

"The first night…" Laurel echoed, even more incensed. She shoved at his chest with both hands, pushing him away. "And already you were planning to tell me that you loved me, and to convince me to stay on permanently as your wife?"

"No," Cade sighed, aware by now that Laurel was not going to listen to a word he said in his own defense. "Those two items on the checklist came later."

"Well, they never should have come at all." Her curt tone rattled him more than the contempt in her gaze. "Because they just aren't true."

"The hell they aren't!" he snapped back.

Laurel let out an exasperated breath. She shook her head at him, the silence between them more awkward than ever. "You can't just decide to love someone, Cade."

"You're right." He nodded affirmatively, as determined to salvage their relationship as she was to end it. "Love is something that occurs because it was meant to happen." Like it had happened to them.

Laurel looked at him with unbearable sadness. "And it didn't happen to us."

The hell it hadn't! Frustration rose in his throat, sharp and bitter. "I. Love. You." How much clearer could he make it?

Again, she wasn't listening. She censured him with a deep, penetrating look. "You need me to help you make your business life a success." She turned away. "There's a difference."

He moved so she had no choice but to look at him. Anger bubbled up inside him. "I want you in my life for a lot more than that."

"Oh, yes." Laurel rolled her eyes. "Let's not forget the hot sex, shall we? I fit the bill there pretty neatly, too, didn't I?"

More hurt than he could ever recall being in his life, he leaned in until they stood nose to nose. "Our marriage is more than that."

She stabbed a finger at his chest, frowned. "You forget who you're talking to, Cade. I've been down this road before, remember? I had a fiancé who only wanted me for reasons relating to his business success. Once those reasons were gone, he was out the door. And the sad truth is, even if you can't admit it to yourself just yet, you will want to walk away from me, too, once the controversy clears."

He wrapped his arms around her, hoping his touch would get through to her even if his words didn't. "You honestly think me capable of using you that way?" he asked her softly.

Her face grew pale, her shoulders even stiffer. "You never pretended to be anything but ruthless when it came to business, Cade. You never pretended our marriage was anything but an arrangement."

Stung by the aloof look in her eyes as much as her words, he reminded her hoarsely, "I asked you to stay on permanently." He had asked her to be his wife, not just temporarily, but forever!

She stood still and lifeless as a statue in his arms. "And I'm telling you I can't."

Cade had thought the two of them had everything either of them had ever wanted or needed. He'd thought they had found the kind of love that would last a lifetime. Instead, his whole world was being turned upside down by Laurel's lack of faith in him, in the same way it had been when his parents had kept splitting up and then reuniting, again and again, during the tumultuous years of his childhood. He had worked hard to get his life in order and avoid that particular pitfall himself, even if it meant being without a love interest in his life. Laurel had caused him to change all that—she had given him reason to hope that he could have the kind of happiness that had always eluded him. And now, having tasted just that, to have it all falling apart so unexpectedly was almost more than he could bear.

He let her go, stepped back, shoved his hands in his pockets. His mood dark and brooding, he warned, "I don't want the kind of off-again, on-again marriage my parents had all those years, Laurel." He didn't want to love with all his heart and soul, only to be pushed away. "You walk out on me now, it's over."

She gave him a pitying look, then shrugged and continued in a cold, calm voice Cade found much more disturbing than her anger. "It's *been* over, Cade, since the moment I first heard that tape."

"I HEARD YOU WERE in a bad mood," Mary Elena said two days later, when she arrived at Cade's house, wedding gift in hand. "I guess Dotty Yost wasn't kidding."

"Do you have a point here?" Cade grumbled, reluctantly accepting the large silver package with the ribbon on top. "Because if not I have work to do."

"Thank you, I think I will come in." Mary Elena breezed past, as if invited. Since making up with her father, moving back home, dating Manuel and resuming her charity work full-time, she acted as if she were on top of the world. "Hello, Beast." She bent down to pat the Labrador retriever's large black head. Beast's tail barely thumped. "What's wrong with him?" she asked in concern.

"He's depressed. He misses Patches, Laurel's puppy."

Mary Elena gave Cade a sage look. "Probably Laurel, too. Just like you."

Cade didn't even want to think about how empty the house was. The only saving grace was that Laurel had decided not to quit her job at DDF. Although all she did there was work her fanny off—and avoid him. To the point it was hard for him to get even a glimpse of her. "The marriage is over, Mary Elena."

Since admitting her feelings for Manuel Garcia, Mary Elena considered herself an authority on romance. "Tell that to your heart."

"Look, I gave it my best shot."

She gave Beast a final pat and stood gracefully. "You were certainly organized in your approach, from what I hear."

Figuring he might as well confide in someone, Cade led the way to the sun porch at the rear of the house. He stopped en route to get a couple of bottles of water from the fridge. "Laurel told you about the damage control lists."

"As well as the audio tape of you and Trisha Teal."

Cade settled in a padded wicker chair opposite Mary Elena's. Not sure when he had ever felt more tense or restless, he stretched his long legs out in front of him. "That recording is a fraud."

Mary Elena twisted the cap off her bottle. "You're sure."

Damn sure. Tired of being doubted, and suspected of the worst, he regarded her testily. "I ought to know what was said during the course of the conversation, and although those were our voices and I obviously said what I said, I didn't say it all to Trisha." Not even half.

"Then who were you talking to?" Mary Elena asked.

Cade shrugged. "Near as I can figure—Beast."

Mary Elena's eyes widened. "You think the tapes were cut and spliced together in the most damning way possible?"

"Yep." Cade watched Beast lumber in to sprawl between them.

"Did you tell Laurel this?" she demanded.

Cade took a long drink. "Nope."

"Why not?" Mary Elena looked upset.

Cade sighed and rubbed the back of his neck. "Because she wouldn't believe me even if I tried," he muttered.

"I never thought I'd see the day when you threw yourself a pity party, Cade Dunnigan. What happened to the man of action I used to know?"

He ignored her indignant tone. "I wised up," he told her bluntly. "I realized three strikes and you're out. And I've certainly had that. Two failed engagements and one failed marriage." He paused, shook his head in regret. "I'm obviously not cut out for this." Much as he had wanted to be…

Mary Elena scoffed. "You probably aren't if you can't get it together long enough to go after Laurel and tell her how you really feel!"

As her impassioned speech ended, Beast cast a hopeful look at Cade, who scowled. "Haven't you been listening to a word I've said? There is no way, given that audio tape George Jr. made to incriminate me, that Laurel is going to believe me."

Standing, Mary Elena shook her head. "Now, Cade. Since when do you—of all people—give up so easily?"

"WHAT ARE YOU TWO doing here?" Laurel demanded of her two married brothers, Brad and Riley. She did not have the patience for this. She wanted to curl up in private and mourn the loss of the love of her life without hearing any we-all-told-you-this-was-a-bad-idea speeches from her family. Because sadly, they had been right. She had been a fool to give her heart to a man who only had business and money on his mind.

Brad and Riley elbowed their way in, sans invitation. "We thought you might need some help moving your stuff out of Cade's house."

Laurel shrugged as her puppy scampered over to greet both her visitors. "I didn't move that much stuff in."

"Ah, the one-foot-out-the-door syndrome. I know it well myself," Brad said, ignoring the sudden testy glare Laurel aimed his way. He bent down to pet Patches, as did Riley. "It kept me single for many years."

Laurel flashed a smile she couldn't begin to really feel. "Well, maybe it will keep me single, too," she stated lightly.

Riley diagnosed what was really ailing Laurel as easily as he diagnosed his patients' illnesses. "That didn't seem to be what you wanted when you and Cade had dinner at Mom and Dad's

Chapter One

"No."

"No?" Lewis McCabe echoed, sure he couldn't possibly have heard Lexie Remington's stepmother correctly. After all, he'd barely had a chance to say hello, never mind declare his intentions.

"I know why you're here," Jenna Lockhart Remington continued.

"You do," Lewis murmured. Darn it, had his four brothers phoned ahead to make his plan public before he put it into action? If so, there was going to be heck to pay, and then some.

"And although…" Mrs. Remington paused to peruse Lewis shrewdly, head to toe, none of her customary hospitality evident "…I can see your need is dire…"

How could she know how long it had been since he'd had a date? Lewis thought in irritation. Then again, this was Laramie, Texas, where everyone was family, and nothing stayed secret for long, even one's fiercest desires….

"…Lexie is on vacation."

"Exactly," Lewis said, glad they were no longer talking at cross purposes. "I figured since she's in town again—" *for the first time in nearly three years* "—I'd use the opportunity to…"

"Take advantage of her kind and generous nature by putting her on the spot and asking her something that you and I both know you really shouldn't?" Mrs. Remington scolded, clearly annoyed.

Was she intimating he was a pity date? That Lexie would only go out with him if she felt sorry for him? Lewis knew his reputation. At least what it had been when he and Lexie were growing up. Maybe he used to be a bit of a dud, but that was no longer the case. A date with him would not be a waste of time for either of them. "I assure you, Mrs. Remington, I have nothing but the utmost respect for Lexie," Lewis said sincerely, determined to do whatever it took to get an audience with the woman he'd had his eye on for what seemed like forever. "I hold her in the highest regard."

"Which is, of course, exactly why you are here. Because Lexie *is* so successful."

Given the fact this conversation had started off on the wrong foot, and had been going down the wrong path every since, Lewis wasn't sure what to say to that. "Of course I admire what Lexie has done professionally," he admitted candidly. "Everyone around here does." Thanks to her stunning fashion sense, she'd become every bit the celebrity her clients were.

Footsteps sounded in the background. Jake Remington, Lexie's father, appeared at his wife's side, his tall, lanky frame filling the doorway. Jake nodded at Lewis. "McCabe."

"Mr. Remington." Lewis stuck out his hand. After a moment, Jake shook it. Encouraged, Lewis continued, "I was just telling Mrs. Remington that I—"

"My wife is right," Jake Remington interrupted. "There is no way Jenna and I are going to let Lexie see you. Because if we do, if you ask her what you and darn near everyone else around here wants to ask her right now—"

Lewis swore inwardly, stunned. "Other guys have been here ahead of me?" He thought he'd gotten the jump on this, since Lexie had only arrived here from London, via her father's private jet, earlier in the day.

"Let's just say you're not the first to come calling," Mrs. Remington replied. "And the answer to everyone was the same. Lexie is not receiving guests at this time."

"Well, then when will she be?" Lewis asked, doing his best to maintain a positive outlook. Not easy, given how quickly and thoroughly and damn unfairly he was being shot down.

Jake and Jenna looked at each other. "As far as we're concerned, not at all," Jake said, "at least during this visit."

The thought of letting Lexie go without seeing her—again—did not sit well with Lewis. Maybe because so many chances to connect had already passed them by. Deciding he wasn't going to let the Remingtons' assessment of his chances with Lexie decide the matter, he insisted as politely and firmly as possible, "I just need a moment of her time. I won't stay. I promise."

Jenna sighed, looking thoroughly conflicted. She ran a hand through her short, red-gold hair before frowning deeply at Lewis. "She'd say yes, you know. All it would take is one look at you, and she'd be agreeing to whatever you asked."

Lewis only wished that were the case. But he had no such confidence that Lexie would indeed go out with him on an actual date, even if she saw how much he had changed over the years. Which meant he had to handle this very carefully....

"And that would not be good for her." Jake Remington clapped a firm hand on Lewis's shoulder. "You need to go, son."

Lewis dug in his heels. He did not want to leave it like this.

"Maybe the next time she's home," Mrs. Remington offered gently but firmly. The door shut. Silence fell on the wide front porch of the elegant limestone ranch house.

Lewis stood there a moment longer, aware he hadn't felt so foolish since he was twenty-three, trying—and failing—to get up the nerve to talk to nineteen-year-old Lexie Remington, when she was home from college on fall break. Eight years had passed and little had changed. Swearing silently to himself, he turned and started down the porch steps to his SUV. He was almost there when he heard a tapping noise. He turned in the direction of the house and saw Lexie framed in an upstairs window, looking as heart-stoppingly beautiful as ever. She motioned to him and pointed urgently toward the rear of the house. Then, with one last glace over her shoulder, to see if he was following, she disappeared from view.

With a mixture of anticipation and excitement roaring through him, Lewis hesitated for only a second before heading in the direction she had indicated. Keeping to the early evening shadows, he strode around the ranch house. At the rear, Lexie was standing in an open second-floor window in what appeared to be an old-fashioned white nightgown, with a high neck and long, billowing sleeves. Her strawberry-blond hair flowed in untamed waves around her slender shoulders. She looked like a princess in a turret. All she was missing was the tiara, and he wouldn't have been surprised if she'd had one of those around someplace. Arms on the sill, she leaned down toward him and invited in a soft, mischievous voice that further fueled his dreams, "Come on up."

Lewis didn't know whether to laugh or try and wake himself up from what was obviously the wildest dream he'd ever had. "How?" he whispered back, aware it was only seven-thirty, and already Lexie was dressed for bed.

"Climb up the trellis," she urged merrily, her soft, bow-shaped lips curving into an even sexier smile.

Blood rushed through Lewis's veins. Had her breasts always been that curvaceous and full, her features so delicate and sensual? "You're kidding." He couldn't take his eyes from her face.

Her delicate features took on an air of challenge. To his disappointment, she tossed her head and shrugged as if it didn't matter to her in the last. "Do you want to meet with me or not?"

Lewis didn't have to be asked twice.

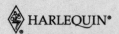

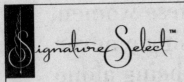

If you enjoyed what you just read,
then we've got an offer you can't resist!

Take 2 bestselling
love stories FREE!

Plus get a FREE surprise gift!

Clip this page and mail it to Harlequin Reader Service®

IN U.S.A.
3010 Walden Ave.
P.O. Box 1867
Buffalo, N.Y. 14240-1867

IN CANADA
P.O. Box 609
Fort Erie, Ontario
L2A 5X3

YES! Please send me 2 free Harlequin American Romance® novels and my free surprise gift. After receiving them, if I don't wish to receive anymore, I can return the shipping statement marked cancel. If I don't cancel, I will receive 4 brand-new novels every month, before they're available in stores! In the U.S.A., bill me at the bargain price of $4.24 plus 25¢ shipping & handling per book and applicable sales tax, if any*. In Canada, bill me at the bargain price of $4.99 plus 25¢ shipping & handling per book and applicable taxes**. That's the complete price and a savings of at least 10% off the cover prices—what a great deal! I understand that accepting the 2 free books and gift places me under no obligation ever to buy any books. I can always return a shipment and cancel at any time. Even if I never buy another book from Harlequin, the 2 free books and gift are mine to keep forever.

154 HDN DZ7S
354 HDN DZ7T

Name _____ (PLEASE PRINT)

Address _____ Apt.# _____

City _____ State/Prov. _____ Zip/Postal Code _____

Not valid to current Harlequin American Romance® subscribers.

Want to try two free books from another series?
Call 1-800-873-8635 or visit www.morefreebooks.com.

* Terms and prices subject to change without notice. Sales tax applicable in N.Y.
** Canadian residents will be charged applicable provincial taxes and GST.
  All orders subject to approval. Offer limited to one per household.
  ® are registered trademarks owned and used by the trademark owner and or its licensee.

AMER04R   ©2004 Harlequin Enterprises Limited

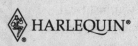

HARLEQUIN®

American ROMANCE®

COMING NEXT MONTH

#1113 MASON'S MARRIAGE by Tina Leonard
Cowboys by the Dozen

When the sheriff from Malfunction Junction discovers he's a father, he's delighted, even if the news comes four years late. Naturally, Mason assumes he'll finally have the only two women he's ever wanted. But Mimi Cannady expects to be wooed, and for a lifelong bachelor that's a tall order—like being asked to do the two-step with two left feet.

#1114 ONE DADDY TOO MANY by Debra Salonen
Sisters of the Silver Dollar

Kate's ex-husband wants joint custody of their daughter, but Kate can't forgive his betrayal. She hires lawyer Rob Brighten to fight the case and finds herself falling in love. But little Maya only wants her "real" daddy. Now, what's a good mother to do?

#1115 TEXAS BORN by Ann DeFee

Olivia Alvarado, vet and local coroner in Port Serenity, Texas, can't stay away from sexy sheriff C. J. Baker, even though she wants to. (Or does she?) She and C.J. are professionally connected by murder—and by mutts (once C.J. gets a dog). And if he has his way, they'll be *personally* connected, too. By marriage...

#1116 CAPTURING THE COP by Michele Dunaway
In the Family

Thirty years of good behavior was enough for anyone, even perpetual virgin Olivia Johnson, minister's daughter. And that was an understatement! Fortunately, it took just a glance at handsome detective Garrett Krause for her to get a few good ideas about some bad behavior—and how to make up for lost time.

www.eHarlequin.com

HARCNM0406

Laurel smiled as he stretched out next to her. "Sounds good so far."

He lifted her against him and kissed her with leisurely heat. "Followed by many more of the same."

She arched against him hungrily. "That really sounds good."

"And eventually—" Cade slipped his hands beneath her T-shirt to caress her skin "—when we're ready…a little one of our very own."

Her eyes lit up with joy. "Definitely a little one of our own," she told him blissfully. "Or two or three…"

"Agreed." Cade made fast work of undressing them both, then brought her to him for another long kiss. "In the meantime, it's probably a good idea for us to hone our skills in that area."

Laurel nodded, stroking her hands down his thighs. "Practice does make perfect," she murmured as Cade set about making her his wife all over again.

Afterward, they held each other tightly, loving the closeness, the tenderness flowing between them. "Have I told you how much I love you?" he murmured.

Laurel nodded. "Every bit as much as I love you."

Cade tightened his hold on her possessively, acutely aware at long last that all his dreams were coming true. He pulled her so close they could feel their hearts beating in tandem, framed her face with his hands and kissed her in a way that let her know they would soon be making love all over again. "Welcome home, Mrs. Dunnigan," he told her contentedly.

Happiness sparkled in Laurel's eyes. Wrapping her arms about his neck, she held him even tighter. "I'm so glad to be here. And Cade?" she whispered in a voice filled with love and tenderness. "This time it's forever."

and splicing was," Kevin explained, like the sheriff's department detective he was. "The voices are real, Laurel. But the conversation, as portrayed, is a fraud."

"In other words," Riley announced merrily, clapping a hand on her shoulder, "you've been duped. And quite well, I might add."

Brad nodded in agreement. "Seems to me you owe this husband of yours an apology, little sis," he told her gravely.

Laurel looked at Cade. His assurance had faded, replaced by a look that said he knew how much was at stake, just as she did. "I'd settle for some alone time with my bride," he told everyone dryly.

Laurel's brothers nodded in support. "Good luck, buddy." Brad slapped Cade on the shoulder.

"Got your work cut out for you," Lewis concurred.

"If you need backup, let us know," Kevin drawled.

"She can be a little stubborn," Riley added as he strolled out the door.

The door shut. Cade and Laurel were alone. As if realizing something very important was happening, Patches sat back on her haunches and looked up at them expectantly.

Guilt flooded Laurel. Realizing she had tried and convicted Cade on false evidence, she swallowed hard. "I'm not sure where to start," she said in a low, trembling voice.

"Then suppose you let me," Cade said gently. "I did a lot of soul searching during the two weeks we were together. Most of it late at night with Beast by my side."

Recognition dawned. "And that's who you were talking to on the tape," Laurel said, realizing it made perfect sense.

Cade nodded, taking her into his arms. "For years, I thought love was just another project to be selected and managed. I thought it was something I could dictate and control. You showed me I was wrong. I know now that love is something precious, that it comes into your life when you least expect it, and turns every plan you have made completely upside down. I also know it's worth it." He stroked a hand tenderly through her hair. "I love you, Laurel, and I always will."

"Oh, Cade." Laurel went up on tiptoes and delivered a long,

heartfelt kiss. "I love you, too. And I'm sorry for not believing in you."

He gave a crooked smile. "It looked bad."

She touched an index finger to his lips. "I knew better than to trust anything George Jr. brought forward." Laurel took a deep breath. "I was just scared." She clung to him tightly. "I've never loved anyone the way I love you."

His gray eyes took on an even darker hue as he swept her even closer. "But you do love me."

"Oh, yes," Laurel whispered as Cade lowered his head for a long, soulful kiss. "Most certainly I do."

They kissed again, sweetly. "Then that leaves only one thing for us to do," Cade decided when the languorous kiss came to a halt.

"What's that?" Laurel asked breathlessly.

"Takes Patches and go home to Beast where we all belong," he told her, with all the love and tenderness she had ever wished for.

BEAST, AS IT TURNED OUT, was very glad to see his little friend Patches.

The two of them romped into a state of exhaustion, while Cade and Laurel sat beneath the star-filled Texas sky, sipping champagne and celebrating the rebirth of their marriage. Cade had never been happier than he was at that moment. Laurel looked the same. He knew life was only going to get better.

"Think it's about time to call it a night?" Laurel said contentedly at last.

"For those two." Cade winked. He whistled for Beast. The big black Lab came running, Patches at his heels. Short minutes later, the two dogs were cozily ensconced on the sunporch. Both were curled up on Beast's large round dog bed.

"For the two of us," Cade continued, as he took Laurel by the hand. "I have other plans."

"And those would be?" she teased, allowing Cade to steer her toward the master bedroom upstairs.

He paused to kiss the nape of her neck, then drew her down onto the bed. "A long night of lovemaking."

strode toward her purposefully, looking handsome as all get-out in a pair of slacks and an open-necked white shirt. Wishing she had on something better than the cutoff shorts and yellow T-shirt she had put on the moment she arrived home from work, she angled her head at Cade contentiously.

To her dismay, his triumphant smile only widened. He regarded her like some big-screen hero, out to claim his errant bride.

"Too bad. You're going to hear what we have to say," he told her implacably.

"I'm surprised Will isn't here, too," Laurel said dryly of her only missing sibling.

"He would be," Kevin told Laurel happily. He shut the door behind them and bent down to take charge of her scampering puppy. "But Will's piloting a charter flight."

"For the record, Will thinks you should listen to Cade, too," Lewis said.

Laurel knew she would never get rid of her siblings unless she at least pretended to hear them out. "Fine. Say what you-all have to say." Laurel paused to aim a killer look at Cade, letting him know, brothers or not, that he was not going to use her that way and then come back into her life as if nothing had happened, no matter how much she loved him. She sucked in a tremulous breath. "Then get out."

With the passion he had felt for her gleaming in his eyes, Cade bowed his head respectfully. "Since Kevin is the detective, I'm going to let him do the demonstration."

Looking all too happy to oblige, Kevin slid the cassette into the recorder, and turned it on. Seconds later, a staticky sound filled the room. Then she heard the sound of Cade's voice, followed by Trisha's. And throughout the conversation Laurel had already memorized by heart, lots and lots of little clicks.

"Do you hear all that clicking?" Kevin asked.

She nodded, though she wasn't sure what the point was. So they had a bad recording. So what? "Practically every other sentence. But those sounds weren't on the tape I had."

"That's because it wasn't enhanced to reveal where the cutting a week and a half ago," he said, watching as Patches raced over to pick up a nylon chew bone.

Laurel curtailed the urge to kick both her brothers in the shin for their temerity. "That's because I was deluding myself into thinking Cade loved me then," she announced sweetly.

Brad leaned in. "I have news for you, baby sis. You can't fake the way Cade looked at you. It was the real deal."

"How do you know?" Laurel asked.

He placed a comforting hand on her shoulder. "Because Lewis talked to Cade yesterday, and Lewis said Cade looks as heartbroken as you do."

"You should make up with him," Riley agreed softly.

Abruptly, Laurel was near tears again. "It's not that simple," she said dispiritedly.

"Sure it is," Brad said, his grip on her gentling all the more. "If you love Cade as much as we think you do, Laurel, then you can forgive him anything. Forgiveness is an essential part of any marriage."

"As are love and acceptance," Riley agreed.

Laurel wished she could believe that. "You didn't hear that tape recording," she argued.

"She's got a point." Riley let go of Laurel and looked at Brad.

Brad looked right back at Riley. "You think it's time?" Brad asked.

Riley nodded. He opened the front door of Laurel's apartment and gestured broadly. Seconds later, Kevin, Lewis and Cade sauntered in. Kevin was carrying a portable tape player, Cade, a small audio-cassette.

Of course, Laurel thought. Seeing no way to get to her on his own, Cade had enlisted her family.

"Whatever you men have cooked up, I don't want to hear it," Laurel said stubbornly, ignoring the fact that her heart was now racing at breakneck speed. It had been only two and a half days since she had come toe to toe with Cade. It seemed like a lifetime. Up close, he, too, looked as if he hadn't been sleeping much. Unlike her, there was a determined, victorious aura about him. He